Swimming with Big Fish

Julie Haines

ISBN 978-0-473-27793-2

Orakei Press
264 Kepa Rd. Mission Bay, Auckland 1071
julieryan@xtra.co.nz

Website: julieryanauthor.blogspot.co.nz

Cover by SelfPubBookCovers.com/GraphicPro

Acknowledgements

I thank my husband, Frank, Eirlys Shand and the Hubcaps writers' group for their support and all contributors to this story, especially Lesley Marshall of Editline and PEN NZ. for editing, and for her accounts of writers in prison. Tom Lodge and Bev Robitaille acted as midwives to the book, Aaron Lam embellished the cover. Ali Akil, Gerald Koszegi Ryan, John Heynen, Gary Bold, Dennis Pivac, Helen Munneke, Bill Ryan and John Cranna gave me specialist knowledge, and Val Nutley, Inna Shibalova and Mercia Henderson helped with translation.

Chapter 1

The Glass-Bottomed Boat
Leigh/Matakana, New Zealand and St Petersburg, Russia. 12 October 2006

The morning after the funeral is fine enough for beach cricket but Dennis Bogdanovich refuses to leave the old couch.

His wife shrieks and the umpire on the verandah - his mother, nags, but Dennis only stares up at a patch of ceiling his father would never finish painting. To him the mildewed blobs are clouds of blue maomao at Goat Island.

Dennis lives to fish. The womenfolk would not let him go today but he has now escaped to his happy place in the Marine Reserve. In his head he is snorkelling over waving seaweed in a cloud of the blue nomads. He's with some girl - probably Barry's kid sister - when they hear the old glass-bottomed boat puttering towards them. He is still struggling to undo her bra and turn her into a mermaid, to give the tourists a thrill, when they are run over, the boat swerves and an old woman falls out.

She should have learnt to swim. Everybody should know how to swim in New Zealand. The boat should have had higher sides. It was a terrible old dunger, anyway.

In the cricket, someone has been run out.

During that moment of hubbub Dennis has an epiphany: he will spend the money his father has left him on a glass-bottomed boat to show tourists the fish they are no longer allowed to catch. He is up in a bound.

"Are you coming?" his mother asked. "They need you to stop the ball going in the water."

Dennis was already on his way to the computer. Too soon to blog the boys in the Fishing Forum, so he keyed 'Glass-bottomed Boat' into Google, and after trawling through various sites finally struck gold - in Russia. Incredibly, the best and cheapest boats, with the shortest delivery date, came from Parritet Ellips in St. Petersburg. Instead of a glass bottom they had developed a curved screen of modified acrylic, highly resistant to scratching. This boat looked like something out of Disney - a plump, powerful, snub-nosed dolphin cruising on top of the water.

A blue Russian dolphin was going to carry him out of the sewerage business he'd been trapped in for thirty years. Even though his nails stayed clean these days and he was now the contract manager, the Fishing Forum bloggers still called him "Stinky", in spite of the mansion on Omaha Beach.

And if that had to be mortgaged again?

"Too bad, Diane." It would still be there for her to polish - a shiny granite bench being better than sex to her. She won't cook fish any more, the smell is so bad for the curtains, but for the rest of his life he would spend every day among the fish - the Fish Forum boys will be ikied when they see him cruising the Gulf at the wheel of this Russian 'Looker 30'.

His mother was doubtful about taking the money her husband had scraped together and use it to invest in some boat. She had forgotten how to spend money – her lumpy couch was proof of that – though it would forever be "Plenty good enough in the old country. On Korcula Island it would be flash." However she would be glad to phone Tonka in St Petersburg, the young cousin who had married so well。 She had to anyway, to tell her which of their relatives had come to the funeral. Also, Tonka's son, Young Serge, could be Dennis' man on the spot and help negotiate the purchase, since the poor boy was out of work.

"Educated - educated, to be the rocket scientist - and now..." the mother wagged a slow finger at her son. She'd had a fresh bandage on it at the funeral, but it had turned soggy and brown from peeling potatoes as she watched the cricket.

No one in this family was afraid of work but they would all die of it: his father had died with a paintbrush in his hand, and Dennis could see himself stiff in his own coffin, wearing sewer waders. No. Now was the time to think bigger: his daughter could wait a bit longer for her horse. All would be sweet when the Remuera stormwater contract kicked in next month.

In a few days the deal was as good as done. Dennis was so pleased he bought his mother a box of chocolates.

He decided to go to Europe himself, to collect the boat, and check out the sights. Dennis had a very good eye, especially for female landmarks, and distance was no trouble to him – in fact he found it usually lessened trouble. As it was to be such a rushed trip his wife decided not to go - Dennis would be well home by Christmas.

From the plane, green fields and kiwifruit orchards, steelworks on the creek and the creamy cliffs at Awhitu were soon washed out by cloud. He was free.

He had one stopover in Bangkok for two hot days and three exhausting nights. No elephants were involved in his activities, but he saw a great many geckos and a variety of fans on several styles of ceiling, drank plenty and ate a minimum of curry. He resisted all temptation to buy pink diamonds, extraordinary rubies or cheap sapphires, on the grounds his daughter was too young, his mother too old and his wife never went anywhere to show them off. Among other possible recipients there were none Dennis expected to see twice. He nearly bought himself a thick gold chain but knew immediately the fun the Fish Club bloggers would have with it – "Slip the anchor" would be only the start of it.

Another long sleep on a plane and he was tipped out into Frankfurt Airport.

In the toilets he shaved and checked his money belt. Reassured, he went to change a few traveller's cheques into roubles. Then he stepped onto the travellator and put his one bag between his feet for the long trip to the Aeroflot terminal. Trading on the internet was turning out enjoyable as well as cheap. Globalisation is good!

He didn't have long to wait for his flight to St. Petersburg. The Aeroflot hostesses spoke English, were slim and had short enough skirts but they still looked a bit dumpy coming so soon after the Bangkok dolls. He got a window seat. The seatbelt baulked but after he applied pressure for a moment it clicked into place.

Fortunately the American beside him wasn't too gabby. Dennis was able to tell him all about New Zealand: "Nice little green country, but works too hard. Needs to get out and see what the world can do for it." Like trading on the internet. He told him about some of the great bargains you could get: New Zealand was part of the global community, and even Russia wasn't far behind now.

There it was down below, actually. Dennis got quite interested in the wide river and the black squares of burnt wheat fields striped with snow. You could see how they'd hacked the forest about too - more like cropping in the way it was replanted and obviously managed. He would have expected just endless miles of scrappy pine woods being mown down, burnt and maybe dug over for gum as the New Zealand bush had been in his grandfather's time.

Then they were descending into St. Petersburg. It was a fair landing. Dennis was not the first out of the plane – that's the trouble with window seats – but he was one of the first through customs. No luggage meant no trouble from the swamp-green customs army, and they probably thought his name was Russian instead of Croatian. As he lined up for a taxi he realised why the customs officers had been wearing fur-lined forage caps inside. It was freezing.

He was sixteenth in line. Eventually an old brown car flung a door open for him and he got in. Then his troubles began.

The driver claimed to be an industrial chemist, unemployed, but his only other English phrase seemed to be "Nevsky Prospect". Dennis didn't want to be a tourist; he wanted to see his new boat. He kept showing the driver his printout of the firm's address but at last realised the man was unable to read Western writing. Dennis unlocked his bag and found the Global Sat. picture of the factory.

Then the driver, who was being tooted at for blocking the way by other more official-looking taxis, started his motor and set off. He kept gabbling in agitated Russian. Dennis picked out the odd word recognisable from Croatian. The driver held onto the picture and waved it about as they went, first along wide streets and then turning and twisting down smaller streets, often reversing and setting off back the way they had just come.

At each fresh start there was a pause when the picture was stabbed repeatedly and turned about and the whole predicament explained again. Dennis gathered the photo was an old one. He could only repeat over and over the name of the firm as his mother had taught him to say it.

After an hour and a quarter they stopped at a shabby brick building a good way from the river. It looked quite mediaeval to Dennis but high on the side in very small Western letters beneath the Cyrillic was the name: *Parritet Ellips.* Dennis went to the door to check it was the right address before he would pay. There was a poster from the Dusseldorf Boatshow 2003 on the wall behind the receptionist.

The taxi fare was surprisingly little when Dennis converted it into New Zealand dollars. He gave the man a small tip.

The salesman who was summoned to meet him was effusive in his welcome, all in Russian, but Dennis understood showroom palaver. He accepted a glass of tea – could have done with a doughnut alongside it after his taxi ordeal. They went through a back corridor to the showroom where they examined the Looker 30 in every part, both talking in boatman's language by waving their arms about.

The smooth twin hulls were made from material originally used for jetfighter planes. They had a sharp V- shape that would slice through waves like two knives, minimising roll or turbulence that might disturb the underwater view and ensuring the boat would not slap down after each wave the way a flat-bottomed one would. It would be a comfortable ride. There was a good German engine and excellent upholstery. No chance of losing a passenger overboard here - the fourteen passenger seats were inside the cabin, arranged in a circle around the viewer lens. The acrylic was very clear and, yes, 'guaranteed scratchproof'. All just like the specifications on the website.

Dennis was handed over to the manager or cashier, a very much grander person than the salesman. The new man showed signs of speaking

English, though very sparingly. "The money is very important!" was his most polished phrase.

He examined Dennis's letter of credit minutely. "This document is quite correct. Delivery will be in three days. What is your address?"

Dennis was flustered. He had not yet spoken to Sergey Mikulitsin but felt it unlikely there would be a front lawn outside his house available for parking a boat. The money had now been handed over and Dennis would have only a receipt to wave about in case of trouble, in this fearsome city where he could not speak the language.

"I will have to get back to you. Er...Zelim poc doma."

The manager raised an eyebrow. "To New Zealand?"

"No, no. To my cousin's, house in St. Petersburg. He's going to be arranging the transport. To Hamburg, I think. We'll get back to you."

"That is quite satisfactory. We will expect your information. Thank you."

The manager stood, gave a firm handshake and opened the door for Dennis. The salesman was waiting outside.

Dennis was grateful when the receptionist called a taxi for him. It arrived with a light on top saying "TaCKN" with the N back to front. Presumably that meant "Taxi" to Russians. The salesman kindly read out Sergey's address to the driver from Dennis's notebook and he felt able to sit back at last and enjoy St. Petersburg in the rush hour.

The cars were not the small square kind he'd expected. He saw all the European brands - plenty of Mercedes and even a flashy Bentley convertible among them - but every driver seemed desperate to get home for dinner. Dennis especially enjoyed the spectacle at intersections, as good as a night at the stock cars: when the lights changed cars charged in to fill every inch of space, facing in all directions, as if the next change of lights might be their last chance for getting onto the road to home. Between intersections the four lanes of traffic often came to a complete stop. Once there was a canary-yellow Lamborghini bogged down two cars ahead. Dennis was very tempted to get out and have a chat with the female driver.

Pedestrians were making better time than the cars. Most of them were women in high-heeled boots that did their figures a lot of good, even in coats. Shoes like that would probably also be practical in winter by stabbing into icy footpaths while keeping the foot partly out of the snow.

There were more minibuses than buses. Dennis noticed a taxi two lanes over: the driver kept getting out and standing up on what was once called the running board to look ahead and calculate the duration of the stoppage. Twice he even ran ahead to get a better view, but after ten minutes' stoppage all three of his passengers leapt out and marched away through the traffic, leaving the doors wide open. Dennis made a note to add this procedure to his repertoire, but did not try it that night.

His young driver tried to entertain him with jokes about generic Russian architecture: "*There was this bridegroom whose friends got him drunk in Moskva and put him on a plane for Sankt Peterburg. He woke, landed and took a taxi to 379 Fifth Soviet, Apartment 149, Block 6, Leninskaya. The lift was still broken so he walked up six floors as usual, got out his key, opened the door and went in to find he was already married with a wife inside, waiting for him with a rolling pin.*"

Dennis found some of the buildings were pretty flash on the main drag but was very pleased to turn off into quieter streets in a district of large, older buildings that the driver said was Kirovsky zavod. He delivered Dennis to Cousin Tonka's apartment in Elizarova Prospect 7.

She lived four floors up and Dennis thought the lift looked shonky, but occasional squash games kept him fit enough to manage stairs - even these, which rose endlessly through a green-tiled well - though by the time he reached Cousin Tonka's floor he was glad he had packed only a small satchel. The concierge had buzzed her and she was waiting at the door to meet him.

"My cousin Marinka's boy from so far away! Come, let me kiss you!"

She did manage it, although she was so little. She wore very high heels for her age and plenty of perfume. Dennis gave her a box of German chocolates and a letter from his mother.

"Come, meet your cousin, Sergey - a fine, big man, just like you. This is your cousin, Dennis Bogdanovich, from New Zealand."

"Young Serge" was a prosperous-looking fellow about his own age. The whole apartment set-up was flasher than you would expect from the street. There were shiny red and white curtains hung right from the ceiling with extra stuff drabbling on the floor, and gold trimmings on all the furniture. Marinka would have been jealous but she would have approved of the icon of Mary on a shelf, with a vase of carnations in front of it.

"That is my Red Corner," said Tonka.

"Yes, President Putin sent it round," said her son, hands in his pockets and rocking on his heels. His mother batted her hands at him and beamed to reassure her cousin's child it was only a wicked joke.

Serge was a bit taller than Dennis but much balder, with a fair, bushy moustache over the mouth of a trout. He was a muscular forty-five.

"Welcome to St. Petersburg," he said. "Did you bring your boat? It's not far to the water from here." He spoke confident English with an American accent.

"No. I've seen it and paid for it, but you're right: getting it to the water is my big problem."

Dinner was served on beautiful plates by a tall blonde girl Dennis hoped would be introduced as a very distant cousin. She was smiley but well buttoned-up.

Tonka noticed and said, "No, no: that is Natasha." Her English would not allow further elaboration. Sergey was amused but did not help.

The girl must have been a servant because she did not re-appear till she came to clear away the plates after a very good meal of meatballs and noodles with plenty of mushrooms, in just Marinka's Croatian style.

They all had a good laugh over his taxi adventures.

"For twelve roubles," said Serge, "you could have taken a minibus to the Metro Station. Then for 45 American cents, one token would have brought you to Elizabetskaya Station at the corner of our street!"

Dennis said he hoped Serge would lead him to many more bargains. Then he explained the photos his mother had sent, passing to Tonka those of the funeral, then others of weddings and babies, and showing Serge the ones of Dennis and his friends posing with big fish or racks of duck. He tried to explain how a kontiki submarine took fishing lines out but submarine seemed to be a dirty word. He also tried to give Tonka his famous recipe for duck and pukeko soup, but that was way above her head.

Over blinis - pancakes soaked in raspberries and sour cream - they discussed options for taking the new boat home. Train to Hamburg and then ship was the obvious solution. Serge opened a bottle of sweet Turkish wine. Natasha had offered him a corkscrew but he preferred to use his Swiss Army knife. Behind him there was a photo of his father, the General, wearing a high helmet and many medals. They had the same mouth but army regulation had flattened it out, turning him into a bronze whaler.

"Turkish, eh?" Dennis said when he'd tasted the wine. "You'd never get my mother to drink Turkish wine. She'd say it might be poisoned."

"Ah, Dennis, the world has changed quite a bit since our mothers left Dalmatia. Especially in the last few years. I got this on a nice holiday in Cappadocia – a business trip, you know. How long is your boat?"

"Eight metres."

"It's possible I could help you. My friend has a very big truck he wants me to drive to Amsterdam next week. Do ships sail to New Zealand from the Netherlands?"

"Probably. Do you have an internet connection here?"

"Sure."

Chapter 2

A Jaunt for Cousins, St. Petersburg, 20 October 2006

On Wednesday Dennis took Sergey to look at the boat, checking to see if it would fit into his friend's truck. They made a handsome pair. Going down into the metro station old women approaching on the up escalator noticed them from far away. *Never too old, even in Russia,* thought Dennis, but towards the bottom, when a video screen showed the two of them advancing, he felt a bit of a hayseed in boat shoes, and a sheepskin coat with wool oozing from every seam, alongside Sergey in his shiny black leather. Even Serge's moustache was glossy - though he wouldn't have looked so good without his cap.

Call me Action Man, Dennis thought and squared his shoulders.

They stood waiting for a train in an enormous golden mosaic of a harvest scene guarded by great statues of men with machineguns and women with spanners. There was no litter at all, but instead of the scent of hay there was an oily underground smell. It was very hot.

Dennis took off his coat. "We must have come down a hundred metres?"

"One hundred and five. It was designed as a bomb shelter." Serge gestured at the arches over stainless steel blast doors that shut off the train tracks from the waiting passengers.

To distract his cousin from embarrassing old troubles Dennis dug into his trouser pocket and pulled out a narrow slip of paper. "Natasha's given me her phone number."

"You dog... Hey, let me see that!" Sergey had snatched the paper. He turned it over. On the back there was an ink signature, *Michael P. Bernardin.* He crushed it in his fist.

"Where'd you get this?" Sergey's face was turning red.

"You keep a very tidy office. If you could see -"

"When was this?" Sergey's lips had taken on the grim shape of his father's mouth.

"Just now, while you were getting your coat. Your mother went out of the room for a minute and whammee - she's hot, that maid of yours! When she wanted to give me her number I looked in the bin for a bit of paper, but Natasha flipped up the lid of the scanner and found you'd left a bit of Russian stuff there. This was under -"

"Where is the letter now?" The lips were white all around. Definitely a great white and closing in.

"Natasha took it. Is she the tidy freak, then?"

But Sergey had run off through the crowd, along the platform and back up the escalator, pushing past ascending passengers. Dennis raced after him, and as he got on at the bottom the supervisor in the glass box beside him was shouting at Sergey through the microphone in Angry Russian Woman but Serge kept thrusting upward.

Back beneath the chandeliers in the marble ticket lobby Dennis found his cousin weaving among incoming passengers at the entrance, making a call on his mobile phone. Sergey wouldn't even look at him, and kept moving away. As Dennis struggled after him, feeling peeved, Sergey's call was being passed from one person to another, the message more urgent with every repeat, but also more deferential. Each time it ended with Natasha's full name, three names at least – "Natasha Marshmallow Marshmallow-lova" or something. Then finally, in English, "Thank you, but not like Politkovskaya - not in the lift!" and Sergey snapped the phone shut.

"There was no reception down there," he said by way of apology to Dennis. "Come on," and he headed once more for the escalators. This time the fierce woman in the glass box paid no attention.

They were no sooner back on the wheat field than the steel doors opened and their train was waiting. They were pushed along in the tidal rush of passengers and found seats. Sergey seemed to have got over his tantrum but he'd kept the bit of paper - probably fancied the girl himself. With those Sharapova legs anyone would - but now here he was, explaining tourist posters to The Kiwi Conqueror.

"That is the Church of the Spilled Blood."

"Whose blood? The architect's? None of those towers match."

"No, no, only Tsar Alexander's - he got assassinated there. You should take Natasha there; it's just at the end of the Nevsky Prospect. Girls like that sort of thing." Sergey stared through the poster. "I took a girl to a monastery once. It was on a little mountain near Moscow. The path goes very steeply, backwards and forwards, up through birch woods but there's a spring at the top and I knew we'd both really feel like a swim by the time we got there. They have separate pools for men and women. It was a bit earlier than this, though. We went in September. It was before she was my ex-wife - before she was even my wife..."

"Any kids?"

"One son, Ivan. She never lets me see him. He would be six next month. Anyway, I was boiling hot and jumped straight into the pool. The water was so cold I had hiccups for a week. Very romantic."

They got out at Yaroslavl and found Parritet Ellips. The letter of credit must have worked because the manager was much more chatty. In fact he was delighted to meet them both. He and Dennis vied to impress Sergey with the Looker 30's extraordinary features: the huge 2x3 metre spheroid underwater viewing screen, the modified acrylic it was made of, the hydraulics of the skipper's pop-up canopy, the two refrigerators, the GPS, the special aerodynamic shape, and the twin engines producing forty to sixty knots.

"It goes like a cut cat!" said Dennis.

Sergey looked sharply at him.

The manager continued smoothly, "...but gain the highest level of comfort to the passengers, a feeling of soft flying without strikes. The Looker is wonderful, be sure. Our boat is in the centre of attention of any beach or marina." His glasses were steaming up with the effort of his recitation. "That's why Looker boats always find their market and really effect business –

United Arab Republic, Maldives, Madagascar, Tortola, Egypt..."

"And Goat Island!" said Dennis.

"What are the outside dimensions?" asked Sergey.

Diagrams were produced and Sergey took notes. He seemed sanguine about the boat fitting into his friend's truck, providing it could be put on a low cradle.

"Of course, sir. Of course," said the manager.

Dennis was very pleased and there was a lot of handshaking. Then he was keen to get home to attend to his email and introduce Looker 30 to his blog. Sergey surprised him by handing him back Natasha's number copied onto some Parritet bumf. Dennis folded it and put it carefully away in his coat pocket.

In the train Dennis entertained his cousin with a recent Fish Club blog - instructions for catching multiple turkeys using nothing but a forty-four-gallon drum and a crust of bread. "You put it under a tree near their roost. One jumps in and can't get out. He makes so much noise the others come to investigate and they see the bread..."

Sergey eyes were glazing over.

"You see, it's not all just fishing. They're a great bunch of guys – and we'd none of us ever met till we joined the Fishing Forum. Occasionally you get a message to meet at a pub on a Friday night - if you're within range - and we had a really good Christmas do last year: a pig on a spit, smoked marlin and 'Filth Dog', a heavy metal band. We have a moderator,

Skotty. He makes sure nothing gets onto the website that shouldn't. Bit of an old woman, really."

Dennis had paid for the train tickets but Sergey said when they should get off. They bought mushrooms and apples from a peasant woman at a little stall outside the subway station.

At home Sergey insisted on getting into the lift with the groceries but Dennis raced for the stairs. See your father turn from farmer to scarecrow inside six months and you'd have the motivation, my boy.

As he got near the fourth floor he could hear Tonka howling. The door of the apartment stood open and from the hall he could see her in the main room, wrapped in her son's arms, weeping loudly and sometimes jerking out an arm, explaining to him - and now repeating over her shoulder to Dennis - some tragic Russian business.

Sergey was smoothing her hair but looked at Dennis as he spoke to his mother in Russian. Then, "Shut the door," he told him.

They were still standing there when Dennis came back.

Over Tonka's head Sergey told him, "Natasha has been in an accident. At the market. She was run over."

"Is she all right?"

"No. She died in the ambulance."

Tonka fairly bawled then.

"Shit!" Dennis blushed a bit.

He put his hands in his pockets and went to the window, and looked up and down the street at the traffic. When he turned back he said, "I'm very sorry about your loss, Tonka. We bought some mushrooms at the station. I could cook lunch for us. Do you have any bacon?"

Tonka gulped, nodded, and unwound Sergey's arms. She tottered off to the kitchen and Dennis followed with the groceries.

Sergey went to his room and shut the door.

Chapter 3

In Hamburg, Germany, 23 October 2006

Sergey arranged to meet his boss, Zaheed, at a Hamburg pub he'd seen on TV, one that had a bouncy castle outside the door. He figured that if the staff missed seeing children being abducted from it last year they would take little interest in adult customers this year.

Zaheed was already sitting with a beer. Sergey recognised his old friend immediately in spite of the short frill of red beard he'd sprouted in the two months they'd been apart.

"Hi, un bier for mein friend?" Zaheed gestured to the barman and they moved to a table near the window.

"I see you have kept the cap but you've had a shave," said Zaheed. "I have given up shaving. Habenze gut times im Hamburg? Do the girls like you without your moustache?"

"Don't know yet - I cut it off only this morning, before I had my passport photo taken. Didn't want to shock my mother when I went home to get the truck."

"I've changed my name to Frits Breijer in my grubby new Dutch passport and on my cigarette lighter as well."

"You have all your gear ready?" Sergey asked.

"Everything we'll need to find our way. You got the suitcases?"

The barman delivered the beer.

"Danke." Serge paid and waited a moment. "Yes, three suitcases and the Easter egg. Herman will be very pleased. You had no trouble getting the...er, map?"

Zaheed shook his head and smiled. "Is the truck all finished?"

"Yeah! It is a beauty!" Turning his shoulder a little towards the wall, Sergey held up six fingers, three times.

Zaheed didn't look impressed.

"An eighteen-wheeler!" Serge mouthed. "Good fittings too, it has. Excellent. Works like a clock - no commissariat rubbish! I tell you, we're working for a very good firm: anything I say we must have, we get. It's like the Americans say, everything that opens and shuts!"

Zaheed nearly laughed. "When do we leave?"

"Tomorrow at six in the morning. Be at the corner of Rathaus Strasse. You know, of course, we are working for 'Crown Removals'? And you should know, in case anyone asks, we are moving a glass-bottomed boat from St. Petersburg to Amsterdam for my cousin - he is a clown from New Zealand but he was very useful distracting the guards at the borders yesterday and the day before. We'll lose him in Amsterdam."

"Does the boss know?"

"No, but he leaves all operational decisions to me and I say the boat is necessary to fill the truck until we get to Herman's. Three attaché cases and a box would beg for inspection, but now if anyone looks inside we can blame all the hardware and even the hydraulic legs on the boat. It's a glass-bottomed hydrofoil, so it looks very unusual."

"You had no trouble with customs?"

"No, the boat came with all the right documents. The only trouble was my cousin's big mouth. We came down through Luga and Pskov to cross into Latvia at a little country place the boss recommended. I didn't want to go through Estonia - I was keeping well inland to avoid anyone who knew anything about boats - but unfortunately it turned out Dennis was also an expert on road-building. He wouldn't believe we were on an important highway and for six hours kept telling me it wasn't up to New Zealand standards, that it wasn't fit for a milk tanker, let alone his precious boat. He cursed every pothole and kept making me stop while he cleaned mud off the headlights. He nearly went hysterical over donkey carts, and then he started on the border guards, jabbering away at them. So at each crossing I just let him go on, poked the documents at the guards now and then on their little table and turned the pages, till they just stamped everything and let us go."

"How did you get on going into Lithuania and Poland?"

"The same. Except at the Polish border he tried to make the guard admit he was related to some Pole he knew in New Zealand. 'He's a farmer and a great fisherman. He's got exactly the same bushy eyebrows as you!' I kicked him in the ankle as he was about to pull the guard's sunglasses off to check his eye colour. The guard turned very frosty and demanded I open the truck. Dennis had only to start his spiel about his wonderful boat and they were glad to slam the doors shut, but I knew, having seen the boat, they were going to tell the Polish Mafia we were coming through."

"Did you see any of them?"

"No, but I kept looking. We were dead tired but you can't take a truck like ours into the secure car park at a big hotel. That meant I didn't dare stop till early yesterday morning when we got to Neuruppin, well inside Germany. Then I slept like a stone. Dennis had snored most of the way across Poland so he went off, ramping about the town. Pity he didn't get lost."

"Where is this cousin of yours now?"

"Down the docks for the afternoon, looking at boats and girls. He likes both. Don't worry, Zaheed - it's too early for worrying. So you have taken up smoking? What did your wife say about that?" Serge offered him a Belomor.

Zaheed lit one for him too, using the new lighter. "I will tell her it is for business - you give a man a cigarette... This is why..." He put the lighter down, turned it over and tapped the engraving, to help them both fix on the new name. "You must always call me 'Frits' from now on, 'Frits Breijer'. I had it engraved today. It was a present from my uncle in Afghanistan. There's been a new fatwa against tobacco, or perhaps he thought he would never be able to afford tobacco again. I think he also wanted to show he was pleased I'd brought the girls some dresses from London. I did not tell him, none of the family in Karachi wanted them. What name have you chosen?"

"I am 'Piet ten Broeke'. I found it on a salami packet. Sound like a quality sausage-maker to you?" He beamed and signalled to the barman. "Another beer?"

The only other people in the bar were three old German sailors. Two of them had black pipes cheerfully steaming. Sergey and Zaheed sat back and inhaled as if they too had retired, enjoying virtual success - an assured and satisfying windfall, and the prospect of entirely new and trouble-free lives - even before their drinks arrived.

Sitting there, contented, smoking and listening to the noise of the wind generator that served the bouncy castle they heard trouble coming up the street towards them. On the wall in front of Sergey was a mirror that showed four or five tiny men pounding up the street, waving their arms. As they grew larger he recognised Dennis in the lead. The others looked like Turks or Armenians.

Dennis jumped through the bouncy castle, the towers reacting violently, and burst open the glass doors of the bar. Seeing his cousin he took refuge on a seat the other side of him, gasping and sweating. The barman put his cloth down on the counter and wiped his hands on his apron. He came out from his counter to deal with the invaders who filled his bar, shouting at Dennis and accusing him in three or more languages of not having paid enough.

Zaheed stood up and cut through the brouhaha in a few quiet words of Arabic.

One of the Turks responded, angry but rational.

Zaheed paid him many euros. Then, with a final bit of moral advice for Dennis, the chief took his squad out. They punched the towers of the castle as they went, glowering at Dennis through the window.

He shouted back, "And tell her to cut her toenails!" Then, slumping into his chair, he told Zaheed, "You shouldn't have paid them. She was worth about a dollar, tops!"

"Come!" said Sergey, hauling his cousin up in spite of his size.

"Hey, I could do with a drink!"

The other two pushed him out into the street.

The barman shut the doors after them and the old men ordered another round in appreciation of the entertainment.

Chapter 4

Oud-Zuilen,
the Netherlands, 23 October 2006

Things were duller that evening for the rest of Sergey and Zaheed's team, waiting for them not far from Utrecht, in an old sausage factory. It stood in ragged parkland near the brick castle on the outskirts of Oud-Zuilen village, For two months they had been assembling a rocket, preparing it to receive the warhead Zaheed and Sergey were bringing across Europe. Herman, Anton and Hans were now killing time.

None of them was Dutch: Herman, much the oldest, was a tubby American with a shock of faded, bristly hair. He was feeding long rolls of plans into the firebox of a boiler, listening to the boys quarrelling in the loft above him. They sounded like kids at summer camp, only with North London accents. Hans was doing most of the talking as usual but Anton always had the last word.

Both boys had been very careful and willing helpers with this jihad, which required meticulous technical skill. Herman had expected the work would be far beyond them. Yet on the gantry inside the silo at the back corner of the building there now stood the first stage of their rocket, looking like a thick-necked astronaut, glad to be free of his helmet yet a while.

The nose section lay beside the bench, waiting for its payload and guidance system.

Herman looked at the name, *Radio Luximbourg,* running down the two sections. His Tennessee friends probably misspelt it deliberately as an excuse for diverting it into Herman's hands. The first stage had come from Colorado, but both sections had been ordered through the same mujahideen unit in New York and everything had fitted together perfectly. Herman was looking forward to showing Sergey the finer points of their assembly work - where things might have gone wrong but had not. He glanced at the bench to check the wiring plans were still there. It would have been a catastrophe if he had burnt those – or even if he did not present them in their original folds, the way Sergey would expect.

Herman pushed a last bundle into the furnace and shut the door. Zaheed might be the boss but to Herman he was just a mountain man, always taking the long view, whereas Sergey - not even Muslim, and only Soviet-trained - could sit down and explain to Anton and Hans in simple English how an electro-magnetic pulse bomb worked and how it could-*would!* – paralyse every electronic device in Britain as long as their rocket was perfectly assembled. He'd let them handle a blob of melted black plastic and copper from a similar explosion in Dzhezkazgan. It had set a power plant on fire and melted wiring eight hundred kilometres away.

Herman knew this was the damage that had scared Kennedy and Khrushchev in 1962 into ending the Cuban missile crisis. It was still capable of inspiring two city boys to hold servo switches steady for freezing hours or fetch and carry gyroscopes or tools any hour of the day or night in the months it had taken to get the rocket ready for Sergey's inspection.

That would, Inshallah, happen tonight or tomorrow, Herman hoped, because there was still work for at least two engineers - wiring a warhead is not trivial.

He opened the firebox again and poked at the black ash of the papers with a long wrench. It was labelled *Property of the U.S.A.F.,* a souvenir of the First Battle of Fallujah. There he'd been, in Ranfield, the German NATO base, expertly fitting out bombers for the new Iraqi gig, when he learnt that the previous day's load had been dropped on the town his grandmother grew up in. Herman had suddenly changed his mind about signing on for another tour of duty.

By the start of the next month he was a pizza cook in Amsterdam at Boom Chicago, a theatre café catering to homesick American tourists. It had sounded like the next best thing to Detroit but did nothing for his figure and he got sick of the jokes, repeated show after show, as he pounded dough backstage. He found he no longer cared what happened in the midwest State elections as long as it didn't suit George Bush. Instead he relied on his laptop and Al Jazeera for news of the Iraq war and a nearly neutral view of the world.

Then a Moroccan waiter befriended him. A few dinners, a meeting or two at the mosque and he'd rediscovered his roots: his father's Polish side of the family might have given him engineering and ice-hockey but his mother's brothers had shown him the warmth of the Ummah. The prospect of an afternoon sitting on the floor discussing the Qur'an, in a third-floor walk-up apartment, now made the trip there on the Overtoom tram feel just like travelling through Michigan in back of the family Commodore, going to celebrate Eid with his marvellous cousins at Dearborn.

In Amsterdam Herman had found himself another hero in the young Mahomet. Reading His early struggles Herman saw He was just like a modern man, facing enormous, hostile forces with no other weapon but faith in Allah - and succeeding. The stories in the Qur'an brought this lost American assurance that a man living the right life could do something to make the world better. Nor would submission to Allah turn him into a robot or a eunuch – even in the U.S. Air Force Herman had never felt as much a man as he did with that group of friends, discussing how they could set the Middle East back into true Qur'anic order, and after that the world.

Tonight in Oud-Zuilen Herman leant on the boiler insulation to enjoy the meagre heat and remembered the sunny afternoon when the imam had called him out of the meeting onto the landing of the steep, dusty stairway. Stacks of mail for departed tenants had toppled over on the floor. The two of them stood at the window and watched a woman at the house behind, scrubbing her garden terrace. Then the sheik sat down on the windowsill in his white tunic, arms folded, and asked Herman if he would be interested in helping with a very important project that needed an engineer.

So Herman met Sergey and Zaheed, and then the four suitcase boys. Six months later and two of them were already out on the North Sea, headed for their mission to destroy the submarine base at Clydebank in Scotland, while Zaheed and Sergey were driving across Europe towards this miserable factory, bringing an EMP warhead for their rocket plus three suitcase- bombs for London, lacking only shrapnel.

Here the lucky rest of the party were, stuck in freezing Oud-Zuilen, with three-quarters of a rocket worth hundreds of millions of dollars and nothing to eat. Herman stood up, turning round to warm his hands on top of the boiler. What would it take to turn this into a pizza oven?

The two boys came clattering downstairs. "...like Californians! We'll only be doing recycling." said twenty-year-old Anton. Hans was coming carefully down the stairs behind him. His hair had been hacked off and he was holding two handfuls of black curls. "Open the fire door!" he told Herman.

"You'll make a terrible stink with that," said Herman.

So it proved to be. The boys were delighted.

Anton, who still had his woolly black mass of hair, turned Hans round by the shoulders to show Herman the bare patch behind one ear.

"Eeeh, you've balded me, Mum! I can't go to school like that!" Anton squealed.

"Aw, shut up!" Hans pushed him away. "Zaheed told me I should get rid of it. Remember? When he came to Pakistan to check up on us, at the Masada, he told the two of us, we always had to look different."

"You're different now, all right," said Herman.

Hans sped two rungs up the gantry steps, drew himself up beside the half rocket , glared from Herman to Anton, put one hand inside his shirt front, and turned himself into a moth-eaten Zaheed, Brummie accent and all:

"Remember, yoong lions of the jihad, yow will be carrying this bomb for the boy who stole your jacket, for the Oopen All Hours shopkeeper who follows yow right around the shop every time yow go in his door."

The accent was slipping but the intensity of his gaze had increased. *"Your bomb is for the schoolteacher who didn't even read your essay and for the plumber who would not give you an apprenticeship. Today you are about to avenge the boys of Bourda, those innocents whose masada Blair bombed, because Prince Charles was coming on a visit to Pakistan! When you detonate this bomb, remember them."*

He held up an imaginary mobile phone, drilled in six numbers and glared at his audience.

"You will be saving the lives of countless brothers in Baghdad and Basra and Teheran. Without your help the American devils will annihilate them unless we quickly do what must be done. America's ships, right now, have two thousand ballistic missiles all primed and trained on the Muslim world, but it is Blair who is the dog will give George Bush the courage to bring his finger to the button.

"Allah intended the fruits of the earth He created to be for the people of Islam to enjoy. He no longer

wants those riches wasted on godless infidels. Allah wants your people, in Palestine and Kandahar and Birmingham, to be great and happy and to inherit an earth as beautiful as the Paradise you saints will, at the moment of detonation, be already enjoying. Forever.

"Coom on, lads, gie it a go! Allahu akbar!"

"I'm going to tell Zaheed the shopkeepers in Oud-Zuilen are even worse than the ones at home," said Anton. "They call all of us Indonesians!"

"I know, I know," said Hans, descending to floor level,"It's bad enough to be called a Moroccan - that happens often enough - but *Indonesians*, and *Surinames?* Call themselves Muslim but they're practically savages: their shops stink of incense, and I've heard if they're sick they call in a witchdoctor." Hans's eyes were wide with indignation.

"They might do that in the old Dutch East Indies, but if you had a spare suitcase you wanted taken to London, any of them born in the Netherlands would be just the boys to help you out" said Herman. "Our friend Akhmed and his cousin, getting tossed about with their bombs in their stinking fishing boat right now, they'd tell you the same story: Akhmed was born here but he and Rashid knew neither of them was ever going to be allowed to be a Dutchman. You must have heard the way Pym Fortuyn talked about immigrants? And then Theo van Gogh and his Somali girlfriend started saying worse stuff."

"Yeah, her. She wears denim overalls and rides a bike!" says Anton.

"Aw, there's Muslim girls showing off plenty of denim in Michigan - I bet you two could even get to enjoy it. Nah, that Dutch business is all political. The Somali girl might have got away on her bike for the moment, but the Brothers have dealt to the two men! You know what? I reckon Zaheed looks quite a bit like that chap who shot van Gogh."

"Except for the beard," said Hans.

"Well, that's easy fixed," said Anton. "He could grow a beard. Dutchmen don't like Muslims with beards but the English don't care so much."

"Yeah. Mohammed Usuf is a national cricket hero in England. They don't mind his whiskers, or his religion, either, when he's after Viv Richard's batting record," said Hans

"Like Paresh, eh? He's never a 'dirty Sikh' when he's bowling!"

"Go find yourselves some work, you two," said Herman. "get those lead bags ready."

Sauntering back to their workbench, Hans said to Anton, "You know what? I reckon we should have brought back some of them suitcases from the madrasa at Chingai. Remember, we slept on two rows of them? Big tin jobs, painted a nice cream with brown bands and big padlocks? They'd hold a hundred times more dust than the little bags Zaheed is bringing us."

"You'd stick out a mile trying to take one of them bastards down a subway escalator!" Herman was still listening.

"I've been told to put my bag out near the entrance," said Anton. "My place has a big forecourt with taxis, and a monument and a row of columns along the front. There are a few smokers' tables outside where I'm going to park it. Zaheed says he wants a dirty big hole in the street and the front of the station blown off, for a picture on the cover of *The Sun*. I'll get my father to save us a few copies from the shop. There's going to be clouds of dust, like at 9/11, and they're going to whoosh all over the City."

"Those New York planes kicked out plenty of dust, all right, but yours are real dirty bombs – when you hit the trigger every single particle of their dust is gonna become radioactive!" said Herman. Energised by the memory of 9/11, he had the heavy spanner stabbing all around. "And when you push the button, both of youse, don't you forget to say: *'This one is for George Bush and his Daddy, from Herman, 'cos he can't get there to vote next week. May the election go badly!'* Go to it! Wrap those parcels."

Someone was thumping on the side door. Herman turned, open-mouthed and white-faced, like a sideshow clown. Hans stepped behind Anton and ran a hand over his stubbled hair. Herman gestured to the boys to stand in front of their work bench to hide the rocket cone. He quietly put the monkey wrench on a ledge beside the door and turned the key in the lock as the knocking came again.

It was a postman in an orange fluoro vest. He was holding out a brown paper parcel. "Ishmael Hassan?"

"No one here of that name," said Herman.

"It's me," said Anton, pushing Herman out of the doorway.

"Sign here," said the postman, superior, officious and hurried.

Anton signed. The postman thrust the parcel at him, snatched his clipboard back and left on his bicycle, orange panniers bouncing down the drive.

Herman locked the door and Hans raced for the window. "He's gone."

"It's from my mother," said Anton.

"With Arabic writing on it! Zaheed will kill you!"

"That bit's only, '*Do not put in washing machine*'. I hate how she writes on the outsides of parcels."

"And look, she's told them she lives in Tottenham - you should never have given her your address."

"I didn't." Anton shook the package in front of Herman and pointed, "Look, she's just put *Sausage Factory, Old Village, The Netherlands.*"

Then he tore the paper off and held up a black, hand-knitted jersey, patterned all over with ropes.

Chapter 5

Hamburg to Friesland,
The Netherlands, 24 October 2006

At six the next morning Zaheed was waiting for the truck, as arranged, on the corner of Rathaus Strasse. He got the key from Sergey to put his bag in the locker behind the cabin, then climbed into the cab and passed the key back without acknowledging Dennis sitting between them. Zaheed was obviously still haughty with him. The weather was worsening and Sergey had turned the heat up to keep the windows clear. Dennis was trying to get out of his sheepskin jacket.

"Sorry about this," he said as he elbowed Zaheed at the end of manoeuvres.

"You say 'Sorry' too often!"

"Want a cigarette?" Sergey stretched an arm across Dennis to offer Zaheed a packet.

"I lost my cigarette lighter in that bar yesterday, thanks to your Kiwi savage."

"Why don't you use this?" asked Dennis the Irrepressible, pointing to the lighter on the dashboard.

"It had my name on it!" said Zaheed,

"Sentimental value, eh?"

"It was my new name. *Frits Breijer.* I only wanted to be ready to show it in an emergency." He lit up with Sergey's lighter and puffed out angry spurts of smoke.

"You trying to get the girls to think you're Dutch by giving yourself a Dutch name?"

"No!" they both replied.

"Anyway, it's stupid. I've never seen a Dutchman with little red whiskers like that. You look more like an 'Angus'. And you can't call yourself *'Frits'* with a nose like yours! The girls'd die laughing."

"He did it for business reasons," said Sergey, "Just for business. You might as well know I have also changed my name - to 'Piet ten Broeke'."

"Haugh!" said Dennis. "This trip is turning into a Russian novel. I know your father's name wasn't 'ten Broeke' or anything like it. I think you took a wrong turn somewhere this morning, Young Serge!"

"Do not call me that," said Sergey.

The atmosphere in the cab became frosty again but Dennis was distracted by the truck smoothly accelerating as it entered the autobahn for Bremen. He was as elated as a child with the speed of the traffic. "We should get to Holland before lunch at this rate. How far is it to Amsterdam?"

"I'm not taking this truck into Amsterdam," said Sergey, glancing at his cousin but keeping his face firm. "It's too big for me to handle in the city and I am not licensed to carry boats, or even to enter the dock area. I'll take you to Leeuwarden – it's a port for pleasure boats."

"Shit! Leverton? How far is that from Amsterdam?"

"Only fifty-five kilometres. It will be no trouble for you if, as you would put it, you have a full tank of gas," said Zaheed very sternly. "It will be easy for you to go from there to Amsterdam by water. It's practically a lake."

"Hell. You might have told me – I'm in my good clothes."

Zaheed looked pleased but still scornful.

"We must find a place to launch your boat," said Sergey.

"No worries! It's got a winch built in and you've got the tray, and those loose rollers will do for a ramp. You find me any post out in the water and I'll swim out and fix the cable to it. Piece of cake, man! It has a draught of only fifteen centimetres, you know."

"Nice day for a swim," said Zaheed, cheering up one degree as he watched the windscreen wipers fight the rain.

"Yeah. I've been thinking I might not take it back to New Zealand after all. The ship I'm putting her on calls into a base in Malaysia to swap cargo with its sister ships. A boat like this really needs the tropical waters where it can work all day, every day of the year, even at night - stay awake like fish do on a coral reef. Nice resort in Thailand, Club Med - plenty of people there willing to pay fifty dollars a ride. I'll soon have it paid off and then I'll be back here to buy a bigger one." Dennis beamed.

The other men said nothing.

They saw 'Ausfahrt 55, Bremen-Hemelingen.' Dennis got a lot of laughs out of that; He specialised in

Australian jokes. They struck right through Bremen and followed the A28. Zaheed was enjoying the GPS.

"Yes. We want him to get plenty of practice," said Sergey, smiling.

"GPS is a New Zealand invention, you know: Navman. Made to let the TV viewers see the Americas' Cup yacht races, being sailed way outside Auckland Harbour," said Dennis.

"Oh, it was, was it? That's not the name on this one."

"No, it is, though! The joker sold out for millions of dollars. Made with a piece of number eight wire originally."

"Marvellous!" said Zaheed, looking out the side window.

As they got into the Netherlands' flat, dairying country, the scenery was improving to Dennis's eyes. "Looks like Te Awamutu except for the windmills. Bet this is valuable land?"

"Every Dutch farmer is a millionaire these days. The EU has a machine that turns cowshit into gold," said Sergey.

They passed through Groningen, staying on the A7, and passed Leek.

"Sounds like a good idea to me," said Dennis.

"We'll stop at Drachten," said Zaheed, studying the GPS for a truck stop.

"*That's roight, let's have a noice cup of tea.* You two remind me of Wallace and Gromit going to the moon. Wallace has the big ideas but Gromit doesn't say anything much – he doesn't even have a mouth. That'd be you, Serge."

Nobody spoke till at last they pulled into a car park with a café like a space station. There was a whole shop for chocolates. They had a lunch of bread and sausage and coffee. Dennis also picked out a huge éclair. Sergey took a phone call and left them.

"This is the biggest cream puff I've ever seen," Dennis said and did not look disappointed as he ate it.

Afterwards, wiping his mouth as Zaheed lit a cigarette, Dennis asked, "What business are you two in, anyway?"

"We have a sausage factory."

"Must be in quite a big way to fill a truck that size?"

"Yes. What is your business in New Zealand?" asked Zaheed, eyes narrowed against his own smoke.

"I'm in Pest Control with Auckland City Council. I catch rats."

"Ah! The Pied Piper, eh?" said Sergey, returning. "Nice uniform?"

"Not bad. Not very colourful, because these days we spend most of our time crawling around basements and poking baits into sewers – though in my job you're more likely to get gassed by methane than die of a rat bite. But rats are tough, you know. I reckon rats are going to inherit the earth when we've finished with it."

"Very interesting. Let's go." Zaheed stubbed out his cigarette. "We must get rid of you and your boat and get back to work at Utrecht today."

"I need to be in London on Wednesday," Sergey told Zaheed, squeezing after him into the revolving door so they could talk privately.

"Impossible!" said Zaheed.

"Compulsory. Go round again," said Sergey. "Remember, the boss acted instantly to save us when I told him the girl had found the Bernardin signature. It was with the crucial page of the Baghdad documents, the bit about the optimal altitude for detonation and she'd taken that. We owe him."

"Look!" said Zaheed as the door again delivered them to the carpark.

Dennis had got ahead of them among the cars, pursuing two Dutch girls. Serge and Zaheed had to run to catch him up.

"Remember what the Professor used to say: "*Without torture, no science,*" Sergey said to Zaheed, as he grabbed his cousin,

Sergey steered Dennis away to the truck.

"Hell, you jokers, that was my best chance since Bangkok! The tall one has legs like Natasha. We could have sat in the boat..."

"Good idea," said Zaheed.

They decided to try for a nice quiet beach near Lemmer. Sergey promised Zaheed that at worst they would set his cousin and the boat down on the side of the road since in winter there would be any number of boat transporters available to help him. They expected to see plenty of yachts bobbing in the estuary on the Ijsselmeer, or anchored in Lemmer's marinas.

And there they all were! Dennis couldn't sit still for admiring boats as they went through the port area and turned west.

"We must find a place very close to the sea and far from farmhouses," said Zaheed, tinkering with the GPS. "Go on this road about four kilometres until it changes its name into Sudergoawei. On the left there will be a road called Sminkewel that leads to a village called Oudenmirdum. Go straight through and turn right. There's a road called Huningspaed runs down to the sea. We go past a hospice for the dying and then it looks as though there is a place at the corner where we could turn the truck."

"We're going miles away from the sea," Dennis whined.

"You've cost us hours of lost time. Don't think we'll keep you and your boat any longer than we must," said Zaheed.

Everything lay just as the American woman in the GPS predicted. Huningspaed, running to the sea, was little more than a farm road but it was paved - obviously the fields on either side had been ploughed and harvested by fair-sized machinery – and there was the hospice.

At the corner where the road turned right to run along parallel to the Ijsselmeer Sergey, cursing in Russian and Dutch, turned the truck into short bushes, then backed the trailer towards the beach. A dyke with a low bank ran beside the road above the narrow muddy shore. The rain quietly continued.

"The tide is coming in," Dennis announced, judging by the way the few anchored boats were behaving.

"Funny. The Ijsselmeer doesn't usually have tides."

Dennis never wasted his strength on being embarrassed - it only lowered your work rate. "Put down the tray and we'll set the rollers as far out as we can. We'll push the cradle onto the bank and then shift the rollers down the bank to the water."

Zaheed ran to unlock the back doors while Sergey kept a lookout for traffic, since they were blocking the road. Dennis was inside the trailer - giving instructions, unlocking the wheels of the cradle and getting ready to push his baby into the water for the first time.

"Chocks away! Get up on the rollers, Zaheed, and steady her as she comes. Where's bloody Serge?"

Sergey came to help slow the descent. The wheels were small but well-oiled and the beautiful blue hydrofoil was soon on Netherlands soil. That had Dennis hooting and summoning all help to shift the rollers. Zaheed swore as he slipped off the bank into the mud.

A man emerged from the cabin of a moored launch. In spite of the rain he stood and shouted encouragement and advice in Dutch, and took a photo of the hydrofoil. Sergey and Zaheed pushed the boat out with superhuman strength, then went back to load the rollers on the truck. The cradle they left on the beach.

This set the man on the boat going again but once Dennis had started the motor his cousin hardly paused to wave. By then several cars were banked up behind them, but not tooting - everyone at Lemmer must be a boatie and this boat was not a Looker in name only. Zaheed reported the boat was cautiously nosing out into deep water as Sergey swung at the wheel to let the queue go. Before he was back on the road Dennis had the hydrofoil rearing up and starting to plane.

"We may have just helped him commit suicide," said Zaheed, looking in the side mirror in case he could see the boat, "but he's happy. Lucky bastard. Has he got any charts?"

"No!" Sergey admitted. "He has some sort of GPS though. I suppose we could at least have told him to get over to the other shore and keep right but I expect him to get stuck on the mud. You're going to be at Rockanje and I'll be in London before he gets free. We'll be fine. Nobody will know our names, but we'll be famous and we'll be rich! You can buy yourself ten glass-bottomed boats then. I think they'd go very well in Dubai!"

"Inshallah," said Zaheed, peering through the rain.

Chapter 6

Assembly,
Oud-Zuilen, the Netherlands, 24 October 2006

A few hours later Herman was delighted to hear the truck rumble to a stop outside the sausage factory, and Anton and Hans rushed to open the doors. Even Sergey and Zaheed were smiling.

Two tourists on their way to the castle on the highly recommended meadow path, now draggled with light snow, had to hurry to get out of the way as the truck reversed into the factory. The boys shut the doors as soon as the cab had edged inside.

Herman squeezed past the rocket on the gantry stair to peep through an unpainted part of the window, checking the tourists had gone - sometimes in the summer strangers, noticing the faded signs, had knocked at the door of the old building asking to buy a traditional village sausage.

"They're gone! You two can sleep in the loft. There's coffee and a bit of soup in the kitchen we've been saving. Hans will get it for you." said Herman.

"No babaganoush?" asked Sergey.

Anton and Herman fitted blackout screens to the windows and they all stood around with mugs of soup. They were safely together at last with all the gear to finish assembling their world-shaking rocket.

Herman was anxious to see the warhead. He always tried to hide his feelings about Russian technology, but he asked,

"You had any trouble getting the GPS? Is it American or European?"

"I'm told it originally came from New Zealand," said Zaheed, scornful of his junior engineer's American pride. He felt quite confident as they prepared to open the warhead crate. He had seen the paperwork and knew some of the excellent physicists and technicians who'd checked it over after it came safely through the rocket attack on that remote Sudan camel-pill factory while it was being stored there, at Al-Shifa. He wholeheartedly believed that, Allah Himself had intervened to protect this bomb from the American devils because He had already given it a most important destiny.

This whole mission had therefore kept Zaheed in an uplifted mood for two years. Despite unfitting difficulties, like the boorish behaviour of Sergey's cousin on their journey from Russia, through Germany, to the Netherlands, he knew that three days from now Allah was going to use this innocent but well-travelled silver ball to change the whole political balance of the world in favour of His people, the Unconsidered.

It took all four men to bring the box down from the truck. Herman put on long gloves and a lead apron.

"It's not very shiny," said Hans, on tiptoe as the lid and inner lead wrapping were opened.

"It's like a little kid's football," said Herman. "Just needs two white stripes round the ends!"

"Looks like an Easter egg to me," said Sergey.

"Let no one touch it, or the bricks around it," said Zaheed. "What you see is just the beryllium casing designed to hold in the two explosions long enough for fission and then fusion to occur. It's made to kill, and will paralyse electronics for hundreds of kilometres around the explosion site. It cost more than a Fabergé egg. Close the box."

"The only thing I'm worried about is how the GPS will get on, trying to talk to it in English," Herman lied.

For the benefit of the two boys Sergey said, "That's nothing - you know they both use electronic language. The thing I live to see is whether your Boeing second-stage rocket will properly respond to the GPS commands to control the attitude of the package – after all your good work , we don't want it suddenly heading for Denmark."

"Don't you worry about any of the gear from AeroThrust," said Herman. "My friends got us only the best. Apart from what you can see on the outside, like the 'mistakes' on the signage for 'Radio Luximbourg', inside they fit together exactly, although they came from different States. My Air Force buddies don't make mistakes when they're warehousing. They knew they were helping with something big."

Zaheed handed his mug to Anton. "They were right. This jihad is going to be bigger than the Twin Towers. It also cost more. We are a very small, quality cell, but behind us we have huge support. You were each carefully chosen to make this whole project work together, all six bombs. The effect on Britain is going to be bigger than Hiroshima. And what a pity the United Nations can't see us at work! Isn't it sad they and the BBC are going to be put out of business by such a magnificent piece of multinational cooperation? We'll be making all their dreams come true, but too fast for them to enjoy it."

"Let's take the crate over to the workbench," said Herman.

"When do we get to see our suitcases?" asked Anton, stretching before he bent to the task of helping to lift the crate.

"Wash, get fresh overalls on and we'll say salat first," said Zaheed.

When they came back they wore prayer caps as well as white overalls. There wasn't much floor space now the truck had arrived, but they each found room to spread a plastic bag to kneel on. Herman had his velvet prayer mat. Sergey, in black leather jacket and cap, slipped out the door for his own quiet moment over a cigarette.

"Swartz Piet, going off to give Sinter Klaas a hand?" whispered Hans to Anton, who giggled as the door shut on their second-in-command.

Zaheed called them to order, facing the rocket that happened to stand in the corner nearest Mecca. He gave the salutation and recited a passage from the Qur'an - in English for the sake of Herman, a recent revert with minimal Arabic.

"Praise be to Allah, Who has sent His servants the Book and allowed them no Crookedness. He hath made it Straight and Clear in order that he may warn the godless of a terrible Punishment from Him and that he may give Glad Tidings to the Believers who work righteous deeds, that they shall have a goodly Reward."

He then began a gentle, encouraging sermon, praising their faith and diligence in the spirit of Mahomet's command to seek wisdom and work to the limit of their powers. He promised a glorious success for their project.

"You will bring food to the starving and shelter to two million of our brothers and sisters, still homeless after the earthquake in Pakistan last year. These poor wretches, some of those you saw sitting in rock shelters last summer, think they have been forgotten by the world, but in a few days you are going to bring them joy. Then they will see Allah smite their enemy in the heart of his evil empire! Their ungodly oppressors will die in their sinful pleasures, in their mansions and limousines, drunk and dancing with filthy women. And as they are destroyed, their atomised bodies will be spread all over the city of London by your explosions. Allah will irradiate their bodies, use their particles to cleanse the whole earth and give it another holy beginning!

"The widows and orphans of Afghanistan and Iraq will bless you as you enter Paradise, and young men of Islam will rise in thousands in every country to take up the work you have begun. The world will know from you and from your example that Allah commands science and Islam transcends nationality, as Mohammed has always taught. Peace be to you."

"Allahu akbar!" they responded. They knelt and bowed three times and went on with the regular salat prayers, each man in direct communication with Allah.

They ended with their own petitions, and finally held cupped hands close to their hearts to receive Allah's mercy and benefits. Then one at a time Zaheed called each man, kissed him on both cheeks, blessed him, and gave him a small bag of gold coins and three mobile telephones out of a box at his feet. "A farewell present from Akhmed and Rashid. May Allah bless their work and yours."

Sergey came back and Zaheed gave him some phones also. These had come from a brave ram raid on a shop in Einkhoven before Akhmed and Rashid left for Scotland, but the gold had been sent to the brethren as zakat by the faithful of many countries, a token of sharing in this jihad. Sergey was not of the ummah and had his own ample support but Zaheed treated him as his absolute equal in every other respect. He briefly put a brotherly arm around Sergey's shoulder.

"Now," Sergey said. "Anton and Hans, bring me the carton at the back of the trailer. Be careful with it. Those bags are heavy and dangerous."

When the box was cut open and the lead lining freed, the tops of the cases could be seen.

"A business satchel! I'm not going to carry a thing like that!" said Hans.

"They might look a bit old-fashioned but they're ready to go, dambusters," said Sergey. "We blew two of them up at Leningrad, as a test before we paid for them. They're only radioactive when the different isotopes combine, once the dumbbells are burst by the initial explosion - but they will burst, I can tell you. At Leningrad we used just a couple of charges out of the middle section and we blew up an old stone building ten times bigger than this. Remember, though, in the real thing every atom of the debris also becomes radioactive. It is an enormously powerful weapon for its size."

"We had a friend working at Arzamas-16, the nuclear decommissioning lab," Zaheed told them. "He retrieved them and checked them out for us. Never mind what they look like, you'll just have to try to live up to them – buy yourself a suit."

"Aw-ah!" said Hans and Anton.

"And some decent shoes," Zaheed added. "You've got an excellent device here, they cost millions of euros and they're absolutely foolproof." He looked down, severe but doubtful, at each boy, as if they were his own chicks about to leave the nest and launch out forever from a mountain eyrie.

Chapter 7

On The Zuider Zee,
The Netherlands, 24 October 2006

That afternoon almost at sea level, or not much below it, Dennis had fallen properly in love with his boat. It happened the first moment he felt it floating in a few centimetres of water, while he was jumping onto the prow and still had Zaheed and Sergey at the back, doing their damnedest to push it out.

His cousin must have been impressed with the boat. Good job Zaheed landed in the mud, though. Serve the grumpy bugger right. Last Dennis saw of them, the truck simply hauled itself out of the bushes at the turn and went back the way they had come, followed by an escort of cars and station wagons.

The man in the anchored launch seemed to have changed his attitude, pointing angrily and repeatedly at the cradle left on the beach.

"Too bad, mate. It's all yours now!" Dennis yelled back at the agitated boatie.

It was a good low cradle and Dennis would have liked to keep it but the boys had absolutely refused to take him into Amsterdam to the docks. Ah well, what you save on train freight you have to spend on a new cradle. That's life!

Sergey sure had some funny ideas: the detours he took over those terrible country roads near the Russian border, for instance. It's lucky the boat wasn't damaged, but now at twenty knots the Looker 30 was planing beautifully through the misty rain. The lake was not too rough, but Dennis could feel waves. He headed out into the middle of the bay, happy to dredge up remnants of an old song about being "on the Zuider Zee, Zuider Zee", knowing he was in the newest and most beautiful boat in the world.

He peered down at the main screen below but saw no fish. He did a circle to test the steering and caught the beam of a lighthouse through the mist, a little to the north of where he had started. With plenty of gas in the tank he decided to test the motor by going out to see the main seawall, Afsluitdijk. It must be enormous to have held back the North Sea since 1932 and make this lake, bigger than Lake Taupo. Men with shovels and dredges did the work instead of a volcano but Lake Taupo ended up a lot deeper - much better for fish. No trout to be seen here.

After half an hour of bucking against the wind at forty knots he could see car headlights through the mist, high up on the dyke. It had at least a four-lane highway on top of it. When the great curved wall of stone loomed up ahead he turned south pretty sharp, to the sound of horns saluting. Dennis could only return the compliment by popping the cockpit cover and standing up to wave, but soon pulled it down again because it was mighty cold and wet outside. After that he motored south till he saw his first lighthouse again and then found another one almost straight ahead, glimmering a caution at him. The first one must be Oosterdijk lighthouse with Enkuizen behind it sticking out into the bay. Another good miss!

He began to pay more attention to the GPS. The American voice (but not a woman like the one in Sergey's truck) wanted him to keep to port and pass through a lock in another dyke just south of Enkhuizen. Dennis hoped there wouldn't be a fee since he had only forty euros and a few hundred roubles in cash. The remainder of his money was in traveller's cheques. Perhaps they took plastic?

No bother. A man in a high control tower like a space capsule shouted at him in Dutch through the loudspeaker but didn't stop him. How could he? He didn't seem to be saying anything complimentary about the boat, however, which was disappointing. As Dennis's side of the lock came up he could see he was floating over a highway sunk into a grassy parkland full of water birds. Classy work! You could shoot ducks while you were waiting for the other lock to open. Retrieval would be a problem, though. You wouldn't want a wet dog aboard a boat like this. A bit high for him to jump, too.

Once back in open water Dennis noticed it was getting windier and darker. At four-thirty a large yacht surprised him, cutting in front only metres away. There had been very few other boats until now and none close. Dennis began to wonder if he should be trying to make Amsterdam in the dark. He heard a foghorn. It was coming closer. Still peering all about, he caught a ghostly apparition up ahead. A giant horse was hooting at him, with a light radiating out from its head! The GPS said he was due for Marken Island: so this must be the Paard van Marken, looking more like a draught horse than a leopard.

There was also a torch waving from the shore. Might be someone in trouble.

Dennis eased the speed down and pulled in as close as he could, idling the engine. "Hello, do you need help?" he called, raising the canopy.

"Welcome," shouted the man. "I heard you were coming. Come to the jetty," and he marched off, waving his torch towards a mooring.

Dennis was surprised he was expected - must be some mate of Sergey. Now it was so late Dennis felt like doing as the man directed and turned the engine power up again, increasing the revs just a little as he circled back, to show what the boat could do. He cruised alongside the jetty and the man came looking for a rope to secure the boat to the posts.

"Sorry, it's too new. I haven't got any lines yet." Dennis shrugged, his hands out.

The man with the torch, a big fellow in white overalls, looked pretty genial - quite like a Kiwi, in fact. He said, "Come. I have a boathouse." This was accompanied by more torch-waving into the darkness, great horizontal gestures indicating a big curve to port. When Dennis didn't look too hostile he offered to come aboard. Dennis opened the port hatch at the back and the man clambered in.

"Zeer luxe!" said the visitor, looking impressed. He turned off his torch and sat down beside the controls. Pointing at the GPS, he showed Dennis a spot round the narrow north end of the island on the sheltered side, where he was apparently very keen to take his visitor.

Ah well, in for a penny, in for a pound, and here's hoping, thought Dennis, but he said, "Right you are, then," and revved the motor. They went cautiously around the point and cruised along, Dennis watching the depth finder and the visitor leaning over and peering into the murk below the perspex bottom.

Until he sprang up and said, "Over here!" and indicated a sharp turn to port. A boatshed rushed out to meet them, and just in time Dennis reversed power. The man let himself out the back hatch and jumped down into the water. He waded ahead of the boat and opened the doors of the shed. The water came up to his waist. Dennis hoped he wasn't doing a knees-bend to trick him and then attempt to steal the boat.

I'll drown the bloody pirate if he tries that on! he vowed, but eased the Looker 30 into what he thought, when the lights came on, was probably the best berth she would ever enjoy. Well, it was their honeymoon night after all. He remembered an old Dally saying about honeymoons: *One month white bread, then...*

Dennis closed down the engine and all the electrical gear. He picked up his satchel and paused a moment, looking at every delightful feature of his boat. They'd had a great first day anyway.

"Welcome to the Island of Marken," said the smiling man with the dripping trousers.

"You a friend of Serge Mikulitsin?"

"Nee. The Water Politie told me to look for a whale and I have caught it!" With internationally recognised gestures he said, "Come, we will have a drink."

Dennis was willing. They trudged up to the lighthouse and entered a door situated between the legs of the ghost horse. Inside was a comfortable kitchen with a woman about to serve dinner. There was a beautiful young girl also.

"My wife, Johanna, and my daughter, Anneke. This is the man on the radio."

"Hello. I'm Dennis Bogdanovich." He offered his hand to all three.

"Ah, yes, I am Frans. I am the lighthouse keeper. My daughter speaks English good. I will get dry clothes."

"So you have a whale on a trailer, Mr Bogdanovich?" said Anneke.

She looked about fifteen, with dimples just like his own daughter, fourteen-year-old Aimee. He hadn't thought of her since the night he showed his family photos at St Petersburg but he remembered she was learning Chinese because her teacher said that in five years everyone would have to speak it. In the meantime Dennis was grateful for this girl's accomplishment. He asked her, "Who told you that?"

"My father heard it on the Water Politie radio."

"Who told them?"

Johanna, the hostess, ushered Dennis to a table with several dishes steaming along it. He was distracted by the delicious, spicy smell of meat but he had to know, "What are they saying about me?"

Frans came back with a high-shouldered black bottle in his fist. "They say you put your boat in at an illegal spot, you left the trailer on the shore and you went in front to a yacht, that is all." He did not seem at all shocked.

"Do they know about me being here?"

"Nee. Have some Bols Genever."

Dennis thought he would have some of whatever it was while the offer was open. "Thank you."

Frans proposed a Dutch toast, which Anneke repeated in English, in her father's fervent tone, "To the freedom of the seas!"

"Amen to that," said Dennis, and the men drank.

Johanna encouraged Dennis to serve himself with stew. Frans passed the potatoes. It was hard to worry at that moment about anything.

Chapter 8

Marken and Amsterdam,
26 October to 1 November 2006

In the morning Dennis woke in the dark, quite refreshed, and was surprised to see it was already half-past eight. Maybe he had crossed a time zone yesterday in crossing the Ijsselmeer? He found a shower, shaved and put the same clothes on again, resolving to buy fresh ones when he next saw a shop.

Johanna brought him coffee and a bread roll, and by then it was getting light. He looked up and down the coast. Amsterdam was not so far from here. There were houses on the far eastern shore and some marinas. The mist was gone, but a fair wind was blowing and a row of chilled ducks sat hunched at the water's edge.

Dennis tried to remember what he and Frans had last night settled on as today's best course of action. It was all a bit of a blur, what with occasional language difficulties and starting on the second bottle of gin. That stuff must be thirty proof. He pulled on his sheepskin jacket and went to see Frans in the lighthouse, hoping to check his email and also hear the local police news about him and his boat.

Frans was busy on the phone when he arrived but gestured consent for Dennis to check his inbox. No word from the office about the Remuera Stormwater Separation contract. He almost regretted not bringing his cell phone but you wouldn't want to get a call about sewerage when you were busy in Bangkok. Or from your wife, complaining about her kitchen drains. Or the mortgage. Luckily, she never bothered with the computer.

There was a message from Bill Sellars: *You might think you're a Looker First Class but you're way more than 30. The boat's fat enough - call it 'The Bloated Pig'.*

Bloody Sellars would say that sort of stuff about the boat. Maybe he could get her name changed before he put her in the container.

When Frans was free Dennis asked him for a few more minutes on the internet to see what hits he'd had on his blog from St Petersburg with photos of his boat. Frans gave cautious assent and watched as Dennis logged into the forum, hoping for replies admitting '*Nothing like that on the Waitemata.*' There were twenty posts. Most were very complimentary, especially about the hull shape and the viewing screen. Squab advised him to photograph his next catch through it.

But Bush Pig also objected to the name on the grounds that Dennis was "*a Looker, right enough, but hadn't been thirty for nearly that long again.*

He was just copying Bill Sellars. *He can talk!* thought Dennis. Jealousy is the desired response to most fishing blogs, but this really rankled.

Skotty said, "*Congratulations. Call your wife or your lawyer.*"

Dennis's blood ran cold. Diane had found out about the mortgage and wouldn't sign.

Or she might want a divorce - or had frozen the bank account. He could lose the boat.

He closed the Forum site and thanked Frans. He should have checked his work site but wasn't in the mood. He had to think how to deal with Diane.

"See all this news about you and your boat in my logbook?" said Frans. He translated many entries from the Water Politie concerning their search for his curious boat. They were calling it "The Whale". Frans sounded serious and amused by turns as he recited Dennis's Politie record, mostly maritime parking and speeding offences. Then he took Dennis over to the window and pointed out something significant in the distance – no doubt the docks where his ship would be waiting in two days' time. Next they went to a large map of Amsterdam on the back wall.

"Looks like half an onion," said Dennis.

Frans looked offended on behalf of Amsterdam's canals, though the docks definitely resembled roots of the onion, trending mostly to the Noordzee Kanaal. Frans showed him where his boat would be lifted onto the quay.

"What about the trailer?" said Dennis. "Could you get the Oudenmirdum Politie to deliver it to Amsterdam?" Dennis described an arc, way left from Leeuwarden, up and over to the city on the right.

"Very unlikely," Frans said, but he had a more cunning plan that took him to the telephone and kept him there, chortling and cajoling in Dutch for several minutes. In the middle there was a long pause before he told Dennis, "My friend says you must go to a different wharf." Then more Dutch.

"One thousand kroner?" Frans asked Dennis, stabbing one forefinger at a point on the map very close to the target dock. "My friend says he can do it. For 1,000 kroner, to the dock in Amsterdam. On Wednesday your boat is on a new trailer, inside a container. Then it must go by rail to your ship, the *Estelle Maersk*, at their base in Rotterdam."

"Ja, ja! Done! OK!" said Dennis.

Frans went back to the phone and concluded the deal. Hanging up, he said, "My friend, his daughter: she lives in New Zealand. Hamilton!"

"Hamilton, eh?" and the two men had a good laugh, each wondering if the other was laughing at the same thing.

"Do you know anyone who could change the name on my boat?" Dennis asked Frans. "Are there any panel beaters on Marken who put can pictures on business vehicles?"

"You want television in your boat?"

"No, I want to take off the factory name - cover the place with a sticky plastic cut-out and put a new name on it."

"I think I know someone. What name will you give it?"

"I think '*Godwit*'."

"You are religious?"

"Nah! It's just these Russian birds that fly to New Zealand every September to eat mud crabs. Thousands of them come down. By the end of March they're so fat they feel sexy. So up they get and fly back - seven days non-stop to Siberia to breed. And they go on that way, backwards and forwards, every six months."

"Good story your grandmother told you, but that is many thousands of kilometres."

"No further than I've come, or the boat is going."

By the next day Dennis had been in touch with the shipping agent and confirmed in English arrangements for getting the boat onto the trailer, into the container and on board the *Estelle Maersk* at Rotterdam. Johanna said he was welcome to stay on a few more days and took him to buy new clothes from the Marken village shops: a bargain teeshirt wishing everyone a Merry Christmas 2005 and souvenir Dutch underwear. Dennis was vain enough to believe his personal charm did not depend on fine feathers.

He refuelled the *Godwit* from Frans' tank, added some ropes, and cashed in traveller's cheques to pay for the new trailer and the container charges.

He still couldn't decide what to do about phoning Diane. He'd be home in a few days. Better to deal with her face to face. Show her the boat, or the pictures of it, and that would calm her down.

Frans's friend came to the boatshed that afternoon, removed the offensive logo, and cut and polished the bow section to a perfect finish. The next day he returned with the *Godwit* decal. Dennis was very pleased to report the new name to Skotty, Moderator and Registrar of the Fish Club Forum. He didn't mention Diane. Bloody embarrassing to discuss her with Skotty. And all the boys will have read that she and the lawyer were after him. He'd phone the lawyer as soon as he got to Amsterdam and had boat on board the ship.

On Wednesday Dennis took a grateful farewell of Frans and his family. "If ever you come to New Zealand…" he said with deep feeling.

Amazing, he thought as he stowed his bag and looked over the controls, *that Frans should decide in the dark to do all that for someone he didn't know from a lump of coal.* He backed out of the boatshed into rain again for the run to the docks. *Mind you, it is a pretty flash boat.*

The work of changing the name was undetectable. Frans's mate had done as good a job as anyone could, back home in the Viaduct Basin. Good old Frans, he did seem to appreciate having had the *Godwit* in his shed, even for a couple of nights. He and Johanna came out of the boatshed to wave him off.

As he rounded the point of the island of Marken he came abreast of the lighthouse again and gunned the motor to make the boat plane higher, in a salute to Frans, back in his office, standing at the window.

There was more traffic on the lake today. He overtook a tug with a chain of barges and then had to pull in behind two yachts sailing together. Craft coming in from the sea kept to their port side – Frans had said those buoys were red because fishermen coming home always had blood on their hands. Nice touch. There were no more manicured strips of farmland here but only continuous marinas to starboard and wharves to port. One of the yachts gave way and Dennis pulled ahead.

He was now gaining fast on a large vessel whose decks were stacked with containers. Crewmen leaning on the rail came to attention and he sped up. Still grinning at their excitement, Dennis saw an oncoming launch with radio masts like a Waikato power pylon. From Frans's office charts he recognised the markings of the Water Politie.

With the instinct of a rat he turned sharply to port and entered the sluice gate of Amsterdam's canal system. The water was gushing out and the *Godwit* bucked horribly between the gates, close and high on either side. He got clear and saw in front the narrow point where the road under the Ijsselmeer emerged from its tunnel onto a ramp. He again chose to go to port and picked up speed.

He looked back and could see the Water Politie were foiled at the sluice gate by their launch's mast. They couldn't follow him but Dennis knew they would radio news of his arrival to the rest of the boys in blue. Did all police wear blue in Holland?

As he travelled up the narrow canal cyclists on the road alongside were cheering and trying to keep up. Cars on bridges tooted. He realised he must slow down to five knots because his wash was rocking houseboats and there would be other canal boats ahead. Spilling a pot of coffee might be added to his charge sheet.

The sixth bridge, where the canal met a river, was a traditional Dutch bridge with high arms like a pergola to lift the roadway for taller boats to pass. Here Dennis had to ease over to allow a little motorboat pass by into the river, towing a waterlogged green sofa. What a great place this would be to have a glass-bottomed boat. You'd never know what you might see next He'd been wasting business opportunities, Garbage men would love it.

Dennis went to starboard for a change, towards a flash stone bridge with gargoyles and three arches. On the railings there were lanterns with crowns on top, held up by pillars like church candelabras. A tram rattled across the bridge while he passed underneath it. Then he heard faint sounds of police sirens on both sides of the city as he rounded a bend and drew level with a flower market. Here the river had many pleasure craft. He could hear the tourists chattering, and a rowboat ahead had a family in it, paddling and squabbling.

"Come on, Daisy. You're just being lazy. Put your back into it, girl!"

"Pull into the hotel, Daniel, and I'll dash up and get the camera."

"You gotta hurry, Mum - we've only got twenty minutes left!"

It was the Hotel de L'Europe. *At last a sign in English*, thought Dennis.

The rowboat pulled in beside the hotel terrace and the grandmother sprang out of the boat, clambered up three steps and opened the terrace door. Two coffee drinkers looked on in amazement.

Loud, multiple klaxons were coming down the side street towards them. Dennis was out of the boat with his satchel in his hand. He slung a rope over the terrace rail behind the rowboat, tied the world's fastest bowline and dashed into the dining room after the woman. To avoid the maitre d' he headed towards the reception desk as if to book in, but then saw blue uniforms in bulk outside the main entrance. He flung himself into the still open lift holding the old woman from the rowboat. He made it just before the doors shut. They ascended to temporary safety.

"Gidday," was all he could manage.

"Australian, are you?" the woman asked. "Don't you just love this seat?" patting the red velvet cushion beside her. "I think it's the best thing about this hotel – lovely when you've been shopping. I went off for a ride in a rowboat and forgot my camera but if I'm not back quick enough it's going to cost us another ten dollars on the hire," she confided, like a chatty old woman on the bus to Onehunga.

"If I don't get lucky I'm going to lose my boat altogether," said Dennis, getting out of the lift after the woman. "I'm in Room 160 and my wife's gone off with our key. Could I possibly make a phone call from your room? I need to call the ANZ Bank urgently – it's just the Amsterdam branch." He looked imploringly at her.

She examined the yellow sheepskin jacket and his good boat shoes. He seemed honest enough if a bit desperate. She opened the door, picked up the camera off the bureau, put it in her bag and held it close while she looked around. There was nothing left in the room for him to steal – he'd hardly want her clothes. "All right. Just don't make any toll calls and shut the door after you." And she let him in.

Even Australians deserve a break sometimes, she thought as she retraced her steps, threading through a crowd of policemen in the foyer and so back through the coffee shop to the rowboat. Politie were inspecting the blue rocket ship that had tied up behind them. She hoped the Aussie she'd left upstairs in her room wasn't a boat thief.

As soon as she was back in the rowboat her son pushed off, wielding the oars manfully to try to save ten dollars.

Up on the third floor Dennis could hear knocking progressing down the corridor toward him. The Dutch Politie were two rooms away. He caught sight of himself reflected in two huge mirrors, surrounded by green brocade drapes:

Louis XXV dreading the onset of a levee.

"Perhaps the wig, sire?"

"Nah. I think the old hair's holding on quite well, don't you?"

Behind his left shoulder he saw another door and whirled to try it. He turned the knob, opened the door a crack. The adjoining room was strewn with clothes and toys. On the bed sat a woman with long shiny hair hanging over her face, She was bent over, elbows on her knees, slowly snatching from hand to hand a soft, black-and-white toy.

"Hello, Mum," she said, low and grudging, without looking up.

"That's a killer whale, isn't it?" said Dennis.

The woman sprang up and backed to the window. "It's *Jennifer.*" She dropped the toy. "What are you doing in my mother-in-law's room?"

"Dennis Bogdanovich. Can you see my boat from here? I've got it tied up at the coffee shop." He had his face pushed against the window to look along and down the building.

The young woman backed further away. She was spunky but too tall.

"Your mother said I could use her phone. The police are after me – only for traffic violations, on the Zuider Zee."

"Bloody Dutchmen. You're a Kiwi, aren't you?" Her mood had changed. "Come and look down from my room. It goes round the corner."

Dennis hurried after her into the next room of the suite and saw his boat. It was navy blue with Water Politie. "They're coming along this floor looking for me. I've gotta go."

"Here, put on this stupid check hat my husband bought. There, you look like a Turkish carpet salesman. You could do with a moustache. But take this." She took a small carpet off the back of the sofa, rolled it up, and thrust it at him. Then she shed her hotel scuffs and burrowed into a pair of high heeled shoes standing by the door. Dennis checked with the mirror and ducked back into the grandmother's room for his satchel.

"Here we go." She snatched keys from the table, opened the door into the corridor and stalked out, like a countess escorting a departing guest. They walked slowly to the stairs and hurried, giggling, down to the second floor where she again led him, sedately chatting, to the lift. There she left him the hat but reclaimed the carpet, shook his hand, and pushed buttons to send him down to the car park.

Dennis emerged, tipped the gate attendant a euro and walked off in search of a taxi.

Chapter 9

To London from Oud-Zuilen,
31 October 2006

That evening in Oud-Zuilen, Anton's father, Ibrahim Hassan, drew up outside the old sausage factory at the wheel of a taxi, come to collect the two boys and Sergey for their London mission. Anton ran out to welcome him.

His father fell on his shoulders and kept saying, "My son, my son." He looked absolutely exhausted. "I got lost in Utrecht. The GPS kept talking Dutch. The Channel was very rough but it should be easier going back, with the change of tide."

He refused coffee. He'd left his boat tied up at the mouth of a canal seven kilometres upstream from Rockanje, at Hellevoertsluis, where he'd borrowed the taxi.

Hans brought him a glass of water. Mr Hassan could hardly spare time to look at the rocket lying inside the truck. "Very nice. How will you get it out if there are only the two of you left?"

Zaheed hastily explained about the hydraulic hoist and the hidden legs. Then he gave a shortened version of his planned farewell, thanking Mr Hassan for his excellent son, for bringing him up in the love of Allah, and thanking the whole team for their work over the last two sleepless days. He sent them off with these reassuring words of the Prophet:

"It is Allah who hath created the heavens and the earth and sendeth down rain from the skies and with it bringeth out fruits wherewith to feed you, it is He who hath made the ships subject to you, thus they may sail through the sea by his command and the rivers also hath He made subject to you."

Mr Hassan still looked nervous. "The tide will have gone right out by now. I hope I've left enough rope."

Zaheed and Anton tried to soothe him.

"All will be well, Ibrahim."

"It will be a much smoother ride, Father, going home - you'll have us for ballast."

Sergey and Herman were having a last engineers' huddle, Sergey assuring Herman everything would go off OK as long as he reprogrammed the logic controllers to suit the new specs...set the servo switches and gyroscopes... rationed fuel consumption...

Zaheed reminded everyone to throw their phones away, preferably into a river, after every second call. They would be given new ones in England.

Herman told Mr Hassan, "In the Netherlands you have to keep them turned off between calls because they can track your position within metres by -"

"Not now, Herman," Zaheed said and resumed, "Always use the phones in the order you received them, and I will know - "

Bash, bash!

Both main doors vibrated to the roof.

Herman pushed Mr Hassan aside to get to the light switch and flick it off. Zaheed and Sergey whispered in the darkness. Then Zaheed felt his way to the side door. Hans handed Anton the big wrench and they edged around the truck, stumbling after Zaheed,

"Ees ziss Zee Olde Dutch Sausage Factory?" a voice outside whined. Then, "It's bloody Zaheed! You having an orgy in there? Where's my cousin?"

Everyone crowded out of the little doorway. Behind the Mr Hassan's taxi a second one stood, its lights shimmering in the mist. Sergey grabbed Dennis and frog-marched him over to pay off the driver. The taxi backed away down the drive.

By that time Mr Hassan had his engine going. Anton and Hans got into the back with their briefcases. The taxi turned. Zaheed handed Sergey his suitcase, saying, "Do **not** leave him with me!"

"Come on, Dennis," said Sergey. "You got here at just the right moment - we're going fishing." Ignoring protests, he shoved his cousin into the back beside Hans, got in the front beside Mr Hassan and shut the door as the taxi moved off down the drive.

Haram! How did that devil find us? thought Zaheed. *I never once mentioned Oud-Zuilen. Sergey must have let something slip coming through Russia or Germany. About the brick castle and the 'old village' perhaps? Someone might have mentioned Utrecht. Curse all taxis with GPS. Haram!*

"Allah, destroy the infidel before he can destroy us!" he said.

Fog swirled around the departing car. Zaheed had trusted Sergey from their earliest days at the laboratory - he would freely borrow anyone's lab coat or pen but was also quick to steer a newcomer away from dangerous colleagues. Zaheed had just now been praying the detonation of his precious bomb would give the dear unbeliever the one taste of joy he had ever asked for or could ever expect: all he had ever wanted was a chance to see his rainbow bomb in action. But now Sergey had brought his imbecilic cousin into their jihad. Zaheed and Herman stared after the taxi lights bobbing down the driveway until it disappeared, turning into the traffic along the street.

He said aloud, "This jihad was in the hands of Allah; now it is in the hands of an idiot - a djinn, come from an island at the bottom of the earth to destroy us. Sergey will have to dump him in Utrecht, get rid of him somehow."

"Inshallah," said Herman, who had not managed to get a good look at Sergey's cousin. His only concern was that the job would not be finished in time. He went straight back to work.

The rocket was now bedded down on the gantry inside the trailer, fully armed, but the launch gear still had to be integrated with the other controls. Herman was sacrificing his laptop. He wriggled under the truck, dragging it with him, along with a wiring loom for connecting it to the truck's hydraulic system. That was how they intended to command the truck canopy to open, get its stabiliser legs put down, and operate the ram to haul the rocket upright. The laptop would also relay commands for modifying the rocket's trajectory to suit weather conditions above and ahead of it. Finally, it would give the command to detonate the bomb.

Impressed by Herman's faith in engineering certainty even in the teeth of disaster, Zaheed stopped pacing about, threw the Dennis problem to Allah, and became Herman's gopher, reaching under the truck with pliers and multimeter on command. He shifted lamps, turned switches on and off, and made coffee. Kitchen supplies were again down to stale bread and Edam cheese but the coffee was still Arabica.

"Would you like me to make it the Ethiopian way, over a few coals in a tin?"

"The hell you will! It's bad enough me soldering this close to the fuel cans!"

In spite of Dennis's irruption, the nearer they came to lift-off the more frisky Zaheed became. To divert Herman he kept delivering imaginary newspaper headlines for 5 and 6 November 2006.

"*London Times*: "23.05 FROM CHARING CROSS TO TOFFEE-NOSED SUBURB DELAYED INDEFINITELY BY AL QAEDA"

"*New York Times*: "SEE, SADDAM HUSSEIN DID SO HAVE THE GOODS!"

Glasgow Herald: "CLYDEBANK WORKING GIRLS DEPLORE WORKING CONDITIONS"

Then, right on cue, Zaheed took a call from the Mull of Kintyre. Akhmed and Rashid were still seasick, they never wanted to eat another fish of any kind but they were almost within sight of their target and their parcels were dry.

"You've done all the hard part," Zaheed told them. "The rest will be easy. Once the crew get into port they won't tip you out of their bunks any more - they'll be off to spend their wages. Stay on the boat and sleep. The others who were here have gone off tonight on their holidays and we're packing up too. Until we meet…"

Lying under the truck, Herman felt the full weight of the suitcase-bombers' lives as well as the rocket upon him as he installed and fixed each wire, soldered the ends and tightened bolts around them. After the lift-off, if he got safe to Marseilles, he thought he might head for Morocco. In the grease and shadows and freezing cold he practised saying *"H'lah!" (hot)* and waggling his fingers as if they'd been scorched by the sight of gorgeous girls passing in sunlit streets. This exercise also helped free them up for his next feat of precision engineering.

There you go! Allahu akbar! He has indeed thought of everything, before we even know we need it! Serve the jihad!

Around midnight Zaheed made him stop. "We have three days to check everything. Everything is going to go off perfectly, inshallah!"

"Especially the rocket, I hope you mean." Herman crawled out from under the truck, both hands full of tools.

Zaheed thought the man looked like a frog but he kept a straight face. "Yes, especially the rocket." He took the pliers and lamp from him and helped him up. "When you're ready, I've got something for you from Sergey."

Herman came back from the workbench wiping his hands on a rag. Zaheed was sitting on the gantry step, a handkerchief spread on his knees, chawing with pliers at a blob of melted copper and black plastic.

"Good old Sergey. My own souvenir from Dzhezkazgan." When Zaheed gave it to him, Herman sniffed at his piece, then suddenly held it out at arm's length, asking, "Is it still radioactive? It's only been forty-four years."

"No, no, that's heat damage. But London is much less than 800 kilometres from here and the English Channel is full of cable. There will be plenty of melted wire lying around here next week, even in Oud-Zuilen, only your bit will be a genuine antique."

Both men put their treasure into their breast pockets.

Chapter 10

A Fishing Trip,
Hellevoertsluis to London. 31 October 2006.

The delivery boys and Dennis were travelling towards Utrecht.

Mr Hassan said, "I don't want to go through there again! Took me two and a half hours to get to Oud-Zuilen. By the time we get back to the boat it might have broken free - or it might have been stolen!"

"My boat's already been stolen - by the Dutch Politie. And for nothing." Dennis leant over the front seat. "That's why I was coming after you, Serge, so you could help me get it back. I need to call my wife too."

"Ah, yes. As soon as we get back from the fishing I will phone them for you."

"Haven't you got a mobile?"

"We can't use them in cars here."

"Pshaw!"

"Herman said to keep to the A2," said Anton, taking charge of the map the taxi owner had given Mr Hassan, "and then we'll be able to pick up the A12 at Gouda."

"I could do with some cheese. And a piss, too" said Dennis.

"We will have food at the boat." Mr Hassan was sitting up straight, hands high on the wheel. Although the rush hour was past, traffic was still running fast and close. He nearly missed the turn into the Botlek Tunnel. All the passengers kept quiet, except for Dennis. He wanted to know what sort of boat they had, why they all had matching bags, why the cases were wrapped up in plastic, were they full of lures and what size fish were they after.

Sergey began by responding to each question with a minimum of new information and then feigned sleep.

Anton took over by giving out fascinating historical titbits off the map about the "former islands" they were travelling across.

"Just find me Hellevoertsluis where the canal comes out at the river," said his father.

In a little over an hour they were on the dock beside the lock gates looking down at the boat. It was still there, at the limit of its rope, nose up on a steep mud bank. Mr Hassan took a look and went off to buy food and return the taxi.

"That boat's far too small for this many of us," said Dennis.

The others were silently marvelling that Anton's father could have come all the way from England in a flimsy inflatable that size. What with the gas tank – and Mr Hassan was bringing more gas - and a plastic box full of lifejackets there would scarcely be room for their feet, let alone space to lie down as they were all longing to do. There was only one seat, apart from the inflated side cushions, and no shelter.

"Do you think it might have deflated a bit and shrunk while your father was away getting us?" asked Hans.

"Yeah, could have," said Dennis. "Schoolboys with fishing lines could have got in it, to be closer to the main channel. A fishhook can do a lot of damage on a boat like this."

"I never caught a fish," said Hans, looking down into the river in the shifting mist.

"Never been fishing? You haven't lived, man. I could show you right here – there's bound to be something coming in with the tide. What bait have you got?"

"We're getting it up the coast a bit," Serge said, untying the mooring rope. "Here, take hold of this."

Dennis sprang to catch it, understanding the job at once. Still holding the rope, he climbed halfway across the wooden lock gate on his stomach to get a better angle and managed to drag the boat off the shiny bank and round into deep water in front of the sluice gate. Then he threw the rope back to Sergey, who pulled the boat to the post and climbed down into it by a ladder of rusty steel loops.

He prodded at the inflatable's sides, while Dennis joined him and felt around the engine for any sign of oil leakage, checked the fuel gauge and topped up the tank. Sergey found a hand pump and a bailer. Then he handed the boys up a lifejacket each, took the suitcases on board, and stowed them and Dennis's satchel in the empty locker.

"I'm sorry, there isn't a lifejacket for you, Dennis. I presume you can swim?"

"No worries, mate. I've got my sheepskin for warmth - and anyway, you never hear about treasure-hunters diving round a wrecked inflatable, do you? They're pretty tough."

After that the boys climbed down and fooled about in the boat while Sergey went up onto the dock and finished off his last pack of Belomor cigarettes, while planning how to get rid of his cousin in London by tourism, boat shows or murder. The mist was turning into drizzle. Only pleasure boats were allowed to use the canal nowadays and this was not a pleasant night. Yet even though there was no one around, Sergey kept his back to the cameras that covered the floodgate.

The taxi dropped Mr Hassan back with two more jerry cans of fuel, containers of rice plate (nasi goreng), a stack of Turkish bread and bottles of drink. Sergey passed them down to Anton and Hans for distribution. Mr Hassan started the motor, and they were out of the canal and well down the estuary before the last finger had been licked. Sergey collected the food containers, and after only a moment's thought knotted the bag, put it overboard and held it under till it sank.

"You're not saving the world tonight, Serge?" asked Dennis.

"No point." He paused. "But I might pick it all up again one day on a beach in Florida. On a day off from my new job."

Hans laughed and then looked at Anton and stopped. Anton sat up straight and stared out to sea.

Mr Hassan told the boys to wash their hands and said he would lead them in salat as he steered. First he solemnly reminded those who could they must take hold of the rope that ran along the sides and not let go till they got to…where they were going. Dennis, sitting on the locker fixed in the middle, would have to hold on to the ridge around its lid. Then Mr Hassan invoked Allah's help:

"In the Name of God, the Compassionate Source of All Mercy, all praise be to God, the Lord of all the worlds, and Master of the Day of Judgement. You alone do we serve and it is to You alone that we look for help. Guide us on the Straight Path; the path of those who have earned Your favour, not the path of those who have earned Your anger, nor of those who have gone astray."

Anton recited his sura: *"We gave Moses the Book and made it a Guide to the Children of Israel, commanding, 'Take no other than Me as Disposer of your affairs.'"*

Hans followed on: *"They were the seed of those who were carried in the Ark with Noah! Surely he was a grateful servant."*

"Ameen," said the father and the two boys,

Dennis squirmed in silence, storing all this away as material for Fishing Forum blogs. He could make a big thing of it, with Skotty as Imam: telling how to kneel in the bottom of the boat, and bow (never confusing it with the prow of the boat) doing it with one hand on the rope and the other hand on the locker, and trying not to be distracted by the boat's motion. Dennis did not discern and would not be able to convey to Skotty the crew's identical personal prayer, the plea to be allowed to live long enough to complete the task Allah had set them, though Skotty did have a similar firm idea at the start of every fishing trip.

Now the sea was beginning to rock into the estuary, the waves splashing everyone's jackets, wetting their jeans and augmenting the bilge water. Dennis slithered about on his box, commenting on the amount and size of the shipping he saw.

Anton's father sat on the petrol tank, peering into the rain, steering with one hand and making dhikr. As he mouthed salutations he counted them off on the fingers of his other hand resting on his knee. The boys on the side cushions watched him work up and down each joint of every finger. As last he finished and their questions burst out.

"How did Australia get on against India?" asked Hans.

"Beat them by six wickets!" said Mr Hassan.

"Whee!" said the boys.

"How did Fatima do in her Cambridge exams?" asked Anton.

"She got two As and three Bs. Eighty-nine for chemistry!"

"Will that be enough for pharmacy school?"

"If she keeps those marks up she'll fly in."

"Were you there last week to see Mido make his goal?"

"Nan! It was a beauty! He picked up a low cross from Edgar Daniels, fooled Ferdinand and slammed it right into the far post!"

"That makes it five wins in a row for the Spurs, doesn't it? And seven losses for West Ham!"

"But this Sunday we're playing Chelsea. The champions!" Mr Hassan looked serious.

The boys froze and their questions dried up.

"The All Blacks are playing at Twickenham on Sunday," said Dennis. His words melted away in the drizzle.

Through all this Sergey had sat silent on the seat, peering into the rain in a ceaseless pattern - first ahead, then from side to side and lastly, behind. Soon after they'd set out he'd pointed out lights of the little town, Rockanje, over to the right, and as they left the estuary he indicated the dunes. Anton and Hans nodded, and contemplated the broad beach where early on Sunday morning Zaheed and Herman would be sending up their rocket. Sergey looked very proud but soon resumed his maritime duty. The sea slapped at the inflatable as it bucked along. Every third wave - felt but unseen in the dark - threw in a seawater sample, distracting the men from prayer and even their concern about the health of the motor each time its note changed.

It was a wet, bumpy, anxious night. The boys bailed continuously. Visibility was low, and there was plenty of traffic - Mr Hassan told them sixteen hundred vessels passed through the Channel each day. Most ships had foghorns and all had lights, but their little boat was threading diagonally through them with no lights at all.

"Stupid place to go fishing. Like looking for marlin in Hong Kong Harbour," said Dennis.

"We'll be all right when we get further up the coast," said Sergey.

"What about trying to catch some bait?"

"We're going to buy it when we get there," said Hans. "It's too wet now."

"What are ya?" Dennis stood his collar up under the brim of his hat.

Mr Hassan kept to the tiller all night, steering by a compass, and from midnight on hoping that a certain low light ahead was the Southend-on-Sea beacon. The boys took turns with hand pump and bailer. They drank Dutch Coke at first, and later cold coffee from an English thermos.

Suddenly Sergey yelled, "Chert! Go right!"

The boat heeled over on a hill of water that rose beside a throbbing mountain of deeper darkness, punctuated by lights nearly at the waterline.

"Poker, boys?" shouted Mr Hassan as he surfed the wave. The old seadog in him rejoiced in feeling the ocean at work. Then they were tossed down into the wake. The bow dived. Sergey snatched Anton's hair as they went underwater. The father grabbed his son's leg with both hands. The boat slewed and caught them both like tossed pancakes.

Hans went hysterical and sprayed everyone with the pump while Mr Hassan fought to get boat and motor back under control.

Sergey had folded into the bilge at the bow, bald and sodden as a blin. He was coughing and spitting but soon resumed his watch, now keeping one hand on the rope and the other across the seat.

The boys mouthed thanks to Allah for preservation. Anton checked how much hair he had lost and rubbed at his ankle.

The boys had given up all hope of sleeping in the slop at the bottom of the boat where each splash and bump would remind them how few tenths of an inch of metal there were between their wet cheeks and the ocean that had so nearly claimed them. Queasy in the wet, they settled back against the inflated sides and resumed their duties, sucking at or scooping up the bilge water that endlessly reappeared from under the locker in the middle. Inside it their three dark cases and Dennis's bag showed dimly through the plastic as dawn came on behind.

"Where's your cousin?" asked Hans.

Sergey gaped. "Chert poberi," he whispered.

Mr. Hassan stood and turned the boat. The coloured lights of the ship that had tipped them over were now barely perceptible. Sergey knelt up at the locker and hoped not to see a floating mass of yellow sheepskin somewhere between them and the ship. It was enough to make a person believe in Allah. But what would he tell his mother? And what would she tell her cousin? Someone must have loved Dennis.

They made three wide circles but saw only a couple of plastic bottles. Their nemesis ship was gone, along with several others passing to and from Rotterdam.

"Gas is low. I'll have to stop and fill-up," said Mr. Hassan. "Keep a watch out - he would have gone east."

It was hopeless in the lingering darkness. They could barely see the foam on each wave before it hit them. The re-fuelling was accomplished with some spills.

"We must go on," said Sergey. "I have to be in London before lunchtime."

"Yes," said Hans. "Like Zaheed always says, 'Serve the jihad'."

"The Kiwi said he could swim and it will soon be light. Someone will pick him up," said Mr. Hassan.

He started the engine and set out on a straight westerly course again, scanning for the Southend beacon or any fixed light in the west. It was nearly day and he began saying fajr. There was no question of ablutions, or standing between salaams. Anton kept his eyes on the sea behind, but Sergey resumed his radar sweeps. Each thought of the man lost in the rough sea while giving thanks for their own deliverance. The last prayer of fajr, asking God to bless the noble efforts of both Mohammed and Ibrahim, put new heart into everybody.

"My father's name is Ibrahim," Anton told Sergey.

Sergey nodded. The story about Ibrahim and his son was familiar, one of his mother's tales. A relic, perhaps, of the Turks occupying Croatia? Obviously Dennis was the sacrificed son. He tried to remember what Dennis's recently dead father had been called. And what was Dennis's wife's name?

Prayers finished, they were rewarded with the sight of the Ramsgate ferry coming up behind and then leading them towards the south head of the Thames estuary.

"Get rid of your phones, boys," said Sergey, slipping his over the side.

"I haven't even used mine," said Hans, hurling one after the other as high as he could. Anton tried to make his skip the waves.

Between waves, Sergey opened the locker and pulled out Dennis's satchel. He dropped it over the side, where it disappeared instantly.

"Here's one for you, Sergey," said Anton to distract him from his bereavement. An enormous Maersk tanker was coming on from the north with huge letters, half the height of its castle wall, saying: *NO SMOKING*. They managed to sneak across in front but the ship took minutes to pass behind them. Its network of waves and wake seemed inescapable, yet by seven they could see the surf at Broadstairs, and as the town lights came closer they were able to pick out the pier.

"Here we go, boys! Allah akbar!" Mr Hassan was weeping as he turned the boat into the rough waves. He gunned the motor and ran at the beach. Then he jumped out with a rope and the two boys tumbled over the sides. Sergey pulled the motor down to keep the propeller high, steadying the locker with one leg.

Hans was dragged into the water but kept hold of the rope and straps on the side. The next wave threw him and the boat further up the pebbly beach, and the shingle running back to the sea gnashed its teeth at their second lucky escape.

Sergey patted his pockets in search of his lost cap, smoothed down what was left of his hair, and resumed command. "Leave nothing in the boat but the life vests. Take the plastic off your cases now, roll it up and take every bit of it with you."

Mr Hassan was slapping himself warm and urging them to hurry. They ran along the beach, up steps near the pier and down a side street to the entrance of a garage. Mr Hassan pushed the doorbell and a little, low door opened immediately.

"Salaam! This way, please," said the garage man and led them into a tiny staffroom.

Mr Hassan brought them each a bulging plastic bag. "Give me the plastic you took off your cases. Put them here under the table. Go through there and have a shower. You first, Hans. You'll find dry clothes, a razor and two cell phones in your bag. Be careful with the phones." He draped blankets over the shoulders of Sergey and his son while they waited their turn.

"Please, have some food," said the garage man.

On the table there was one plate of fresh bread rolls filled with warm scrambled egg and another heaped with Chelsea buns. Someone passed a coffeepot through the door and the garage man filled steaming mugs.

Hans came back looking warmer and happier in jeans and a red jersey. Anton disappeared next.

"Your van is ready. You should be in London in two hours," said the garage man.

"Terrible traffic at this time of day," said Mr Hassan.

"As long as I'm in Piccadilly by eleven," said Sergey firmly.

Anton drove while Mr Hassan slept, and by 8.45am they were fighting trucks on the A28 though most of the commuter traffic was ahead of them. The fields were dank, the trees almost hidden in mist.

"I reckon we'll need coats as well as suits, this weather," said Anton.

"Sure, sure!" said Sergey. "Go to Marks and Spencers. Go to Harrods! You can afford it."

"I can get you very good coats in Tottenham," said Mr Hassan's sleepy voice from the back seat.

"Fine! Spread the money around among the brethren – but don't talk!"

Chapter 11

A Piccadilly/Tottenham Interlude,
London, 1 November 2006.

Anton stopped the van and let Sergey off halfway down Piccadilly outside Fortnum and Mason. He waved them off, then went in and bought a small packet of smoked eel. The girl tied it up with red ribbon.

Back on the street he was caught up by the crowd, backpacks striking his shoulders and shopping bags bumping his case. The Christmas Shopping Festival must have started already. With nearly half an hour to spare, he turned into the market beside St. James-in-Piccadilly. Stallholders held out to him teddy bears dressed as Santa, tartan scarves, and postcards in the shape of double-decker buses. He bought a paper cone of chestnuts and retired to a bench to enjoy a taste of home. The top nut was already peeled and tasted pretty good.

Peeling another, he saw the very thing he most needed poking out from under the canvas skirt of the stall beside his seat: a box that looked exactly the right size to hold his case. He nudged it with his foot and found it very light. He spilled the chestnuts, and while pretending to pick them up, went round the back of his seat, grabbed the box in one smooth movement, and was off into the church of St. James to rationalise his burdens.

A few people were wandering about - reading marble memorial plaques for Lord This and Lady That, and generally enjoying the airy, peaceful space. There were lots of clear windows in what had been a fashionable church for those who, having survived the plague and the Great Fire of London, were attempting to cook up a bit more history. Sergey had a vision of Peter the Great, in smock and knee breeches, looking at him through the wrong end of his spyglass.

Recalled to national duty, he went down the main aisle and saw two pews were occupied by recumbent victims of a modern plague. Two seats further on he sat down to open the box and found it full of silk flowers – no contest with an atomic bomb. He put the suitcase on top of them and the lid fitted tightly.

Then he undid the packet of smoked eel on his knees, took a small metal phial the size of a cigarette lighter out of his shirt pocket and salted the fish liberally with the contents. He had put away the phial and was re-tying the festive string when a pair of elderly tourists came round in front of him to enjoy the floral altarpiece. Sergey gave unspecified thanks, buttoned his jacket, gathered his two parcels and hurried out of the church.

He had eleven minutes to go three blocks to Itsu, a certain sushi bar. At the door he swung the box up on his shoulder, entered and marched through to the kitchen, where he slapped the small parcel on the bench. "Special order for the Italian at Table Four," he told the sushi-roller, and left by the back door.

Outside, he took a taxi to the Millenium Hotel in Mayfair where the concierge kindly supplied him with an envelope. He addressed it to a friend who was a guest, sealed the phial inside it and handed it in at the reception desk. Then he walked to Veronkowsky's, a security firm nearby and collected a packet containing a fat wad of euros, his pay for the morning's work – little enough considering the cost of the phial he'd been carrying for the boss, 14.5 million roubles.

He thought of treating himself to a new grey suit from Saville Row. He turned into the street and found Norton and Sons where Veronkowsky probably had his made, but the braided military jackets up in the window twinkled a message: *We were not made in a day.*

Round the corner, another shop window displayed a leather jacket very like the one ruined on the boat. He stopped for a long look. There was no cap with it but when he enquired they showed him a "superior," or adequate, model. Sergey bought it and wore it into the next shop, where he found a satisfactory grey suit with a subtle, inbuilt stripe that made him look tall and English – taller than his cousin?

Poor Dennis and his sheepskin; it would have drowned him in a minute.

In the changing room Sergey abandoned the Folkestone op-shop gear Anton's father had given him. He found the palm of his left hand rather itchy – in his mother's stories was this a sign of money coming in or going out? Either proposition was plausible considering the price of this suit. Or the itch could have been from a stray molecule of the isotope. If so, at least it showed the phial hadn't been harmed by its dunking in the Channel.

He next sent his mother part of his windfall; there were exchange bureaux everywhere. The rouble exchange rate would make any amount of euros look good but Sergey did his filial duty. His mother would find a way to trickle some of it to his son.

Afterwards he caught a tube to Tottenham and made his way to the Hassan residence in Northumberland Street. The houses were all alike – three-up-and-two-down, post-war rebuilds, mostly full of Africans by the look of the passers-by. From the street outside Number 25 he could hear shouting, and furniture falling. As he opened the gate he heard Hans's voice: "You can't be Shane Warne - they're both on the same side!"

Sergey thumped on the door, which fell open. He rushed inside, and into the room on the right where the noise was coming from. A wet towel and a pair of tights descended on him. A wad of crumpled paper hurtled at him and dropped at his feet.

"Why are you making so much noise?" he said as he peeled the tights off his face.

Five young Pakistanis were playing office cricket.

"That's nothing. It's quite normal round here," said one.

"I'm Stephen Waugh, so he couldn't be Shane Warne! They're both Australian," said Hans, red-faced.

"What are your cases doing in the middle of all this?"

"That's the wicket," said Anton, brandishing an upside-down, rolled umbrella.

"Your mother's coming!" shouted the man in the outfield, against the window. The cricket game stopped, the extra players faded out the door, and Hans rushed upstairs with the two cases: Sergey handed his box up to him over the banister. Anton started to put the furniture back in place and Sergey helped shift the table. A flower vase had been broken. Anton was standing at the living-room door, very contrite, holding a bunch of mangled yellow chrysanthemums, when his mother came bustling into the hall. She put down two bags of groceries and stepped out of her sodden shoes.

"I'm sorry, Mama. I'll get you some more."

"Bishmillah ir rahman ir rahman. I know - I saw the boys rushing out the gate. Come here, boy!" His mother hugged him as if she would never let him go. "You're not wearing your new pullover, Ishmael - that's a terrible old rag you've got on. I'm glad you've come early. You're back in time for Fatima's prizegiving!"

Over his shoulder she saw Hans and Sergey. She patted Anton/Ishmael's back with both hands and hugged him some more.

Then she put him aside and started on Hans. "Allahu akbar. It is good to see you boys alive and well and looking so smart - but you need a haircut, Warith. And this is Sergey? I am Aisha. Welcome to England and welcome to my home. Sit down. Rest,

rest! Put the carpet straight, Ishmael, and take the flowers to the kitchen. Would you get the groceries, please, Warith. Put the meat and milk in the refrigerator while I get changed?"

She tore off her wet hijab and coat to hang them behind the door and her hair burst out - long, shiny, lightly streaked with grey. She was a forceful little person, clearly mistress in her home. "I'm sorry about the washing, but you know the English winter!" she said to Sergey, doing a quick circuit of the room, gathering in a bundle of more personal items before going upstairs with them.

When the boys went to the kitchen Sergey walked round the living room, now largely free of strings of washing, to examine the family photographs. There were old ones in fancy frames - one of a man in a djellabah and several of women draped in black. Newer ones showed the children at various stages. In the latest, Anton ('Ishmael', as his mother called him – and Hans was 'Warith'!) and a beautiful girl in a veil were both wearing school uniform. There were several certificates for sport and for a prize from a bank, awarded to Ishmael Hassan for a Thrift Essay in 2000, and one for Aisha Hassan who had qualified as a member of the Tottenham Citizens Advice Bureau in 1996.

The living room ran the full depth of the house, from the bay window at the front with its view of the street, to French doors at the back opening onto a garden with the brown remains of a vegetable patch. The furniture was old but not worn out. The television set was new. It had an Arabic scroll hanging above it, no doubt a text cautioning about programmes that would not suit the Muslim code. The red floral carpet was probably Persian, and a small green mat patterned with white calligraphy hung along the back of the sofa.

Sergey thought Mrs Hassan had given him and 'Warith' a very warm welcome. He wondered what Ibrahim would tell her about them all, especially about their strange choice of transport from Holland. Would he tell his wife about Dennis? They should have told the Dutch coastguard about him. Or someone at Broadstairs. Really, he was just collateral damage in yellow sheepskin. The project was too big to stop for one man.

He puzzled over what role he should adopt with Anton's mother. Until Ibrahim came home he would say as little as possible, pretend he didn't speak much English. The father had gone straight to the shop after his double ordeal on the Channel. He must be a good provider. Not like Sergey's father, who came back from the Afghanistan war to vodka himself to death. Though perhaps he would have approved of - even helped - this jihad?

A good smell came from the kitchen. Sure enough, Anton and Hans brought in small cups of coffee. Mrs Hassan put her head round the living room door, nodded approval of Ishmael's hospitality, and bustled down the passage to the kitchen. Anton turned on the TV and flicked through news, children's cartoon programmes and *Neighbours*, looking for the game on which the sun never sets.

Sergey could tell Mrs Hassan was frying meat in the kitchen. He'd seen enough cricket so he went to watch the cooking.

It was going to be a lamb stew, strewn with rosemary and crumbled cinnamon stick. Now Aisha was grating nutmeg over it. Sergey bent to enjoy the aroma, and Aisha warned him against getting his tie and good suit spattered.

He perched on a stool by the small, high table and examined the kitchen: gas stove, deep square sink and a yellow plastic washbowl, refrigerator with a microwave oven on top of it, Dutch toaster, Chinese rice cooker, rows of spices - and the crippled flowers, broken short by the boys and jammed into yoghurt pots in front of the steamed-up window. Beside it was a door to the garden, cut in two pieces like the door of a stable.

He inhaled the smell of the cooking. "My mother cooks that. From Croatia - Rizot od Janjetine. With tomate."

"You are from Croatia? I thought you were Dutch."

"My father, yes. My mother, not."

"I don't put tomato in mine. I put lemon, and sometimes saffron. How far is Croatia from Kosovo?"

"Oh, many, many kilometres. My family does not know anybody from Kosovo."

"There are lots of women and children from there at our mosque and I see them at the Citizens Advice too." She stirred the pan. "Do you have any washing? I'll be taking a load to the laundromat tomorrow. Or I might send Ishmael down tonight, after we pray. Are you Muslim?"

"No. I am nothing."

"That is sad!" She turned to have a good look at him.

"Is OK." He smiled his best and she went on sprinkling rice over the fried meat and then poured a jug of hot water on top. She put the lid on the pan and glanced up at the clock. "Dinner will be at six o'clock when Fatima comes."

"Ibrahim?"

"He won't close the shop until seven-thirty. We sell plenty of magazines and cigarettes to workers coming off the train at night." Aisha climbed on to a stool with a cup of coffee. "I sell buttons and knitting wool and things like that there too. I taught a few women to knit and then I started to give sewing lessons. Now we have four machinists sewing out the back of the shop. We make covers for ironing boards. Nice bright covers. The English say the road to Hell is paved with good intentions, but I think Hell is full of ironing – that's a woman's joke for you!" Aisha beamed.

No, this was not a woman who was aware her son had three suitcase bombs under his bed.

"My girls are from everywhere: Ghana, Libya, and two from Palestine," she said, drying her hands. "And we've had them from Chad and Afghanistan and Tashkent. They have to speak English to each other, and they get on fine. Two of them have gone to start training to be nurses."

"That is very good," said Sergey.

"How has Ishmael been at learning the sausage business?"

"He is a clever boy. He will be good."

"I hope you don't use pork meat?"

"No, no! No pig meat at all in our sausage! That is why it will be so popular."

"I want Ibrahim to get the council to build a proper industrial kitchen for women round here to use. Then they could go commercial with the sweets and dukkah they sell at the markets, and maybe frozen lamb tagine as well." She got down from her stool to check on the dinner.

At sunset Sergey took a walk in the garden and smoked three cigarettes under the meagre eaves of a shed while the others did salat. Through the French doors he could see Anton leading the prayers in the living room - bowing, standing, kneeling, and bowing to the floor again, in seemingly endless repetition, presumably with passages of Arabic scripture in between. It looked the same performance as with Zaheed in Oud-Zuilen, only longer.

Sergey did his own meditation. He lit one cigarette for his cousin, thinking how appropriate death by drowning was for such a keen fisherman. Silly as he was, Dennis the fisherman must have prepared for death as often as any rocket engineer. Jihadis prepare five times a day, as Anton and Hans were doing right now.

Tomorrow they'd go to reconnoitre Hans's chosen place of death - at Croydon in the south - and the following day's excursion was to inspect Anton's new site at St. Albans in the north. Charing Cross, now

Sergey's site, he had visited today and found everything as Anton had described, though he hadn't been able to see any escape route. Sergey would follow Anton's plan, although he'd have to bring the time forward to eleven at night, as Zaheed required for propaganda purposes. "Inshallah!" he found himself saying, and laughed.

Anton banged on the window to summon him for dinner. Sergey reminded himself Anton's parents called him *Ishmael* and Hans had to be *Warith.*

Fatima was coming in the front door as Sergey came in the back. Aisha, going up the passage with a pile of plates, introduced them. They were going to eat in the lounge.

"Hurry, daughter," Aisha told her. "We will wait for you."

Fatima hung her coat on a hook and dashed up the stairs in a grey hijab and a blue Lycra gym suit. She was a very pretty sight.

When Ibrahim came home at seven-thirty - parking the van so close the front window rattled - they were still drinking coffee around the table and picking at sweets. As soon as he'd washed and sat down at the table Aisha brought her husband his dinner. He sniffed and seemed to approve, and Aisha sat down, gratified.

Ibrahim ate quickly at first, and then asked Fatima, "How did you do in the competition?"

"I passed. The judge liked my mat routine. I am repeating it on Saturday."

"There you are, Ishmael, you have a famous sister – well, famous in Tottenham, anyway. She was worth a good few votes to me in the borough elections."

"Don't forget the Mosque boys. They poked thousands of pamphlets in letterboxes for you, and my Bureaux girls helped too!" said Aisha.

"Good girl, sis," said Ishmael.

"Have some Turkish Delight, daughter." Ibrahim passed her the plate.

Fatima took a piece and looked down modestly.

She was still pretty in denim. She had short, dark hair, finely arched eyebrows and a glowing complexion without any makeup. Warith stared wordlessly across the table. Sergey had to dip another piece of bread in the oil and dukkah.

Ibrahim took a drink of water and tried to finish his lamb. He had not touched any bread or salad. "We'll say Isha early tonight. I am tired. You will please excuse us, Sergey?"

"You can have the spare bed in Ishmael's room," Aisha told him. "Warith can sleep here on the sofa."

Sergey could hear the prayers beginning as he started on the stairs. They were over by the time he'd had a shower and he heard Ibrahim going to bed.

Anton heard Sergey begin to snore. His mother seemed to like him. She had given them all a good welcome. A real good mother he had and still looking very spunky. He wondered if his father had told her anything at all about them –even how they got over from Holland. She hadn't asked about what food was available on the ferry or if it was a rough crossing.

They could never tell her about losing Dennis. If only he could tell her how he and Sergey were nearly swept out of the boat too, to be churned under in the ship's wake, chopped up and drowned as Dennis probably had been. His father would have searched for him forever – or until he ran out of gas. Still, Allahu akhba, for giving him a father strong enough to grab his foot and save the two of them. Sergey's father would have been useless, a man who famously "only came home from Afghanistan to drink".

Exhausted as he was, Ishmael fingered through his hair to assess the damage. Some broken hair came away on his fingers and there was a swollen patch as big as his palm that was very tender. Lucky it was on top and not behind his ear like Warith's disastrous bald spot.

And if the hair fell out before Sunday he would get to see how he would have looked, middle-aged...

Chapter 12

Dennis Afloat,
English Channel, 1 November 2006

What Dennis remembered was: Hans shrieked, the boat tipped, the motor ROARED out of the water and they were thrown deep into the boiling bow-wave of the oncoming ship. The engine noise underwater was total.

He surfaced at the last gasp of his lungs. The sodden mass around him was the sheepskin of his jacket, holding his arms down. *I am alive inside the carcass of a drowned sheep.* Waves slashed noiselessly through. No one answered when he tried to call. One shoe was gone; he kicked off the other and paddled feet and hands through three more waves to get round with his back to the seas. It was black night with just a few lights flickering at the peak of each wave.

He called, "Serge, Sergey!" Then, "Hans!" Even the names of the others had gone. "Serge!" The ship's noise was gone too. Just faint foghorns, far away, between waves.

The water was freezing – so much for "wool keeps you warm when you're wet". He couldn't move his arms except where the waves insisted. He was floating just under water – "drown-proofing" didn't they used to call it? After each wave he had to force his face up to the surface to breathe.

The coat had to go. When a wave forced his elbows out he was able to pull the lower edge apart. The bottom button popped, and after the next wave receded he got the top one undone with one hand.

I might be able to sink out of this deathtrap but I can't raise my arms out of the water. And I dread going under again. I might be trapped. Forever.

Several more waves passed.

No Bogdanovich has ever drowned. No one from the Fish Club has ever been shipwrecked – oh, yes, Boulder! When his fuel lines ruptured and he had to swim for it. Spent two days on the littlest Poor Knight. That's how he got his name. If I want my boat back I need to swim. Like Boulder. Only he had insurance on his boat. I have to get mine back from those bloody Dutchies.

He ripped two more buttons out in pure rage, took a huge breath, threw himself back and pulled up his knees. The coat fought him all the way but at last his right arm was out and he was on a win. And on the surface again. He dragged his other arm free and pushed the coat under. It spread out and sank.

Dennis rested with his back to the waves. *Trailing my flippers - like the seal Blfish and I saw that time at the Kings, happy and contented at 5am, resting, miles out at sea. Me, I've had enough of it. I want to get back to dry land. Back to Europe. Denmark would be nice. All those blonde chicks.*

He rolled over and started to freestyle. His fastest stroke. *"The one sport that can save your life,"* as Mrs.

Moore, the coach, monotonously said. One hundred and I'm done.

A low plane with a dark bottom and a broad orange stripe appeared. Dennis waved but it went on.

Wish I'd looked in the coat pockets before I let it go. There might have been a cough lolly. Or a whistle. Or a bus ticket.

Another hundred, breaststroke.

Always sounds more fun than it is. Easily becomes dogpaddle. It's damned cold, The English Channel.

Crash, scrape, dong, bash, slash.

His nose and forehead were bleeding and there was something hard everywhere in front yet hidden under a layer of short seaweed. Rocks! No...metal.

Here it comes again!

He was slapped onto the thing a second time. It was covered in tiny barnacles among the weed- only the size of coffee crystals but every one vicious and a man-eater in training. He found a vertical bar with some bare patches, and gripped it as the next wave grated him upwards, then he got a second grip on the bar.

I might be crying tears of blood but it's hard to tell in the conditions. Wouldn't want to be caught crying in front of barnacles after what I say about them every winter, up on the hard at Leigh. It was never as cold as this, though.

Finding a second bar with his shoulder, he realised he'd hit a sunken container, end on. *Legend of the Seas.* He grabbed for the other door bar with his left hand and swung his legs sideways. Maybe he'd be able to get on top, wave assisted.

He nearly made it, but then was twisted and all but scraped off into the sea again. Regaining his hold - both hands on the same bar this time - he floated, waiting for the next wave.

Hoping.

Only a refrigerated container could float for the six weeks it's taken to grow barnacles this size. Wonder what's inside?

Another wave. Here goes!

Success, but there were more barnacles waiting for him on top. He got himself sorted with a good hold down onto both door bars, then raked for a toehold, wedging his feet against the fins of two ridges just in time for the next wave to sluice him, scarifying him through his Sinterklaas teeshirt. *Diane always tried to make me wear a singlet like my father. I'm lucky I still have my strides. The coat would have been useful now. The money belt is the most protection I've got. Pity it wasn't bigger - or lower.*

Next wave he was head down, under again, but it was worth it for the intervals between swells. Apart from the rain and the cold you could almost feel saved.

Like the original animal marooned on Goat Island as food for castaways. Wish I was there now.

The container was wallowing like a harpooned whale. He had to stay at the sunken end because of the door bars, but sometimes when it reared up he could see lights. That had to mean land was near. Then under he'd go again. It was all right as long as he got his mouth shut in time. Still, now he could see the waves coming as the sky lightened above his feet, and he began to hear more planes. Some of them would be flying low on Channel hops so one was bound to see him.

If the sky is brightest above my feet, that means the sea is taking me and the container east or nor'east towards Holland or Germany or Denmark. Denmark is full of blonde dolls. Only the passport'll be a washout by now.

Dennis rolled a little and felt the money belt squish. The notes were plastic but the electronic ticket and the travellers cheques would be goners.

I wonder if there are any fish hanging around. I saw a little starfish on my last dowsing. Floating logs attract fish at home - Skotty regularly circles if he sees a big one adrift when he's out looking for marlin. The next time I go under I should keep my eyes open. There was that kingie those capsized yachties caught a few years back under their catamaran. Those jokers, though, drifted for three months - halfway to Chile and back, I've only got a bit of seaweed, one starfish and the barnacles for bait whereas the cabin of their catamaran turned into a hanging garden. I'm not that ambitious.

They all got home safe, but lots of people still won't believe their story. I bet the Forum boys won't believe me either. Until I show them my scratches.

Here comes another wave. How many more can I take?

Out again. *Ugh.* He spat.

Sixteen hundred ship movements a day: surely somebody should be passing. Sixty-six times an hour, more than one a minute. And then there are planes.

Most are too high - I can hardly see them - but there will be lots doing short, low hops from England. They've gotta see me here, stretched out like a squid on a slab. My hands are cold.

These containers are dangerous to shipping. Someone should be on the lookout for them. Damned uncomfortable too. And I could do with a drink.

Dennis turned his head and stuck out his tongue to catch the rain. Another wave caught him.

His hands were so cold he knew he was going to lose his hold on the poles soon. *Though the barnacles along the edge will probably have cut me off at the elbows before that happens. Someone must spot me soon.*

Out here the sea was the horrible colour of school ink - watery on top and dead underneath.

I wonder if Sergey or any of his mates have survived? That boat was dangerously overcrowded - an inevitable disaster. A fish is going to eat Hans before he has ever caught one. They were all hopeless fishermen anyway – whoever sets off fishing without bait?

Dennis could hear an engine. *Sounds like Skotty coming to get me in the* Westcoaster *– after all his lectures about container danger he's going to run me down.* He started to kick up his legs.

Three more waves and when he looked back over his heels he could see a blue ship as big as a tug with a strip of orange paint up the bow.

Down he went and then up. *Shit*! The container was rocking sideways and his legs slid away, hindered only by the barnacles.

A lion with a crown had stopped beside him. It said *Nederlandse Kustwacht*. There were four sailors at the rail above, one of them whirling an orange bag over his head.

"Wait!" Dennis yelled as he saw another wave coming.

Too late. As he spluttered out of the wave he felt the rope of the throwline across his legs. He kicked up his calves and risked one hand to rake for the loop of buoyant line floating near his head. The orange bag bobbed towards him, he let the line belay round his wrist and grabbed the beautiful bag with both hands.

Goodbye, barnacles.

He got his arms through the strops of the bag and in only two last waves was being hauled up the gleaming blue side of the vessel and into the hands of the Kustwacht.

Chapter 13

Hamburg Barman, 1 November 2006

Glad to be home, Carl Jellouschek took off his socks and rubbed his feet. Tonight the bar takings were up but tips were down. Rain makes people mean, he reflected, and tomorrow it was going to be worse - probably with snow. Those customers who reached the bar would stay longer but then they might fight.

He picked up the cigarette lighter he'd found after the last bit of trouble, flicking it and watching the flame for a minute. It was an unusual lighter - not new, made of metal in Pakistan. He wondered how "Frits Breijer" had got it. He could be a sailor on a Dutch ship that had called in to Karachi. Is Karachi a port? Or he could have just found the lighter – or even stolen it. The name was definitely Dutch, but on the day the Armenians attacked the bar the only customers who'd looked to be Dutch had been his old regulars. None of them was called 'Frits'.

At least one of the defenders was definitely fluent in some Eastern lingo, but then crews often included quite a bit of poor scum that might have been scooped up anywhere in the Middle East or Asia.

If business didn't pick up soon he might sign on himself. Some ship sailing into the tropics would be good. Or he might start smoking again.

Carl dropped the lighter and switched on the TV for a snatch of news before bed. A picture came up of a curious blue hydrofoil being launched on the Dutch Inland Sea. The picture was gone in a flash. There was plenty of sport news but he was too tired to care, even about football.

Chapter 14

Recce to Rockanje,
the Netherlands 2 November 2006

At the same late hour, in the old sausage factory at Oud-Zuilen, Herman turned his computer on to scan CNN for anything about the ice hockey match, Detroit Red Wings against the Blackhawks –nothing! *The New York Times* offered only election news. a tirade about the Senate race in Connecticut and brave Ned Lamont. Who could care? Defeated, he tried the local news to get the weather report. More drizzle for tomorrow but not bad in the Channel, and the further outlook was good for Saturday.

The Netherlands news was disappointing as usual. It rarely offered him much about Iraq or the US elections. Tonight the bulk of it was a big blather about the Water Politie catching a little blue hydroplane in a canal in Amsterdam. It wasn't even speeding! Probably didn't have the correct coloured sticker or something. *What a bunch of old women they are. We'll give them something better to talk about this weekend than how and where to sell drugs and prostitutes. Here they call an election if a lying Sudanese girl cuts her hair off, runs away from her husband and becomes a Member of the Dutch Parliament. Now even Iron Rita's turned on her."*

Herman shut the laptop down in disgust

"She only did it to make trouble for Muslims. The girl's just a hunted infidel but the Dutch are worse fools, they don't know the serious business going on right under their TV aerials!"

Zaheed looked up from clipping his toenails over a newspaper. "My wife usually does this job for me. When they tell you they've found a nice girl for you to marry, be sure to look at her hands. You want one with fingers strong enough for this job but long enough for making kebbe rolls."

"Don't talk about food!" Herman groaned. "Why did Sergey decide to go to London so early? Has he got a girl there?"

"Not Sergey - he's strictly business. I think he had a little side job sprung on him, or something might have become more urgent. Sometimes I wonder if our rocket and everything except him seeing his EMP bomb go off are not just a side job for Sergey. He definitely went off the boil a bit while he was married but he's keen again now. Anyway, remember that last long phone call he had on Friday?"

"I thought that was his mother."

"No! I think it was his boss in St Petersburg," Zaheed told him. "And straight after that he was on to Anton's father to come to collect them earlier. He really wanted to go on Sunday but then we had the trouble with the GPS that took up two days."

"Weren't those boys just dead keen to get to London! No wonder – any place would give you better last days than we're having, shut up here, freezing, in an empty sausage factory," said Herman.

"We should have a break too." Zaheed crunched up the newspaper before pulling on a sock. "I think we'll go over to Rockanje tomorrow morning and have a look at the launch site - see it in winter conditions."

"OK – but what say we get us a good breakfast in Utrecht first?"

By midday Thursday they were driving through Rockanje, a tidy little town that looked to be full of retired people. They went straight through to the Duinen, past the sewerage works and into the wildest country in the Netherlands, with little shrub-covered hillocks that were once dunes. In World War Two the Germans had chosen the same site for launching rockets on London.

When the team had visited last September the roads and car parks had been packed; a city of striped canvas covered vast sands and the sea was full of bathers. Today in the mist they had it pretty much to themselves except for a few dog-followers. They visited all the car parks and selected a medium-sized one near the sea that provided fair bush cover so the truck wouldn't be seen from the road.

"No lights here," said Zaheed, imagining it at night. "You'll have to rig up some lights on the gantry – and underneath the truck too, if you're going to put your computer down there. The trouble I foresee is that this place is an ideal spot for lovers – you know the Dutch, commit zina in any weather."

"You're only jealous because you didn't have weather or girls in Afghanistan. If you'd grown up in Detroit you'd think this was a pretty likely spot."

"Oh, we have weather in Jalalabad, all right. There's no chance of those bushes catching fire, is there? I wouldn't want the Fire Brigade joining the party."

"Nah! This isn't a V1 or V2 rocket – always blowing up or falling over. I heard the Dutch called them '*Verdonk* 1' and '*Verdonk* 2' - That's 'Dud 1' and 'Dud 2'. Ours they will call 'The Ten-Minute Miracle'! Could be 'Five-Minute' even."

"The English'll call ours 'Iron Rita' if she brings down a second government!" said Zaheed. "Just the same, we'll park in the middle. Now, let's go back on the road north - see if we can find a way to bypass the town on Saturday night."

As they retraced their route Herman pointed out across the wild land, towards a port in the distance. "You see, it's not far to Rotterdam from here. How's about we fly to Marseilles after lift-off?"

"We'd have to use this truck to get to the airport."

"It'd be a darn sight less conspicuous to park there than the launcher. Weren't we going to bring it anyway, packed and ready to drive down through France?" Herman steered over into the bushes and put on the brake. "What say we change over? You drive and I'll have a look on the internet, see if I can find us an early flight."

He was out without waiting for a reply, and round holding the passenger door open before Zaheed had gathered up his map and scarf. Zaheed walked around to the other side of the truck as Herman opened the laptop. "Do you want a window seat?" he asked, preparing to search for airlines.

The Netherlands news came up and Herman's fingers stopped in mid-air. "Look at this! It's the boat I was telling you, got a speeding ticket in Amsterdam." He turned the laptop towards Zaheed, who was getting settled behind the wheel, "Made in Russia, with a glass bottom! What have they got to look at?"

Zaheed shifted the gear and glanced over politely.

"That's Sergey's cousin's boat. Haram! That's Sergey pushing it out. And me on the other side!"

"What were you doing fooling around in the mud?"

"The man's a stupid pig! Look at the way he is waving!

"We had to put him off in the Ijsselmeer, Sergey couldn't risk going in to Amsterdam to unload at the docks. He is a Kiwi, can never keep his mouth shut, and thinks every word that comes out of it is a great joke. See him showing-off to the man in the other boat! We are ruined!

"Allah, protect us in our great need. Protect the work you have begun."

Chapter 15

Kustwacht and Port Politie,
Rotterdam, 2 November 2006

"Oiy!" yelled all the Kustwacht men as Dennis reached the handrail. One more pull on the derrick and he was over the rail and flopping on the deck at their feet. It was smooth and warm. He could have lain there forever.

"Thanks, boys," he said into the deck.

The sailors' shoes squeaked to make room for an officer.

"Hello. English, are you? Congratulations. Get him to the sickbay. Drop two buoys with flags, radio Rotterdam-Rijnmund the position and call the Water Politie to collect our castaway."

Dennis raised his head at once. "They've got my boat."

"Then how did you get here?"

"I was going fishing."

"I've heard fish come around flotsam - but a container? Tell the Water Politie to bring a doctor."

Dennis was helped up by two sailors and led to the sickbay. One gave him a blanket, the other sweet coffee. Then they let him lie down and sleep.

Minutes later, it seemed, he was being stripped and blanket-bathed. All his barnacle scrapes were painted with soothing cream. The sailors were gentle, silent nurses, and Dennis was glad to keep his eyes shut. The engine engulfed him in a perfect male lullaby.

Then he was being rolled onto a stretcher and looked up to see a Politie in a hooded seagoing jacket. The man was walking backward with a whistle in his mouth, carrying him feet first out onto the deck. The wind and rain were back. They were going to tip him over the side? BYO board?

The Politie and a sailor attached him and the stretcher to the derrick again and Dennis was swung out to blasts of the whistle and lowered onto the deck of the Water Politie launch tied alongside. Sailors hung over the rail of the Kustwacht boat and waved to him. Dennis got one hand free and waved back as he was being carried into the cabin. He saw the Hooded One descending onto the launch in a sling, to his own whistle accompaniment. Then the engine revved up and the Water Politie launch pulled away from the larger vessel in a wide arc. Once the cabin door was shut Dennis found the launch quite cosy but the stretcher was an encumbrance, taking up all the seating.

"I could sit up," said Dennis to the three uniformed men above him, staring down, fascinated by all his wounds. He turned on an elbow to begin sitting up and then changed his mind. Even the elbow was raw.

"In a minute. First I must examine you," said the one with glasses. "Lift your shirt, please. How did you get all these scratches and abrasions?" The doctor was searching for an undamaged patch of chest to plant his stethoscope on.

"Bloody barnacles on the container. They hate me."

"How long were you in the water?"

"I think about half an hour till I hit the container – or it hit me."

"Turn over, please." The doctor listened at several places on his back, where there were fewer cuts, and then he said, "You were very fortunate. Floating containers are not as common as people think. Can you tell me what day it is?" He was poking through Dennis's hair.

"Wednesday? Yes, it must be. It was Tuesday the 31st when I left my boat in Amsterdam. Where are you based?"

The four-striper said, "We are the Rotterdam-Rijnmund Port Politie. If you left your boat in Amsterdam, what were you doing out at sea?"

"My cousin invited me on a fishing trip in his boat, but about five in the morning a ship snuck up on us and tipped us out. I'm OK. You should be looking for them now." Dennis struggled out of the blanket and swung his legs down.

"How many others were there in your boat?" asked the officer with the notepad.

"Four. Two young fellas, an older chap, and my cousin."

"What is your name?"

Dennis took a little thoughtful pause. The coastguards hadn't bothered to ask him that. His passport was probably pulped but he still had the moneybelt and thought he could remember the booking number for the *Estelle Maersk:* if he could get these chaps to drop him in Rotterdam today things could still be sweet for him and the *Godwit,* but if his name was on their hit list they might not. "Skotty Mulcahy, from Akarana, New Zealand," he said.

"What are your friends' names?"

"One of them was called Hans and my cousin is...Sam Snelgar. I can't remember what the other two were called. They were father and son. All of them had lifejackets."

The officer with the notepad went to speak to the man at the helm, who made a radio call.

"Why were you not wearing a lifejacket?" asked the doctor.

"Aw, I was just a ring-in at the last minute so they didn't have one for me. I had a sheepskin coat to wear that was really good in the boat, but once it got wet the damn thing nearly killed me. You got any food here on board?"

"You are a fortunate man, indeed - we have biscuits. You will get a meal soon, when we get to port. Can you stand up?"

Dennis could, but he had to hang on to the back of the seat even though the launch had slowed down considerably. Looking beyond a passing ship he could see lights flashing on straddle cranes between endless rows of containers. He was nearly safe on dry land.

One of the Politie, the Un-hooded One, brought him coffee and plenty of spicy biscuits. This lot of Water Politie seemed quite decent seagoing jokers.

Perhaps they could talk turkey to the Amsterdam lot about his boat, get them to send it over to him in Rotterdam.

His worst damaged bits were the tops of his feet, plus his face and fingertips – the fingers made it awkward to drink hot drinks or manage biscuits, but on land they weren't such vital parts. As for his face, by the time anyone he knew saw him, the scratches and scrapes would be well healed. Presuming his money was in fair condition he should be able to get hold of the *Godwit*, pay any stupid fine owing, get the container on board the ship and have her underway for Auckland today. He might even be able to wangle a cabin on the same ship. He could then fly home from Singapore, making it back in plenty of time to sign the sewer contract, settle Diane down and get to Skotty's Christmas do. What a story he would have for them. Never mind setting up in Asia just now. Aimee with her Chinese language would be useful one day but there was no hope Diane would let her leave school at fourteen.

There was loud sailor business outside and Dennis could tell the launch was easing into a berth. When he went up on deck he saw several Politie waiting on the wharf and was suddenly conscious of his clothing – pyjamas and no shoes, since even jandals would have hurt his feet. *Who cares?* he told himself.

Perhaps the Politie were there to tell him they'd already picked up Serge - and the others. He might have to hang about for a few days till he heard how they'd got on.

A blanket was dropped on his shoulders. "This way, please."

Among the Politie on the wharf there was a plainclothes photographer. "Congratulations," he said from behind his camera. Dennis worked an unwilling arm out to wave and smile. Several of the policemen clapped.

A Port Politie car was waiting to help Dennis after his ordeal, though the station was said to be close to the wharf. He clambered into the front seat and peered around, hoping to spot the *Estelle Maersk,* but the driver said Maersk kept its fleet to its own section of the port.

At the station, an officer with fancy epaulettes greeted Dennis and took him to meet someone with a crown on each shoulder - Inspector Schleffer.

"Welcome to Rotterdam-Rijnmund. I believe you had a very lucky escape. We are still concerned about your friends."

"You haven't picked them up yet?"

"No. We are hoping you can tell us about their boat and where they were planning to fish."

A blonde civilian with good teeth and a tight skirt brought more coffee and biscuits.

"They had this little inflatable, far too small for the five of us. They were a bunch of absolute amateurs – didn't know a thing about fishing. One of them had never been fishing in his life before. Thing is, I've got a boat of my own that should be in Rotterdam today and I'm hoping you can help me get it over from Amsterdam. It's booked -"

"Is this your boat?" The inspector reached across the desk and gave Dennis a photo of the *Godwit.*

"Gee, thanks. I never thought I'd get a photo of it outside the hotel."

"That is the problem, I am afraid. The Water Politie want to speak to you about tying up there, and there are several other matters. We will be transporting you to Amsterdam-Amstelland Station this afternoon to talk to them. I am glad we were able to rescue you and that you are so well, considering your injuries. May I have the photo back, please?"

"Hell! And what about the meal the doctor promised me?" Dennis shouted, with further variations, as he was hurried out of the inspector's office by two Politie, down a back corridor and into a van waiting outside.

Chapter 16

The Day We Went to Croydon,
Tottenham, London, 2 November 2006

That morning after a good night's sleep, Dennis's cousin woke in London to a quiet house smelling of coffee and fresh bread, and Hans calling him for breakfast. Downstairs he learned Anton's parents had gone to work and Fatima to school. There was washing hanging all around the room again.

"We need to get going - it's a long way to Croydon," said Hans.

"Why did you choose Croydon?" Sergey asked, stirring sugar into a second cup of coffee.

"Because Zaheed wanted me way south of The City and because that sort get all the good jobs in London. For us it's *'No Muslims Need Apply'* except for changing tyres or making ham sandwiches."

Anton nodded. "Have a look at the ticket-takers in all the stations on the way. They'll be black, but the engineers will be white."

"You're coffee-coloured, Ishmael," Sergey said. "You should be able to slip in between."

"How would you feel about a Chechynik joining our team?" asked Anton. "Get your coat."

They walked to Seven Sisters to catch the 9.20, changed at Victoria to the Southern Line and got off at Croydon High Street Flyover.

"It's taken us two and a quarter hours, and that's off-peak," Sergey said. "You're going to have to stay the night down here, Hans. The first train is at five in the morning, but there could be any sort of delay on the way and then you'd be late."

"Where would I stay?"

"There'll be untold places," Anton told him. "Come on, show us your bleeding site!"

Keen shoppers were bearing them along as they talked, heading towards high blocks of buildings, each of them a vertical mall.

"Look at that!" Anton pointed to fashion dummies in a shop window. "You never see girls as skinny as that in the street - or looking as good with so much of them showing. See that slapper up ahead? Thinks she can buy a skanky thing like that to wear and she'll be Justin Timberlake's next girl."

"It's all the shops with computers and TVs and DVDs that I hate," said Hans. "Like the kids on the train with their iPods. Zaheed says that's how djinns travel these days, in iPods. Anyway, these types down here think everyone can afford stuff like that and needs a new model every week.

"This is where I want to do it. At this ATM beside PC World," said Hans. "I'll hang around the station till about ten minutes to – we'll time it on the way back, how long it takes to walk here– and I'll arrive here right on seven. There'll be no one queuing that early. I'll put down my bag and - "

"Excuse me, gents. If you're not wanting to use the ATM, would you mind?" It was a labourer with a bankcard in his hand.

"Of course," said Sergey, "of course," and shepherded his boys away.

They found Hans a private hotel a few blocks from the bus station. The receptionist said there was no need to book, even at weekends, but was even more surprised to hear he wanted to stay all night.

Going home they had to change at Kings Cross. Down on the tracks a couple of mice were fighting over an apple core. The one that had it couldn't eat for having to dash at the other mouse. Twice trains interrupted the show before one contestant was eliminated.

"I guess he'll get eaten now," said Hans.

"You must get almost that hungry at Ramadan?" said Sergey.

"Never! I stock up at breakfast."

Sergey was laughing at him when the phone rang in his pocket. "Good afternoon, Zaheed." The big smile switched off. "When?"

Zaheed had more to tell and Sergey listened, turning away from the boys. "Did they give a name?"

More from Zaheed.

"Tomorrow. Use Herman's." Sergey folded the phone and put it away.

"Is it trouble with the…machinery?" asked Hans.

"Yes. Just a little trouble. And they're a bit worried about the weather. Where can I buy a Dutch newspaper?"

"I don't think my father stocks anything like that," said Anton. "You'd better try here."

Sergey went back into the station to look at the newsstand but returned empty-handed. He knew there'd been nothing about launching of the blue boat in the London papers – he'd read them all on the train coming south, while searching in vain for any mention of Litvinenko's state of health. He hoped there would be no question of returning any money

At Tottenham station the boys bought falafels for a late lunch and ate them as they walked along the streets of identical houses till they came to the one with the broken finial and the green door - Anton's home.

Mrs Hassan was back from the shop early. She came into the front hall, wearing her hijab, when she heard the door open. She had been crying but was brandishing two squashed red silk flowers at them and she looked angry. Before they could even take off their shoes she said, "So you did remember to bring me more flowers, Ishmael! I found your suitcases!" She shook the flowers in his face. Three men towering over her in the little hall did not intimidate her.

She started on Sergey. "How could you dare to use my good boy for such a dirty job? You are a wicked man! Oh, my Ishmael! When we sent you to the grammar school and to the best masada in London we - "

"Go inside and let me shut the door, Mama!" Anton said in a voice Sergey had never before heard from him.

Aisha sat in her husband's chair, with a navy tracksuit hanging above her. The three men sat opposite her, on the sofa.

She began quietly. "If you were living in Palestine I could perhaps understand it. If your home was just pile of stones and your whole family dead and the Noble Sanctuary walled off from you, maybe. But in a nice house like this, with a good life…?"

"Those things you said and worse are happening to our people all over the world. The only way to stop them is to do something that will show Mrs Blair what it feels like. Then she can tell Mrs Bush!" said Anton.

"Those women are nothing to do with you. It's like saying, just because you didn't get into medical school is a good reason to kill people! And what would *your* parents say, Warith?"

"Dad's mother got her leg blown off in August, remember? By a cluster bomb. He and Mum both went back to Palestine to look after her. Now the Israelis have built an eight-metre wall between the house and the farm. That is twenty-five feet - higher than your roof!"

"Are you doing it for money, then?"

"Would you think it was good if there was money paid? My mother's given all her jewellery to Hamas."

"Allahu akbar! And now our sons!" Aisha was weeping. "And Ibrahim knew! He lied to me! He told me he was going to Folkestone to see a friend with a shop who didn't know how to do VAT returns! Oh, the trouble you have brought on us!"

Ishmael went over and drew his mother up to hug her close, sending the others out with a look. He watched over her shoulder as they walked down the garden from the kitchen door. Aisha sobbed and Ishmael kept hugging her and patting her back. Through the clotheshorse he could see the other two men. They had their hands in their pockets and Warith was kicking the brick edging around the withered tomatoes.

"I've been thinking of this for a long time, Mama. I've prayed about it. It was you who taught me to end each day, always, by saying, *'O God, in Your name do I die and live.'*"

"*O Allah, open for me the doors of Your mercy,*" said Aisha.

They said together, "*Our Lord, give us the best in this life and the best in the next and protect us from the punishment of the fire.*"

"What's that in your pocket?" Aisha drew herself away. "Is that something to do with the bomb?"

Ishmael got a plastic bag out of his coat pocket and showed her two rolls of parcel tape. "I saw a cockroach up in the bathroom last night – "*See one, you've got thousands*". I'm going to get you some stuff and fumigate the place properly this time. You've got to seal every crack around the doors and windows to do the job properly."

"I suppose that's another good trick you picked up in Pakistan!" Now Aisha was offended as well as heartbroken.

"Don't worry, I'll do it when you're at work - in the morning, before we go to St.Al..."

"St Albans? Why ever are you going there?"

Ishmael didn't answer, but went straight out of the room and tapped loudly on the kitchen window to tell the others they should come in again.

Chapter 17

In the Cells,
Amsterdam, 1 November 2006

When the van carrying Dennis stopped behind the Central Police station the doors opened onto a ramp with high wire sides. He mentally shrugged – he wasn't really dressed for an escape attempt anyway.

Two Politie hurried him into an interview room and left him there alone. It was a bit warmer inside than the van had been but the seats were still bare plastic. He stood to try the door. Locked. Windows: high, and fitted with bars. Not very friendly after what he'd been through.

The bleak surroundings soon had him thinking about his story. He must avoid saying anything that would hinder his getting hold of the boat and must not mention the girl at the hotel or the lighthouse keeper – whatever his name was. How much could he say about Serge? Or *Sam Snelgar*, as he'd called him to the Politie. He'd given Skotty's name as his own. He'd better have a quick look at his passport before the Politie did - make sure it was unreadable.

Dennis felt for the zip of his money belt with his ripped fingers. Poking about inside the pocket hurt like fury, the edges of the banknotes cutting into the barnacle slits in his fingertips. He couldn't feel the bulk of the passport, and pulled the bag open wider to try and look in.

There was no passport.

Had he left it at the lighthouse? He'd used it at Marken to change money at the bank.

The Kustwacht! Those lovely lads had taken it. When he was asleep.

No good going on with the alias – and he should have used Skotty's real name anyway. "Alistair Mulcahy" would have pleased the bloggers more.

He could go on a bit about the old girl from the rowboat at the Hotel de L'Europe, say he'd been picked up by her in a bar in Amsterdam. He had better say they'd met on the internet - that she'd arranged from New Zealand to meet him in Holland. After all, she sounded Kiwi, like her daughter.

No, leave them out of it. The daughter had seemed grumpy when he first saw her but she'd been very helpful getting him out of the hotel. So he shouldn't be getting them into his trouble. The boat business needed a quick fix if he was to make it to the container depot in time. Did Dutchmen take bribes? He patted his damp belt. At least he still had some money.

He felt for the email with the shipping consignment numbers. It was tattered but he thought he could still remember the name of the wharf where he had to collect the new cradle and the container. Pity his airline tickets were gone – must have been inside the satchel he'd lost in the capsize - but they were electronic so he could print them out again at any internet café. Everything should have been put into the money belt; he should not have worried about a bulge on his abs. But then the rotten Kustwacht would have had the lot.

The door was unlocked and two Politie and another policeman in a grey uniform came in and rearranged the furniture with three chairs around the table and one on his side.

"Please put this on."

Dennis was handed an orange overall. There was a good joke in all this somewhere about William of Orange but he was too busy with press-studs and sore fingers to attend to literary matters just then.

"Sit down, please," said the first blue Politie, who had taken the head of the table. "This is the Supraregional Investigation Forum. I am Inspector Hayden from the Public Prosecution Service of Amsterdam-Amstelland and this is Officer Freiswyk, who represents IJsselland Supraregion. We are here to discuss you and your misdemeanours. You are free to speak or not speak, in either Dutch or English or any other language, and you have the right to ask for an interpreter or for legal advice. Rechecheur Jan Schlaaper, here – " indicating the man in grey, bent over a notepad "is a member of the CIE, the Criminal Intelligence Service, and he will advise you if you need any advice." The man in grey looked up with droopy red eyes, nodded and returned to his notepad.

"I don't mind talking," said Dennis, "as long as you can all understand English?"

"Yes," confirmed the second blue Politie, who had a knobbly red face and big ears. "We will conduct this interview entirely in English. What is your name?" he asked, switching on the dictaphone.

Dennis reassessed his many options. He'd spin them a bit of a yarn to see what they were after and to give himself time for sorting things out. "Skotty Mulcahy, but round here I'm known more as Xavier Hollander."

"What are you doing in the Netherlands?"

"I'm on a working holiday."

"Is that your working name?"

"Yeah. Isn't it great? I saw this film about a famous Dutch madam who made it big in New York - I've always thought it'd be a better name for a man than a woman, but I suppose sex differences didn't matter much in her game. Anyway, I do OK with it in the brown cafés."

"You won't be working for a few days till your nose has healed, I think. You sound like an Australian."

"Yes, I hear that quite a lot. Nice to be a bit exotic in my business, you know."

"What part does your boat play in it?" asked the grey policeman, the bloodhound adviser, abruptly coming into play.

"Well, the customers enjoy a change of scene..."

"Where did you get this boat?"

"My auntie left it to me in her will."

"Is your aunt Russian?"

That changed things - they knew where the boat came from in spite of the new name. Better cut literally to the chase since the boat trouble was probably the most serious charge on their list. The

Russian Aunt option was very tempting but she wouldn't be wasted - he could always revive her for the Northland Fish and Game website. The boys would gobble her up like burley!

He said, "Yeah. She knew I'd need a shallow draft on the canals – there's so much rubbish thrown in these days."

"That is another matter the Amsterdam-Amstelland Interregional team wants to discuss: that you illegally entered the canal system of Amsterdam after 1 November!" said Politie One, looking at him severely. "And you abandoned your boat in an historic section of canal in Amsterdam. Also, that you were seen speeding in an inland waterway, the Ijesselmeer; that you failed to keep a safe distance from un-powered craft; that you launched a pleasure craft from an unregistered launch point; and that you abandoned dangerous equipment in a nationally designated marine recreation area!"

"Is that all me?" said Dennis, very surprised. "Come off it! I've only been in Holland a couple of days."

"I thought you worked here?" Number Two Blue Politie pounced. The wart on the end of his nose wobbled.

"Just tell us where you were between 1800 hours on 1 November, and 0130 hours today," demanded the bloodhound.

"You've lost me, mate."

"I must advise you," the Inspector said, "that you are a person of interest to the Aliens Politie! You are a suspected alien, without papers, in possession of possibly contraband equipment, with military or terrorist potential! You will answer the questions of these officers, and depending on your answers, your case may be referred to the Supraregional Investigation Forum or to another body outside this jurisdiction!" He sat back and laid both fists at the edge of the table in front of him. His glasses shone gold in the last of the daylight.

"What a lot of cobblers! All I was doing was bringing my nice little glass-bottomed boat into the wharf for shipment to New Zealand, where I will take tourists out to see lovely coloured fish! And if it comes to big words, you three are acting in restraint of international trade!"

"We want to know your name, your home address and what you have been doing in the Netherlands," said Number One with heavy emphasis. "Where is your passport - or your Identity Card if, as you say, you are working in Amsterdam?"

"Didn't I tell you? Some old bitch at the Hotel Europe's got them. Well, I told the Port Politie: she said she was going out for rookworst...I want to talk to my lawyer."

"You are a very foolish person," said Number One. "If you were innocent you would not have tried to complicate your story. You would have told us the simple facts of your situation and you would now be on your way. We will not waste any more time on you tonight. You will be detained here in the cells till the morning - by then we will have received your passport and identity card from the Kustwacht. You will appear before another tribunal tomorrow when your future will be decided. Interview ended at 4.28 p.m."

Dennis sprang up, his chair tumbling over, as the officers prepared to leave. "I demand to speak to the New Zealand Ambassador! I am a New Zealand citizen here in the Netherlands on legitimate business and you are treating me as a criminal!"

There was no response to his outburst. Number Two unplugged the dictaphone, sent Dennis a malevolent look and followed the others out.

Dennis wondered if the famous Bogdanovich luck was still bobbing along in his wake, or whether he would have to think of something else to bear his spirits up. It was going to take some pretty hot invention to turn this into a good story.

Chapter 18

St Albans,
North London, 3 November 2006

On Friday Anton looked up the subway journey planner on the internet and decided the route from Tottenham to St. Albans was so complicated and the weather outside so miserable, he'd asked his father to lend him the shop van. Ibrahim looked very sad as he handed over the keys outside the front door of the house and got into the passenger seat.

Sergey, watching his face in the side mirror, thought it wouldn't now take much more than his wife's anguish to make him pull the plug. The boat trip had been a challenge for him to revive lost skills - and to stay awake - but now the sacrifice of his son was coming close. Sergey had seen very few thorn bushes in Tottenham apart from a few brambles along the train track and no rams at all, but Ibrahim was certainly looking for Allah to intervene in his family crisis, perhaps by removing the distributor of the van. They dropped Ibrahim at the shop and Sergey could see him in the side mirror watching them set off towards the London Road, no doubt relieved they had no luggage with them.

The poor man could not know which would be his son's last day. Maybe Sergey should have kept a few grains of the polonium isotope to put him out of his misery, but it wouldn't really have been quick enough. There must be something in the paper today about Litvinenko. If he could buy a Dutch paper in St. Albans he might see that photo of Zaheed - and Dennis. His body might have been found by now.

Today he definitely should do something about Anton's mother. Maybe rat poison? In her coffee? She was the one likely to crack and run to the police - or even just put the suitcases out with the rubbish. She could have left the shop on her little, short legs and be hurrying home to do it at this moment.

Now Sergey was doubly anxious as Anton headed northwest to St. Albans. Apart from the risk of betrayal by Ishmael's mother, his own stupid cousin could have already blown the whole scheme wide open by jabbering what little he knew to someone in the Netherlands, or to someone who pulled him out of the sea. Once the rocket goes off, just a description of the Crown Removals truck will be enough. It would then be remembered at the Polish border and perhaps by people held up in the road when they were launching the boat on the banks of the Ijsselmeer. And someone in Oud-Zuilen might report seeing it go into the factory.

A siren screamed behind them on the outskirts of St Albans and Anton pulled over to let a striped police car swish pass.

"Feel like a jam sandwich?" asked Hans.

Anton laughed at him in the rear-vision mirror. "Nah. Too soggy."

Sergey tried not to show any interest. He lit a cigarette but Anton told him to put it out, saying his father was very strict about no one smoking in the house or van.

"Do you remember that time the cashier was going to call the police on us at that gas station in Birmingham? He thought we were thugs, the racist bastard!" said Hans, leaning over between the front seats. "Slammed the window shut on us because we were all dressed up in our black suits for Farida's wedding."

Anton explained to Sergey beside him, "Plus we'd both shaved our hair off for a joke."

"Yeah!" Hans slapped the upholstery. "We were right out of petrol too, but my cousin looked all right. She showed him some money and he soon came round."

In the centre of St Albans they left the van in a parking building and walked out into St. Peters Street. This was an older market town, more stylish than Tottenham, once catering to tourists crazy about Roman remains, and now making itself into a modern service centre, as well as a trendy weekend market for Londoners.

Sergey said, "On Sunday morning it will look quite different. All down this street stallholders will be setting up the Farmers' Market. People will be queuing up, eager to buy organic vegetables fresh enough to make them live forever, but unfortunately Sergey's bomb will have gone off before the stalls open."

"Nah, antioxidants won't do it for them this week," said Anton.

"Never mind," said Hans. "The news about the radiation danger from your bomb, Sergey, will make all the housewives round here keener to stock up. There'll be hundreds out early."

"That's right, the farmers would already have cut their cabbages and by Sunday morning they'll realise I've turned them into gold bricks. They should wrap them up to get the highest price," said Sergey.

Anton changed the subject. "I'll look a bit silly in a suit, carrying my satchel at six-thirty on a Sunday morning at a Farmers' Market, won't I?"

"Carry a clipboard as well - that'll be a good cover. This Sunday morning there'll be officials running all over England trying to look as though they can tell people what to do next," said Sergey. "The main thing you both need to remember is, do not be late. If you are, Zaheed and Herman will already have got the rocket up and then your mobile won't be any use as a starter. Do it at ten to seven."

"I think I'll stand over by that fancy street lamp."

"That'll be a good place because it'll still be pretty dark at that hour. Put your bag down beside a nice bucket of gladioli, have the phone on your clipboard and make your call. Come on, let's get back home. We need a little lie down to get ourselves straight for tomorrow."

"Don't you want to see the shrine of England's first Christian martyr?" Anton asked.

"Or the Roman ruins?" Hans added.

"No, thanks. We'll make our own," said Sergey, going to pick out an armful of newspapers from a street kiosk.

Anton went into a shop and bought a cockroach bomb for a souvenir. Then they went back to Tottenham.

In the afternoon Anton and Hans prepared the house for fumigation by taping cracks around the doors and windows. They had to go out to buy three more rolls of tape but went into a bucket shop up the high street, not to Anton's father's shop.

Sergey found the suitcases were still under his bed, and lay down to guard them while feverishly combing through his pile of newspapers for anything about a sick Russian in London, his cousin's body found in the Channel or the boat turning up in Amsterdam. The poisoned sushi still hadn't come to notice, but in case it had not found favour he'd left enough powder at the hotel to make the boss's enemy a lovely cup of tea.

He still hadn't been able to find a Dutch paper and there were no pictures of the boat in the German or French papers, but on page three of *The Times'* news section he found a picture of a big blue golf ball, an aeronautical radar installation at Cromer on the east coast in Norfolk that used high-frequency pulses of radiation "equal to a million mobile phones" for tracking incoming aircraft "as much as two hundred miles out across the North Sea." The news story was that the machine had recently gone rogue and was shorting out the electrics in cars passing on the road outside the back fence. *"It gave me a dead dashboard. One fired fuse box cost me three hundred pounds last time, and now it's happened again," said a woman who drove a Nissan Almera.'*

Sergey sprang up. "Look at this!" he shouted as he ran downstairs to show the others, who were watching TV. "Now will you believe what our bomb will do? And look at this article beside it – it's just old rubbish, been dragged off the internet, a forty-year-old blah about an imaginary EMP bomb set off over Kansas that could have crippled the entire USA!"

The boys read it all.

"Well, they can't say they weren't warned," said Anton.

"Does anyone read *The Times*?" asked Sergey.

"Nah," said both boys.

"Not round here," added Hans.

Chapter 19

Morning in the Cells,
Amsterdam and elsewhere, 3 November 2006

Dennis woke again to a policeman shaking his shoulder and staring into his face.

"Good morning. It is six o'clock. Breakfast in one hour," said the guard. Then he slammed the door and the light went off.

"I know that, you idiot! You've been telling me all night!" Dennis yelled after him. For the first time the cell was almost dark. He thought he might at last get a few minutes' sleep. It was absolutely inhuman the way he'd been treated. Every time he'd pulled the blanket over his head the door had opened and he was shouted at for several minutes - they must have thought he was suicidal or something. Another night like this and he would be! He had plenty to tell the New Zealand ambassador about the Dutch Politie. The name was an absolute joke.

"Raus! Raus!" The lights were on again and tin pans were clanked in his face.

Breakfast à la Nazis: a bowl of porridge with a mug of tea sitting in it. No milk. He'd sat up to grab the bowl and save it from spilling on him but was so groggy from lack of sleep he could hardly hold the thing straight. It was enough to make a man weep. The spoon had fallen on the floor. He looked at it, imagining it lying beside a pair of Hotel de L'Europe scuffs, and a little giggle came along with the first tear.

Bush Pig would love this scene - it would remind him of his honeymoon. Dennis began to mentally compose a blog about it for the Fish Club as he tackled the first inch of tea and then picked up the spoon to scrape the porridge from around the bottom of the mug. *A good bowl of porridge, and a man can face anything*, his father always said.

"Would that be without milk and sugar, sir?" squeaked the waiter in his head, and Dennis was back.

He'd show the bastards! You don't mess with a Bogdanovich! He'd march into that court and read the riot act! Today was the day he had to have the boat in the container and onto the ship. The sooner they came for him the better.

He washed his face, swilled his mouth out and tidied his hair in the steel mirror. He'd managed to achieve toileting, get the overalls buttoned up again and was sitting ready on his bunk for half an hour before the hatch opened and a face peered in. He stood up and the hatch closed.

After another half hour he thought he'd do a few press-ups until his sore hands objected. Then he lay down for a while and nearly dozed off, till he heard the hatch again and sprang up, but was too late to see the guard's face.

Dennis leaped two steps to the door and hammered on it. "Take me to the judge!" he yelled, and continued thumping and yelling till he was hoarse and his knuckles were bruised. There was no reply.

All this was repeated six times. No more food was offered, but the hatch opened on the hour and Dennis waited there, ready to punch at the guard's face through the grille and scream his demand for justice. The knuckles on both hands began to bleed over the barnacle scratches but the guard never answered him. In between times Dennis kneed the metal door and kicked at it as long as his joints would allow.

At three-fifty the hatch opened briefly, then the door was pushed inwards and knocked Dennis onto his bunk.

Two guards with truncheons came into the cell.

"Come!" they said and grabbed an arm each. They pushed him out the door, holding his arms behind him. Two Politie in long grey coats stood outside. The guards drove him past them and on down the corridor to a lift that was standing open. Dennis was shoved into the corner face first, and the others crammed in behind him. The lift ascended.

His left knee painfully scraped against the wall as the guards swapped holds on his wrists. "You bastards are going to be sorry for this!" he croaked into the crack in the corner.

One truncheon hit him on the head and the other behind the knees. The lift opened and, slumped over, he was dragged out backwards by his twisted arms. His right shoulder was ripped out of its socket. Someone was screaming. Then the guards heaved him up, grabbed him under the armpits and carried him with his raw feet dragging on concrete. Through the agony of his right shoulder Dennis saw brown boots and recognised the wire mesh of the ramp he had walked up, going into the Politie station the day before. He was dropped on the floor of a van, vibrating from its running motor. The men in coats pulled down dickey seats by his head, the doors were slammed and the vehicle began to move.

When he woke, Dullboot put a water bottle in his mouth. They were still travelling. He had blankets over him but the floor was cold and hard. In spite of the pain in his head he tried to turn over, but his shoulder must have been dislocated. He groaned.

Shinyboot laughed and offered to pull Dennis up onto a seat that he flopped down above his face. Dennis cursed him and shut his eyes. After a bit he gingerly attempted to turn the other way, but what with the pain in his neck and an early warning from the other shoulder, he stopped. He tried bending his knees. That was not an option either. He was reduced to concentrating on the bits of him suspended between the ridges of the floor.

He could tell the van was speeding on a motorway, and remembered the journey across Germany and the Netherlands with Serge. After another kilometre or two he asked, "Where are we going?"

The guards conferred in Dutch.

Dullboot said, "To see the judge."

They both laughed.

Chapter 20

Charing Cross,
London, 4 November 2006

Sergey bought a coffee and a packaged biscuit in the forecourt at Charing Cross Station. At the darkest table, with his suitcase at his feet, he surveyed the scene and pictured it as it would appear in tomorrow's paper, without pillars or monument. It should be spectacular enough for Zaheed. Half a pillar would be a good touch. The bomb by his feet would choose which of them to leave.

Zaheed was always crazy about propaganda. When he'd seen the photo of the double-decker bus with its top blown off, right outside a hospital, he'd looked absolutely jealous. He'd torn the picture out, put it in his shirt pocket and immediately announced he wanted one bomb to go off early so that George Bush could have pictures of what was coming to him. He didn't care that tomorrow's bombers would have a full security alert to deal with.

Sergey was glad he was given the early job. Anton had been forced to give away his site with its escape route, thereby losing his chance for any afterlife on Earth but he was going to get to Paradise much quicker from St Albans than from Charing Cross. For Sergey it meant he did something to help the jihad at ground level and would see the rainbow bomb detonate as well. That was his dream and the culmination of his life's work.

He eyed the Charing Cross monument, wondering whose memory he was about to obliterate. The taxi that had brought him from the restaurant was still waiting for another fare. He hoped Hans wasn't too talkative or overgenerous to his driver, taking him to Kings Cross to catch the Croydon train. Hans seemed to have enjoyed the festive Friday atmosphere at the restaurant and all the Turkish knickknacks but the dinner had stopped being a proper finale once Anton and his father chose to go instead to the girl's gymnastic display. Unbelievable. Zaheed would have known how to fix it – if they'd still had any polonium dust he would certainly have sugared Ibrahim's coffee with it.

Yet the way Ibrahim had saved his son - and Sergey himself - from the sea had to be remembered. Making a return journey in that horrible little boat showed how much the man supported the whole jihad. He wouldn't talk, even if he did survive the EMP bomb tomorrow.

The couple at the next table were quarrelling: "...better than your father and his stinking dogs," she said.

"He loves those dogs. They're all he's got now," said her partner.

"What about us? I notice he's not slow coming to the table when I cook."

"Come on, Sausage, let's go. He'll be snoring by now."

The minute they left, a man with dirty hair and no buttons on his coat swooped on their cups and drained both. Sergey sipped his coffee, and with his foot slid his suitcase a little further into the darkness under the table. He took the biscuit out of his pocket and broke open the wrapper, conscious of the newcomer's attention.

If it hadn't been for his mother he could himself have been homeless in St Petersburg when his wife kicked him out.

I was in the shower when she left the house. Zaheed had sent me home from the laboratory at 2am, I'd had a few hours sleep and was going back to relieve him – we were running long computer repeats, modelling consumption of solid rocket fuel at various trajectories. It didn't matter to us that we weren't going to be paid for the work, but that morning she just stood at the bathroom door slowly saying, over and over:

"Your rocket is going nowhere!"

When I got out of the shower I found she'd left me the boy to mind while she went out to get her hair permanently curled. Those curls are all cut off now.

I was standing by the door, still wrapped in the towel, when I saw her laptop - and her red boots standing there, empty. The Swiss Army knife was on the table beside my keys. I dropped the towel, grabbed the knife and flicked out the major blade.

How the boy cried when the toe of her boot went flying under the sofa. He crawled after it, blubbering, but he cheered up once I started on her laptop - I'd made a game of it by then, popping the keypads out and so on. When I started on the inner works, where she hid her business data, I let him choose which blade I should use next. He was quite enthusiastic about that, even offering to take his clothes off to match me.

Later on, after I'd got dressed, we made the motherboard into buterbrodi (open sandwiches) using her French cosmetics for mayonnaise and slices of lipstick for tomato. I might have gone a bit far there, but she'd never shown any respect for my work. She openly despises science.

People like her are nothing but barnacles on the ship of state, thinking any movement is progress as long as it brings them loot to pile up round themselves. As for ones like her boss, Kodorkovsky - they are more like shipworms; it was his greed that caused the total collapse of the banks in 1998.

That was our ruination too. You can't develop rockets unless you can command the produce of every factory and farm in every state of the USSR. Perestroika - setting the republics loose - was a bigger disaster for our team than the loss of the Columbia was for NASA.

Anyway, it was at very moment when I started slicing up her boots and wrecking her laptop that I had the revelation: the only way our EMP achievement could be saved for science instead of being turned into electric power plants was by using the democratic technique of "going public": we had to demonstrate the bomb's potential by setting off a sample over Europe. I would get my friend Zaheed the warhead he wanted and he would happily deliver it to London- the perfect shape for the experiment. Then the world could judge our work.

Tomorrow...

Early tomorrow morning my wife will remember her bitter words, and in the updraught of our explosions my CV will float on a rainbow cloud to the top of military inboxes on every continent.

Here I am, about to light the fuse on the first charge. Sergey held out his cigarette and looked at the smoke rising. He stubbed it out.

A bunch of footballers came onto the forecourt and went rollicking down the steps, lashing at each other with black scarves. One had a furry brown ball with a throwing handle and big yellow feet. He slung it at a friend wearing a jester's hat. The hat skidded under Sergey's table.

"You didn't see that one coming, Jimbo," the attacker bellowed.

Jimbo retrieved his hat with a dimpled apology and ran after the gang, joining in a loud song about 'Ten Guitars' and a whole lot of dancing that faded away down the street.

No damage.

10.48 pm.

His taxi had gone but the hungry man was still there. Sergey took a bite from his hard chocolate cookie and laid it down, swigged enough coffee to be sure the man was looking, and packed away cigarettes and lighter in his money belt. He walked off, smoothing down the bulge on the brand new suit.

At the last column of the portico he paused to check that the hungry man had taken the biscuit bait.

Yes. He seemed not to have noticed the suitcase. Sergey hoped he would have so few teeth the biscuit would take a long time to get through.

Sergey went into the concourse. The same grizzled Black cleaner he'd seen on Wednesday was swabbing steps near the toilets. The gate was open, saving Sergey 20p.

Then he made for the Staff Door, following a man with golf clubs over his shoulder and a cloth cap on his head. The clubs also wore caps. The man was checking-in at a time clock. When Anton let slip that there was an escape route from his site he had said nothing about any time clock. He'd only said to go down into the engine room and set the bomb off from there.

Sergey watched the man's fingers closely and tried to memorise the code that would produce the magic number, 22. The high gate beside him was closing and Sergey threw himself at it.

Too late.

He tried to repeat the numbers the man had used, listening to him clatter off down the stairs and through a door that slammed below. No luck. He searched his memory for anything he had ever known about common displacement errors. He even punched in random re-combinations of the same numbers. Nix.

He had decided to tackle the gate mesh that would admit only his fingers, and squeeze over the narrow gap above, when another worker arrived.

Sergey went back to the time clock. It said 10 53 but the bomb timer was running one minute fast.

"Having trouble, are we? Where you from?" said a little man with a broom.

"I'm an engineer," was all Sergey could think of.

"Ooh! One of those cushy bastards. Spends nights on a bed in the back of a van with headphones tuned to the cricket, eh? What's your number?"

"They didn't give me one."

"Didn't they? I suppose it's only for the emergency muster - if there's a fire or something - and there usually already would be by the time you lot get here. There you are, you're '23' – wish I was 23 again! 24 wasn't too bad either, but it'd be a bit wasted down here. Come on."

The man planted his broom and held the gate open to let Sergey through, then lead the way into the depths.

Sergey paused outside a door marked *Engine Room* as the helpful man disappeared round a landing and down more stairs, Sergey took his cap off in case Golf-Club Man was inside and remembered him. He opened the door and entered a high noisy hall, full to the roof with large black machinery moving banks of clanking escalators upward and downward. The air was thick with the smell of hot oil. There was a narrow passageway either side, and when he saw the golf clubs straight ahead of him he dodged to the left side of the machinery tower. Peeping down that side he saw two men playing cards on a shelf at the far end of the room. The arrival of Golf-Club Man caused them to pack up and go to join him, somewhere out of sight.

10. 54pm.

The door opened again. Sergey froze behind it against the wall, hoping the door would shield him. A fourth young man, also carrying golf clubs, hurried in. He was greeted with loud jocular remarks about his putting ability and tomorrow's score.

10.55pm.

Sergey took out his mobile phone and made a call. He put the phone back in his pocket and went up the left aisle till he could see the four men sitting on stools They were going to have a briefing. The machine noise stopped, and Sergey's ears and jaw throbbed back to normality. The first golfer was pointing to a wash basin in the corner,

"If you think of this as a Toolbox Talk, that is the most essential tool in your toolbox, right there. It will save your life every day. The greatest danger in this job is not electricity, it is not fire. What is it?"

"RAT SHIT!" everyone yelled.

"Right. Never eat anything, never touch your face…"

Sergey stepped forward. "Send your men out now! A bomb has been set to explode in three minutes."

"Go!" said the foreman, and they went. He leaned back and pushed a button.

Even before the door slammed on the other men, the tannoy was blaring: "Inspector Sounds, will you please go to the Operations Room immediately. Inspector Sounds, will you…"

Sergey moved right to cut off the foreman's path to the door.

The foreman dodged the other way, kicking over the stools as he went round a bank of wheels at the toe of an escalator. When Sergey got to that corner the man had disappeared. He wasn't among the machinery and he couldn't have got to the door. But there was a small, brick-lined opening in the side wall - Anton's escape shaft!

Sergey ducked his head and climbed into it on his knees. A touch of pity for his new suit got through.

For the first hundred metres the tunnel was lit and Sergey saw wires and smoke alarms on the roof, rat droppings on the floor, and the foreman's behind and boots busy up ahead. Then it was dark, but though the foreman was going fast, Sergey - counting down with the bomb - gained on him.

They must have gone two hundred metres when they felt the concussion of the explosion. Bricks fell on Sergey's back and tumbled under his hands and knees as he strove to crawl even faster, expecting to feel the other man's boots at any moment and dreading their way was blocked by the tunnel having collapsed ahead.

The only noise was of squealing rats skittering along the tunnel, over them and underneath them - in both directions at first and then doubling back from the rear. Dennis, his crazy cousin, had been quite right about them being smart survivors. This tunnel must therefore be a good bet. The bricks and soil here might not yet be radioactive and every metre gained improved their survival odds - though some of the rats might have been irradiated in the station behind them. Sergey felt the scratches on his neck afresh.

How much further? The foreman's boots kept kicking bricks back at him.

Sergey fell back a little. It was good to have an expert ahead, even if the man was hostile. He wished he'd bought good boots. Gloves would have been even more useful since his hands were already raw from the broken bricks, but what he'd need most at the end of the tunnel would be a decontamination suit. Meantime he kept crawling, ignoring the pain in knees and back and hands.

Fewer bricks had fallen this far into the tunnel and the rats had now left them far behind. So there must be an exit. There were still wires running overhead. He must be three hundred metres from Charing Cross. If they came out at another station it would undoubtedly be on high alert, and the minute he emerged the man ahead would turn him over to security. Sergey would be caught like a rat even if he crawled back down the tunnel.

He tried to catch up but the other man went faster. The foreman wasn't younger than Sergey, but as a sportsman he was probably fitter. Sergey felt a loop of wire touch his arm and grabbed at it, hoping it wasn't alive. Several metres came loose fairly willingly and Sergey struggled to get his pocketknife out and cut a length free. He had lost ground but gained a possible weapon. Why had he not brought a gun? He put the knife in his mouth, wound up the wire and stuffed it into his coat, then set out to catch his enemy to immobilise or kill him by some means as yet unimagined. Something a caveman would think of would have to do.

Sergey began slithering along by hauling on his elbows. If he lived to tell the tale he would call himself "Sergey, the Siberian Snake". His hands and knees were so sore he had no choice but it seemed he was gaining on his quarry and once he caught up and entangled his feet in the wire then perhaps something could be done.

Light was growing up ahead. Both men were panting and pushing themselves to new levels of desperation. When Serge could almost touch the boot ahead he snatched the loops of wire out of his coat, and the next time a boot lifted off the ground he snaffled it and pulled. The other boot smashed back and struck down the side of his head, nearly tearing his ear off. Serge rolled onto the newly arrived foot, immobilising it, and pulled the wire around the first leg up to the knee. As the other man tried to turn over and get his arms into play Serge was able to wrap the wire round the second leg. The man was bucking and smashing Serge against the roof of the tunnel. The knife cut into his lip.

Holding the wire tight, Serge took the knife with his free hand and began to slice at the captive legs. A scream told him when he had cut something vital in the lower left leg. The body collapsed and Serge rolled over to trap the other boot and stab into the groin. Another scream filled the tunnel. The leg went flat and shuddered till Serge let go of the knife and hauled himself over his victim. The man tried to heave and snatch at him but Serge was free!

"Bloody murderer! Bloody murdering Paki bastard! You'll die too! Bloody murdering devil!" The man's shrieks filled the echoing space.

Serge crawled away from him as fast as he could, into light and the welcome oily smell of machinery. He had arrived in the silent engine room of another subway station very like the one he had just destroyed. Embankment would have been closer. This must be Piccadilly, or Leicester Square.

There was no one to see him emerge in this engine room. He dusted himself down and looked for blood, front and back. There was little visible damage. The creases in his trousers were still sharp above and below the ragged holes over his raw knees. Such sights would not be unusual today.

Sergey washed his face quickly at the basin in the corner and smoothed down his hair. A little mirror showed his grazed right ear and bright blood clogging the bristles around the cut on his mouth. He splashed more water at his mouth and scrubbed the blood out with the corner of his shirt. Feeling stiff and sore, he rinsed the basin before drying his face and hands on a grubby towel. He tucked in his shirt, pulled his cap out of his pocket and put it on, then drew himself up to tackle the climb to the station. He did not stoop to see how long it would be before his adversary in the tunnel could drag himself out. The engine room door closed behind him.

Chapter 21

Cottage Hospital,
somewhere in Europe, 5 November 2006

Dennis woke in a bed. He was wearing green hospital pyjamas and his watch and money belt were gone. Someone was standing beside the window. It was an old-fashioned wooden window like those in the bach at Leigh but this was set deep in a wall of rough, plastered stone. The dark figure at the window turned and came towards him. It was a male in a white steward's uniform.

"How are you feeling today?" He had an American accent rather like Serge's.

"Not bad. It's mostly my head. Where am I?"

"Don't worry. You are just here to get well. How does the shoulder feel now its back in the socket?"

"A bit better. Where are those two bastards who did it to me?"

"Oh, they're not here. We sent them straight back. There's nobody like that here. How did you get all the cuts on your face and the front of your body? And on the tops of your feet?"

"Bloody barnacles did that."

"Seemed excessive, even for... How's about breakfast?"

"Where are we?"

"You're in a safe house. Would you like pancakes and bacon? Or I could scramble you some eggs?"

"Safe from what?"

"I'll get you pancakes. How do you like your coffee? White and sugar?"

"White tea, one sugar and I want to make a phone call."

"Who do you want to call - Serge or Frits or Pete or Zaheed? You were raving about them all night."

"Not Zaheed! Frits and Zaheed are the same chap. I'd call Serge but I haven't got his number. I want to call my wife."

"OK, OK. I'll get your breakfast and then we'll see about your phone call."

Who would he call? The shipping agent's number would be on the slip in his money belt but would the receptionist talk English? The only numbers he knew off by heart were the Auckland office, his wife's and his mother's, plus a couple of fishing mates'. His mother would panic and be useless. His wife wouldn't want to listen... He might try Bill Sellars or Bush Pig or Bob Roberts. Bill would probably be best. What time of the day would it be in New Zealand? Bill wouldn't care but Cheryl was a midwife – she might be peeved if the phone rang in the middle of the night and it wasn't a baby.

The orderly returned with a tray. He set it down as a tray table and lifted Dennis into a sitting position, wedged with two extra pillows. "There you go!" The cup and fork were set on the left of the tray in recognition of his right arm being in a sling, and the bacon already cut up.

"Thank you." Dennis said. He started to drink the tea first, eyeing the stack of pancakes and maple syrup. "Hey, where's my watch and money belt?" he called to the retreating orderly.

"Ah. I'll see about them too," the man said as he closed the door.

Dennis shovelled in the bacon and had hacked away half the pancakes before he pushed the tray down the bed and swung his legs over the side. The knees felt very bad but he had to get to the window. He used the small bedside table as a walker for the last metre and managed to see a snowy garden and wooden gates inside a high stone wall before the orderly came back.

"What are you doing out of bed? You don't like your breakfast?" He came and put an arm round Dennis's chest and supported him back to bed. "I was going to tell you that the ligaments in your knees are quite badly damaged, but you've found that out now. If you ever want to regain full movement you're going to have to rest them for six weeks before you start any exercise at all."

"Where is this? It wasn't snowing that hard in Holland! Where have you brought me?" Dennis was looking right in the man's face as he lowered him onto the bed. The grey-green eyes never wavered. The whiskers in the nostrils were neatly trimmed. He was strong but not young.

"The snow came down very heavy last night, when you were sleeping after the anaesthetic. Now, swing your legs in - I'll help you lift them. There you go. Do you want to finish your breakfast?"

Dennis sulkily accepted the tray back and mopped up the maple syrup with the pancakes. A man had to keep up his strength, especially in dangerous circumstances. Besides he'd always been fond of pancakes. His wife and even his daughter made them, but these were much lighter.

Where the hell was he? He had seen snowy pine-tree tips over the wall. Russia again? The Black Forest? Lithuania? Could be anywhere. When he got his watch back he would know the time and date and might be able to work it out, remembering it had taken him and Serge two days to get from St. Petersburg to that town in Germany (though they had taken a very funny track) and half a day to get from Hamburg to halfway across Holland. Maybe he had just been driven round and round Holland until he passed out, but surely the garden was too big and too wild to be Dutch? He'd also spotted a shiny metal panel for remote-control arms on the gate.

This room was very bare. There was no window catch. The table was new pinewood. There must be central heating since the wooden floor had been warm. There were vents by the window and door – probably hiding movement sensors. People were moving purposefully about upstairs. He was not in a hospital because his bed wasn't an iron job with levers. The sheets were "Made in China" and so was the khaki blanket. There might be a label on the mattress. He began to feel under the pillow and along the side with his good hand, then pulled it out as the orderly came in with the watch and the money belt.

"Thanks." The watch had stopped yesterday, 4 November, at 9.20 p.m. The damned solar battery had let him down again. Trust Michael Hill! "Would you put this on the table over by the window to recharge, please?"

Then he went through the money. The traveller's cheques were gone and the few Russian roubles. The Dutch money he'd changed at Marken village was all there, including enough to pay for the container, but the shipping slip was gone. "There is money missing, and a document."

"I'm sorry to hear that. I'll ask. Do you want to make your phone call now?"

"I'll need the email that was in the money belt, to get the number."

"OK. I'll see what I can do."

Dennis decided he would try the Dutch number without any country code. If he got through he would know where he was and might still be able to get his boat away. If not, he'd know he was in deep shit, somewhere else in Northern Europe - or even Asia.

The orderly returned briefly with the shipping slip and a phone. It was a Nokia. He could be in Finland – or anywhere else on Earth. He dialled carefully and the call went straight through.

A woman's voice answered. "Maersk Shipping. If you wish to speak to someone in Dutch, press 1. If you wish to speak in English, press 2."

Dennis pressed 2.

"If you know the extension number you need, dial it now. For staff directory, press 1. If you want Exporting, press 2. If you want Importing, press 3. If you want burble burble burble..."

Dennis pressed 2.

"How may I help you?" It was the same woman's voice.

"It is Dennis Bogdanovich from New Zealand speaking. I have a booking for a container on the *Thor Heyerdahl* sailing for Auckland this afternoon. The consignment number is 666 P00H 4."

"Val. I have you on my screen."

"What I was wanting was to open the container and add some more goods: a tonne of pinecones and four hundredweight of horseshit."

The line went dead.

Dennis immediately dialled Bill Sellars' number. A sleepy voice said "Hello."

"Cheryl! It's me, Dennis. I'm in deep shit, in…."

Before he could say any more the orderly ran in, grabbed the phone and switched it off.

Their friendship was at an end.

"The Tribunal is waiting for you. I will bring a wheelchair."

Chapter 22

On the Night,
Rockanje, the Netherlands, 4 -5 November 2006

At an early hour, Zaheed, in a sombre mood, locked the doors on the sausage factory, imagining strangers forcing the lock in a few days' time. Maybe Allah would again send spiders to make webs that would fool the Politie into thinking no one had lived here for ages? Herman had turned on the truck engine for him, to warm it up, but kept the lights off.

What had they left that should have been destroyed? Herman had packed two bags of tools last weekend and taken them to the local market. He'd made only 700 kroner, but simply dumping good gear would have made them more conspicuous. No one did that in the Netherlands. Herman had resisted being separated from his laptop, however, even though he knew it was one of the most easily traced devices. He said he needed it to keep up with news from Iraq, but Zaheed suspected the Detroit ice hockey team was even more significant. Eventually Herman agreed his laptop must be used for managing the launch and had wired it into the mechanism.

Now Zaheed stood at the locked door watching car lights intermittently passing outside the park, and prayed. *Inshallah. If You want this rocket to go up You are going to have to help. We and Your newest recruit*

He and Herman had made their last salat here in the sausage factory. By dawn they would be giving thanks for the accomplishment of their long jihad. Next month he would make the Hajj; maybe the whole family would go. He would certainly take his boys – but his wife would probably be pregnant by then. Inshallah. Then he would be on gardening leave for the rest of his life. He might take up orchid breeding.

Herman slammed the rear doors of his van shut and said, "Come on."

Zaheed climbed into the warm cab of the launch truck and let off the brake as the van went winking ahead down the drive. He didn't turn on the truck lights until the road was clear and they were off. A slightly imperfect moon was sinking into a thick layer of mist on the horizon.

By 5.30 am the truck was parked just off the Strandweg among the Rockanje dunes, and Herman backed his van to block the entrance to the empty car park. He arrived at the truck wearing a headlamp and immediately crawled underneath. The rams for lowering the stabiliser legs groaned into life and two by two the legs thudded into the macadam. Each time the Crown Removals logo on the canopy shuddered.

Zaheed crawled a little way under the warm chassis and watched Herman testing the sequence for raising the truck canopy. It would screen some of the ignition flare of the rocket from the town once it was erect, but they would then have to crawl out between the wheels.

By 6.30 Herman had the front wall folded in and was ready to raise the great canopy, something it had been impossible to practise inside the factory. Zaheed scrambled out of the way as the ram started. The metal of the canopy buckled and groaned but rose jerkily erect, the back flaps banging. Someone was going to hear all this. Then the rocket and gantry began to move with an even louder ram noise. When the noise stopped the rocket was left standing gleaming in the moonlight like a queen awaiting her ceremonial moment.

Herman came hustling and flashing out from between the wheels

"Get back!" he shouted, and at 6.58am the rocket was launched. The noise and the heat forced the two men into the bushes with arms over their faces as the shaft of fire slowly rose. Before they could wipe their eyes it had entered the cloud above and the smoke was moving southeast like a wall.

Zaheed stood with his thumb on the remote control, his eyes on the clock. He was counting down for detonation.

The canopy had wilted and crashed. Herman crawled back under the truck as soon as the smoke shifted, and crouched there reading off his computer screen. "Climbing steadily. Ignition stage shut down and... detached! Wind steady west nor'west. 200 mph at 30,000 metres."

Zaheed: "GPS is keyed in."

Herman: "OK at 40,000 metres."

"Whatever are you boys up to?" said a female voice.

Zaheed turned. At his elbow was a short woman wrapped in a scarlet quilt.

"Is that a weather balloon you just launched? I heard the boom."

"Yes. It is for Radio Luxembourg."

"Are you an American? The bugger I'm looking for is American too, but I don't mind if I don't find him, the rotten bastard!"

Herman, yelling: "Altitude 49,700 metres!"

"I threw his clothes out in the rain today, when I found him looking - "

Zaheed: "Madam, we are very busy at the moment. We'll be finished - "

Herman: "Target! Fire!"

"We've done it!" Zaheed whispered and the arm holding the remote fell to his side.

A brilliant glow flared high above to the west.

Zaheed hurled away the remote and threw up his arms in triumph. Herman crawled out from under the truck, pushed the girl aside, and went into a hooting native American dance.

"Boy, you fellas are happy in your work!"

"Didn't know you had any back teeth till now, Zaheed!"

Zaheed hugged him, tears running down his face into his beard. "Allahu akbar! Allahu Allah!"

"Are the both of you two Muslims?"

"We are, madam, we are! It is a great day for us."

"It is his birthday!"

"That's dang right, and we are going to the South of France to celebrate!"

"Oh, that's nice. Whatta ya know, that's just where I was thinking of going myself - in the morning. Do you two want to come with me? I've got the Kombi behind the scrub there. It's a good old van, quite comfortable."

Herman looked at Zaheed, who nodded decisively.

"Has it got a good engine?" Herman asked. "Is it reliable?"

"Bloody oath, it is! We went all round Germany in it and we were going to do Scandinavia – I'm an artist and he's into Nordic skiing, but I don't care about him any more. He's a user and a loser and a thief!"

Zaheed came into the light with two bags. Herman disappeared under the truck once more. The lights went off. Then he crawled out dragging his laptop, dusted it off and forced the lid down, put his rolled prayer mat under his arm, and followed the others into the bushes, guided by the girl's voice.

"I'm really glad to hear someone's doing something about the weather. Don't you get sick of these grey skies? I'm from Aus, you know, so I've had two winters on end. Depressing! Morbid! Can make you lonely. Makes you think about home."

Chapter 23

Sunday Morning,
Tottenham, North London, 5 November 2006

That same busy morning Anton's young sister, Fatima, woke in Tottenham still glowing with the success of her gymnastic display the night before. The only disappointment was that Warith and Sergey had not been able to come and that Aisha, up on the bleachers, had kept bursting into tears. Fatima's coach told her it was probably just her mother's stage of life. Ibrahim and Ishmael, sitting stiff and suited on either side of her mother, were very sober. Fatima thought that in her father's case it would be to do with becoming a Borough Alderman and being worried about the speech he had to make after the display. Ishmael might have been a bit jealous because he used to do gymnastics at school. He always liked the rings best.

But her somersaults and hoop work had brought the house down. Her father gave a little speech and handed out the prizes. He smiled at her when he gave Fatima her cup, which had a regional finals ribbon tied to the handle. Afterwards the family went to the pancake parlour and had pastries and ice-cream sundaes. Her friend Chimamanda was at the next table with her parents and big brothers.

Then Aisha went off to the toilet and when she didn't come back Fatima was sent to look for her.

"She's not there," she told her father.

Ibrahim and Ishmael both got up and rushed out of the restaurant without saying goodbye to their friends. Fatima followed them into the street, carrying her mother's bright-green coat. It was very embarrassing.

She could see her father running far up across the street, nearly to the police station. He must be going to ask the police to help them find her. Ishmael was not so far ahead, on her side of the street.

He looked back and waited for her to catch up. "Dad will get her," he said. "We'll wait here."

It was cold. Ishmael told her to put the coat on but Fatima wouldn't for fear someone might see her. They backed into the doorway of a hairdressing salon. Two cars with flashing lights came out of the police station and turned on sirens that nearly deafened Fatima but Ishmael just squatted down to look at the pictures of a blonde man getting dreads done. Fatima noticed Ishmael had some hair missing off the top of his head.

"I always wanted dreadlocks," he said. He had another good look at each of the pictures, as if he might be going to try to do his own – perhaps he'd already tried and had to cut the bit out - but at the same time he was asking her all about school and what she wanted to do when she left, did she really want to be a pharmacist, blah, blah blah.

"I'm not bothered. It's a pretty good job. I know I can do the chemistry and you get excellent cheap make-up and stuff," she told him, and kept looking up the street for her parents. Eventually she slipped the coat over her shoulders.

When at last she saw them coming her mother was clinging to her husband and looked to be crying still.

"I've got keys. We'll get the van," Ishmael said, and he and Fatima went back towards the Leisure Centre at a fast trot.

"This is a good training run for you," Ishmael said when she complained. "You know, you could be a really good gymnast - maybe even make it to the Beijing Olympics - you've only got to do a bit of running like this every day. It doesn't have to be fast."

Eventually they got their mother home and she and Dad went straight up to bed. Ishmael took her some hot milk and stayed a long time talking.

So much for being an overnight sensation, Fatima thought. When she turned on the TV it was only news. She peeled down a strip of tape someone had stuck over the crack between the French doors, but stopped when some minger flakes of paint came away. She left it hanging. There had been another bombing in the City, at Charing Cross. There was a lot of blah blah about staying indoors - as if anyone would bother to bomb Tottenham. The V2 rockets only landed here by mistake - didn't even hit the concrete works, just a lot of minger little houses.

Very early the next morning she'd heard her father and Ishmael go off in the van. Straight afterwards her mother came in, woke her up completely by kissing her twice, her cheeks wet, but didn't say anything about getting up for fajr.

"*La ilaha illa Mohammed Rasul Allah,*" was all she said. Next thing she was on the phone in the hall - yelling at a minicab driver about going to St. Albans, of all places - and then she went out, too, and slammed the front door.

Fatima wiped her mother's tears off on the sheet. If her mother was going to the Farmers' Market today she should have been told - there was some cool stuff on those stalls if you knew what to look for - but probably it was just an emergency with one of her old nutters at the mental hospital; there they'd all be at six in the morning, prancing around, covered in bling, and waving their handbags.

"*Oh, have you come to take me home? Have you come to take me to the bank vault? I want to see my star rubies!*"

It was hopeless trying to sleep after that. Just before seven o'clock she got up and went downstairs to an empty house. "Nobody tells me anything!" she said.

There was a lightning flash that lit up the garden for ages. When it faded she was in the dark again - the lights were off, the TV wouldn't work, and the battery in her mobile phone had run out on her.

Chapter 24

The Second Bomb,
Beckenham, 5 November 2006

The same glare that lit Fatima's garden in north London blasted into the O'Brien house in Beckenham, spotlighting a pile of hats on top of the wardrobe. Hiria staggered out of bed and joined her husband at the window. A red glow was rising over the railway station. David grabbed her and hugged her so tightly she could hardly see the weird white plumes growing out of the redness.

"Spike Milligan would have something to say about them picking on his corner again," he said. "And this time it looks to be nuclear."

Hiria looked at the crack in the upper sash, wishing they had pasted paper over it last night after the TV warning that Charing Cross had been hit by a dirty bomb. There was thunder on the stairs. If she died it would be deserved, but Jessica was only ten - and perfect.

The door burst open and the girl threw herself at her parents.

"I'm scared. There was fierce lightning in the garden and the bulb has gone out on the stairs."

David reached an arm out to the bed lamp. It was dead. Then he pulled free and tried the television. Nothing.

"Never mind, kitten, it was just another bomb - miles from here." Her mother hugged her. "You can have the torch off the hall table tonight. Come back to bed, David."

Jessica climbed in with them, something she hadn't done for years - not since her grandparents' trip-of-a-lifetime, when they'd taken over her room. It was only to give her parents a good time in London that Hiria first took the money. She'd been asked to make a long trip to visit Mrs Inister in the asylum at St. Albans, to show her the contents of her safe-deposit box and Hiria had the bagful of treasure at home overnight. She discovered it contained enough Boots shares to keep the old lady for ten lifetimes, at a time when she and David were struggling to meet their mortgage on a house that was falling down around them, brick by brick. Now that it was re-pointed it was probably going to make them a flash tomb.

The funny thing was, David thought her parents had left them the money to get it done, as a farewell present. It's lucky that in their mad effort last night to block every crack around doors and windows he didn't find the Tesco bag with the rest of the stuff from the deposit box. Fortunately home improvements always stopped at the top-floor storeroom, and at three this morning, exhaustion ensured the room again remained untouched.

Here she was, chewing the rag about a bit of embezzlement, when a nuclear bomb has exploded over Bexley, with thousands of people already dead, and undoubtedly more deaths to come. There was very little food in the house – she shopped Mondays, and sparingly, in her effort to repay Mrs Inister. Jessica's hair smelled lovely. Hiria reminded herself to take the shampoo bottle out of the top bathroom - acting like her mother in the backblocks of Northland. To think shampoo could have become a treasure in London!

Perhaps Mrs Inister had been killed by the bombing? Hiria felt a nasty hope sprout, but immediately another vision came: she saw the beneficiaries, six of them, all ages. They'd come sniffing around in the radioactive dust in front of the bank, clamouring for the safe deposit box and the legendary necklace.

"I'm sorry, I can't make you a cup of tea if the power is off," said Jessica. Both parents hugged her, and left their hands intertwined till she squirmed free.

Until Jessica spoke David had been lying rigid with worry on the other side of the bed. At eleven o'clock the previous night the television interrupted a sordid Scottish murder story with news of the first bomb, at Charing Cross Station. Very soon there were pictures of a huge pile of rubble in front of the roofless concourse. Firemen were climbing up the brick mountain in a replay of 9/ll, and ambulance officers struggled back over it with bodies on stretchers. Tony Blair came on the scene looking very dapper in a dinner suit to cheer the gallant workers on.

Then came the aftershock, the announcement that it was a dirty bomb. Everyone in London was told to stay indoors until further notice, they should block all cracks around windows and doors, and immediately fill every possible container with water except within the City, where water supplies were already suspect. Hiria and he had set to work the minute they heard this warning but had soon run out of containers, and out of tape for the windows. They went on to use rags and folded paper instead, and shoved cardboard boxes up the four chimneys.

Jessica had woken grumpily when they switched on her bedroom light to start sealing her window and fireplace. "Is it a fire drill?" she'd asked.

"No. Go to sleep. There's been a storm warning on the TV," her father lied.

After that Hiria persuaded him to go to bed.

Now he wondered, how long would the radioactivity last? Had they saved enough water? Would the sewerage still work? Would the power-cut wreck his firm's computer business or make it more essential? How much petrol did he have in the car? Would his smooth, brown wife run away home for good, leave him and England to it. Would she take Jessica? And where, when, would he be able to buy a beer?

He rolled over to pull out the bottom drawer of the filing cabinet beside the bed. He rummaged around, found no whisky bottle, but there was an old transistor radio that might still work if he could find batteries for it. Hiria was always threatening to give his disgusting, chipped, metal cabinet to the rag and bone man, but it might have protected the transistor from the blast.

"Can I have your camera batteries?" he asked.

Hiria pointed to her handbag on the dressing table.

David got the batteries and inserted them in his radio. The only station he could raise was Canaerfon Community Radio, the announcer sounding businesslike: *'Five more suicide bomb strikes including one at St Albans, one at Croydon - "*

"Croydon! Did they say Croydon?"

"Shh!" David nodded grimly, eyes on Jessica and radio to his ear.

" - two at Clydebank. This morning's electromagnetic pulse bomb over southeast London has knocked out the BBC's microwave system, including the backup loop designed during the Cold War to withstand this type of explosion. After the Cold War ended in the nineteen-eighties some copper components had been used in maintenance and so the heat of today's bomb had melted thousands of vital connections over eastern parts of South Wales, England and Scotland."

"Can't bring themselves to say 'United Kingdom' even in wartime!" said David, switching off.

"Who are you at war with?" asked Hiria. She was surprised at the pronoun she'd chosen and hoped David hadn't noticed.

"The bloody wogs, I suppose! There're millions of Muslim petrodollars sloshing around London - you catch the sickening fumes of them in the City. Now they've decided to pump them out into the suburbs."

"There are three Muslim girls in my class," said Jessica from under the covers.

"Oh, it won't be them, Jess," her father assured her. "It's just some religious fanatics gone crazy in the desert in Iraq – or sitting in caves in Afghanistan. They like blowing things up."

"Like Uncle Barry's Buddha statues?"

"Yes. Or it could be a set-up by National Geographic, just wanting some fresh stuff to show on the history channel!" said David.

So there were now five dirty bombs, one of them at Croydon. That was only five miles away. They lay in bed, going over in their minds the work they had done last night to make the house airtight, and their conversation. David had reminded Hiria how he once smelt lightning through the closed windows of his car and she reminded him of the stink of ensilage coming into the car, driving through Matamata to visit her cousins. Nothing would stop this deadly effluvia creeping into the house - certainly not duct tape.

"If we'd taken up your father's invitation for a Christmas trip we could have been safe in New Zealand now," he said. "I should have listened to you. There's no school term to finish now."

"Will Santa have trouble getting down chimneys this year?" asked Jessica.

"You don't believe in that old rubbish now you've got your cell phone, do you?" said her father.

If we get as far as Christmas, was Hiria's thought. What use was her embezzling now? There would be no more holidays. She would never see New Zealand again, and she would never be able to pay the money back - or even use it! Gold rands would be worth far less today than the water they'd saved last night. They had twenty-five buckets and pots and vases and both baths full, but for food they had only the school snack cupboard full of assorted chips, plus whatever leftovers there were in the refrigerator. In the freezer there was only a relic of her birthday cake with its striped cream roses, a pottle of stewed quince pulp, some sausage stew, a few loaves of bread and a carton of ice cream. Better eat that first. For breakfast!

She'd always shopped on Mondays after work and by Sunday the cupboard was always bare. Her stolen hoard wouldn't buy food, either. She imagined herself handing over gold coins to the checkout girl at Waitrose. She would be marched off to the snobby cashier, Tamsin. At least that moment would square off for the way they'd treated colonials at Dulwich Tennis Club. It would give them something besides Italian tiles to talk about at the school gate! But when would that be?

"All the blackberries in the Green Mile will have been blasted away by the bomb, won't they? The poor squirrels." said Jessica. She sounded tearful for the first time.

She was a strong little person. Hiria remembered how she hadn't cried - she could have only been six - when the precious bottle of coloured sands she'd wheedled out of her grandmother at Legoland had dropped and smashed just as she was getting out of a taxi at Kings Cross. She'd just pulled on her coat and run with us for the train.

"The foxes will do all right for a while, then," David was saying.

"Horrible, scabby things!" said Hiria. Then to distract Jessica from her thoughtless comment: "Mind you, I saw two beautiful big ones the other night running down Kings Hall Road. They had rubbish in their mouths and our bag was torn."

No more rubbish days! No work. No pubs! David will go mad, locked up here with just the two of us. He didn't keep liquor at home but never a day passed without a drink.

How could they keep Jessica safe? She would be desperate, cut off from other kids. Hiria hugged her daughter till she squirmed, then turned to her husband. "Your mother was babysitting last night for Cath and Tim, wasn't she?"

"Yeah. She'll be safe for sure, way out at Richmond, but Dad… At least he won't have known anything, poor old sod. The hospital is much nearer the blast than we are."

Hiria wondered if the nurses would have stayed on duty, or whether they would have rushed off to their homes. Des was doomed anyway, with his damaged kidneys – and just when they'd started to visit him again. What a waste of years! And what a miserable life, nothing but short-order cooking and betting on the horses. He'd been quite keen on America, though. Always said he should have emigrated, and now look what the connection has brought us: Blair and Bush have probably killed my father-in-law, in bed, at Lewisham Hospital.

It was seven-thirty and should have been getting light. David got up again, pulled on a jersey and had another look out the window.

"There's a black fog out. It's billowing like smoke and there's ash all over my car." His wife and daughter came to look. "Someone... see, two men are coming out of the station."

One of them was pulling the other. At the narrow part of the pavement they stumbled over tree roots and separated. One came on alone. His face was half blackened. He staggered past the house and on into the roiling fog. The other man was crawling along the kerb using one hand.

David rushed out of the room and down the stairs. The front door opened and slammed shut.

Hiria ran after him, screaming his name, and pressed herself to the door on tiptoe, peering through the tiny pane of knobbly glass. A smell she remembered from a woolshed disaster in her youth was already in the house.

After a short while David thumped on the door. "Let us in."

Hiria opened the door a crack and the two of them pushed it wide and staggered in. They collapsed together onto the bottom of the stairs.

"Get us a drink, Jessica," said David.

Jessica stepped carefully down around them, noticing the palm of the man's left hand was raw. Her father was holding him up. Her mother was still sobbing, sprawled on the floor busy poking paper between the door and sill with a tail comb. Jessica dipped two mugs of water out of a bucket. Then she brought her father a wet towel and a dry one. He was spitting whole mouthfuls of water onto the carpet! The visitor could not hold his mug with his skinned hand and didn't try to use the other. The right arm must be broken. David, still supporting him, held the mug to his lips. He spluttered and gulped and shook his head, his eyes on David, and then opened his mouth again like a huge filthy baby.

Hiria leaned back on the door in her frog-patterned pyjamas and watched, tears pouring down her face. She looked horrified and helpless. Jessica brought a desk chair out of the computer room.

"Good girl, Jessica," said her father. "I'll get him up and you push it under him."

They set out to wheel him slowly backwards towards the dining room with David supporting his right leg. He screamed as they turned in the narrow passage.

"Put him on the couch facing the window. On that side it'll be easier for him to move," said Hiria.

She was back with them. She gestured for the wet towel and spread it gently on the man's cheek. He winced but did not cry out.

"There must have been a fire on the train," said David. "Was there a crash?" he asked the man.

The man nodded and carefully tipped his raw hand over.

A derailment when the power failed? Or a crash into another train or a bridge? The reason was a mere detail in the whole catastrophe.

Hiria finished sponging the man's face. The right ear was raw and swollen and he had a cut at the corner of his mouth, but from the nose up and over the bald part of his head the skin wasn't too bad - he must have been wearing a hat. She examined his left hand, which was badly burnt on palm and thumb. There was nicotine stain between his fingers.

He seemed to be uncomfortable lying on his back and Hiria discovered he had a bulky money belt such as she and her Kiwi mates had worn in the old days on their OE. They called them bum bags. He had his on backwards, but when she offered to take it off he said, "No. No!" quite fiercely.

Hiria slackened the buckles and pulled it round to his left side and that seemed acceptable. The fabric of his suit sleeve disintegrated where she touched it. Only the dark stripes on his shirtfront were burnt, however the tie was baked to a crisp, so his chest underneath was probably grilled too. She draped another towel over his head to keep him warm.

Jessica at the window said, "It's still dark outside. There are more people coming. Do you want me to let them in?"

"No!" said Hiria. "Get away from the window and pull the curtains."

David sat silent in his big chair from which, until yesterday, he could control the world's intrusion with a flick of the TV remote. This evening he'd been expecting to admit his wife's champions, the All Blacks, playing England at Twickenham.

"You said we were going to Hop Farm tonight for the fireworks!" said Jessica.

"I'm sorry, kid: it will have been cancelled - Guy Fawkes came early this year," said her father.

"*Remember, remember, the Fifth of November, Gunpowder treason and plot.*

I see no reason why Gunpowder Treason ever should be forgot." said Hiria. "My brother thought it was better than Christmas. He hoarded Double Happys in his sock drawer all year."

"And then he joined the army? Go on – that stuff happened back about Shakespeare's time. Still, my father told me Catholics shouldn't celebrate it. What do you think, Jess?"

Jessica glared at her father as she pulled the curtains over the bay window. Her elbow caught the arabesque wire screen Hiria had installed to prevent train commuters peering in. Strings of little bells jangled.

"Pakistani?" croaked the patient, eyeing his nurse from under the towel.

"In these pyjamas? You look more like a Paki than I do with your turban!" She lifted the towel off him. "No, I'm a New Zealander. Quarter-caste Ngati Kahu, if you must know. So you can talk, can you?"

"Urrgh."

"No, we're not terrorists," said David, getting up. "We don't go in for Salted Nuclear Bombs - haven't got a bomb in the house, actually. Of course there may be some spare parts on the roof today."

Hiria said, "Help me get his coat off so we can see what's wrong with this arm."

"Cut the sleeve out and pull it downwards," said David. He handed her scissors from the mantelpiece.

"I'll get him something to wear and find a sling and a blanket. You go and get yourself dressed, Jessica."

The man whimpered as Hiria snipped away the sleeves of his coat and shirt. The coat sleeve came off but the shirt sleeve wouldn't pull free. It had to be cut downwards and pulled open. His right arm was revealed, pure white where the skin still fitted but a two-inch-wide strip from the shoulder to halfway down his forearm had turned into ragged brown bubble-wrap - or pork crackling. Hiria decided it was best to leave some of the shirt material stuck to it. It would certainly be sterile.

"You can't put that arm in a sling – a splint would be better." David had returned with a small glass of Hiria's tipple. "Here: give him a drop of Nelson's."

He brought a sip of rum to the victim's lips. The patient swallowed and then shook his head. His throat must be damaged.

"Never mind, mate. We'll see you right. Here's a blanket. I'll put it round your shoulders but we'd better have a looksee what's wrong with your leg now."

Hiria was already cutting up the trouser leg. She could tell she was hacking into a new suit, though it was no sin as both legs were completely worn through at the knee. The trouser material was less rotten than the jacket but the right leg had diagonal slits all down it. Fresh blood was seeping through some of them at the thigh. She uncovered a line of wounds with shards of glass sticking out of them.

"Tell Jessica to bring me down the tweezers."

Hiria found herself doing first aid by scented candlelight, with the front curtains drawn to avoid attracting any more business. David made sausage sandwiches for the family and fed the patient mashed banana and icecream while Hiria probed his wounds for glass splinters. He shrieked at times.

Jessica kept up a commentary from the front room on what people and how many were passing. She saw her friend Imogen's father going home. She banged on the window but he just waved a bit and went on. He must have been on the train too. He was dragging his bag by the broken strap.

After an hour or so she reported that two funny old police vans had arrived. David and Hiria rushed to see. They were not the new white cars with red stripes but very old navy-blue vans. Instead of Keystone Cops, snowmen with gasmasks got out and marched into the station. Two of them wheeled right and went into Dr Lewis's house, next door to theirs. After a bit he came out with them, dressed like the policemen. Jessica could point out which was the doctor to her parents because of his medical bag. Those three went into the station too.

"We'll get Lewis in here when he comes home," said David, "if he's still got that anti-radiation suit."

Hiria decided in the meantime to apply some of her precious manuka honey to the patient's burns - over the strip of shirting on the right arm but directly onto the skin of his neck on that side. Except for a red patch at about the level of the shirt pocket his chest seemed to have been relatively sheltered by a surprising pelt of singed fair hair. She also held a spoonful of the honey for him to suck in the hope it might soothe his throat and help the nasty cut at the corner of his mouth.

At eleven o'clock David went upstairs to the bedroom and put on the radio.

Caernarfon station was still broadcasting but reception was poor. Their batteries were probably running down too. News was scanty and repetitive but they now revealed that the last bomb over southeast London had been detonated high for maximum electromagnetic-pulse damage to communications. That was what had knocked out the television and national radio systems. It affected all electronic components, including those in car engines and planes. There had, however, been no new bombings since 7am.

The BBC was disabled even though it had moved out of town last year to White City. Away from Bush House but not out of the woods, David thought.

An offer to take over The Caernarfon Community radio station had been declined. *Scottish Radio in Dundee is giving Caernarfon what news the BBC teams can supply by shortwave from their auxiliary station in France. The American President, for instance, has sent Britain his deepest sympathy and will be despatching medical and other help. He is exerting all possible pressure on his friend, the President of Pakistan, to find and disable terrorist cells. The Royal Air Force had scrambled defensive and reconnaissance planes at eleven pm after the first attack when the bomb had gone off at Charing Cross but are now grounded since two commercial planes are thought to have crashed at*

Hiria was at the bedroom doorway listening, and fingering a strand of her hair.

"If some subs have escaped I hope they're quietly making all possible speed towards Pakistan!" said David to his wife.

"If it was Pakistan, why would they do Bexley and Catford?" Hiria demanded, dragging the strand of hair out of her mouth and jamming it behind her ear. "There's heaps of Muslims living round there."

Caernarfon repeated the Prime Minister's advice to stay indoors and conserve battery power *because the six detonations detected so far were of the salted type, designed to maximise radioactive fallout over the widest possible area. The effect will last for many weeks. Emergency measures already planned by Operation Square Leg in 1980 would be put into action, starting immediately.*

"Many weeks?" said Hiria.

Then they heard the announcer say, "*Ooh. Er, what's that?*"

There was a pause.

"*I'm sorry*," and with a rising inflection and stiffening rage the announcer continued, "*Radio Caernarfon is now going off the air on the orders of the English police, under a Government D notice prohibiting the media transmitting anything about CNI readiness! Nos da, a pob hwyl!*"

A different voice ended the broadcast with the injunction, "*Stand ready for evacuation and obey any orders that may be issued by your local authority.*"

"What the hell do they think they're doing? That's our only radio station!" said Hiria. "How are we going to *get* our evacuation orders?"

"Fat chance of Bromley Council riding to the rescue," said David, hurling the radio down on the bed.

Chapter 25

Tribunal with Tomatoes,
somewhere in Europe, 5 November 2006

The first thing Dennis saw in the courtroom was the Amsterdam Bloodhound. Beside him at the table was someone sneering in a green uniform and an American major covered with decorations.

The Bloodhound spoke. "Dennis Bogdanovich, following your interrogation in Amsterdam, the Amsterdam-Amstelland Supraregional Investigation Force met to discuss your case, on the morning of 3 November. Your belongings were examined and contact made with the manufacturer of the boat in St. Petersburg. We have seen a video of the boat's capabilities and we received reports from the Water Politie and from Town Watchers in Friesland and Marken Island. Europol had reports of a fracas you were involved in at Hamburg. A witness to that disturbance later recognised you with co-conspirators in a picture on the TV crime watch programme, *Opsporing Verzocht*, and this led to the involvement of an international terrorist committee. The next day the rocket attack on London and the bombings in London and Scotland occurred."

"What rocket attack? I've got nothing to do with that!"

"This hearing is charged with establishing the names of conspirators in the Netherlands terrorist attack on London.

"What's this about a bombing? What's it got to do with me? Or my boat?"

Silence.

"The UTBT - the Counter Terrorism and Special Tasks Unit of the KLPD, which is headed by the Netherlands Public Prosecutor - has appointed me to determine your part in this plot," the Green Man said, looking down his nose at Dennis. "Do you deny this is a picture of you?"

He nodded to a female underling and she brought a newspaper to Dennis. She could be the phony Maerske receptionist, about forty with a bust of around fifty. Dennis was surprised to note he was not in the least attracted.

The picture showed *Godwit* sliding into the Ijsselmeer, with Dennis balancing on the prow and Sergey and Zaheed pushing. The newspaper was not in Dutch. It was called *Dziennik Gieldowy*. Nearly every word had a z in it and half the other letters had ears and tails or dots, but he recognised the name under his picture – 'Xavier Hollander'. The paper was carried away again.

"Yes, that's my boat. It is booked to go on board a ship sailing to Auckland tomorrow. Where is it now?"

"The Amsterdam Police are examining it for fingerprints, and for any traces of explosives or nuclear materials. Afterwards it will be held as material evidence should your case come to court in that jurisdiction over your civil offences."

"I demand to see the New Zealand ambassador at once."

"The New Zealand Government has no representation in this region, and has already deferred all matters pertaining to the bombings to this International Anti-Terrorism Tribunal, granting it authority over any of its alleged citizens who may become of interest in a terrorist investigation. You have become of interest." Green Man sat back and let the charge sink in.

"That's ridiculous! It's a glass-bottomed boat for *tourists*, not *terrorists* – you lot can't spell any more than Americans! And for that I've been beaten up and driven all round Europe and imprisoned by you! I want my boat back. Where is it?"

"I repeat, we are not at present concerned with the getaway vessel. This tribunal is to examine you and establish the identity and nationality of your co-conspirators." He again summoned the woman to present the newspaper picture of the boat.

Dennis scanned the print for clues. He saw a by-line 'Gdansk'. That was in Poland, wasn't it? Or was it Denmark? The date was 4 November.

"Is the man in the cap Frits Breijer?" asked the Bloodhound.

"No."

"Is the other man Frits Breijer?"

"I don't know what his real name is. He's just a friend of my cousin."

"Is your cousin the man in the cap?"

"Yes."

"Is his name Sergey or Piet?"

Dennis briefly turned and gave a murderous look to the orderly sitting behind him. "Sergey. 'Pete' is just a business name."

"What was your relationship with Sergey?"

"I guess he would be a second cousin once removed."

"I mean, what were you doing for him and his business associates?"

"Nothing. They were doing me a favour, bringing my boat to Holland. They make sausages, that's all I know. I can't tell you any more about them except they were both decent chaps."

"We have found their vehicle," said the American, speaking for the first time. "What can you tell me about that?"

"I don't know: it was just a big removal truck. It fitted my boat nicely and it turned out to have a good ramp for launching it."

"Nice choice of word! What did you think of the pull-down legs?"

"What legs?"

"You didn't notice it had supports suitable for a crane fitted under the skirts of the canopy?"

"Nah. But then I wouldn't notice anything like that – I'm more of a tits man, myself."

"I think we have heard enough." The American stood up. "This man will be a great help to us, given a little more encouragement. Ship him off." He nodded to the other two and left.

Green Man wound up proceedings lamely. "You will be removed to another facility for further questioning and held at the pleasure of the United States President."

"What the hell has George Bush got to do with me? I'm a Kiwi!" yelled Dennis.

The Bloodhound gave him a long sneer, standing back at the door for one last hungry look as the Green Man stalked out before him.

A burly new orderly wheeled Dennis out and turned the wrong way down the hall.

"Hey, my passport!" Dennis yelled.

"You won't need it where you're going."

Dennis found he was backed into a narrow room like a larder, full of tins of tomatoes and beetroot.

"Get these on." The orderly dropped orange overalls in his lap, kicked on the brake and went away without closing the door.

His mother would like the big supply of tins, especially the beetroot. It was very cold in here. Staff kept clomping past along the flagstones, carrying bunches of papers, chins held out to indicate they had more urgent matters to attend to than partly-processed inmates shouting about lost boats. Didn't they realise *Godwit* represented his father's life savings? From his sixty years of gum-digging and ditch-digging and twice-a-day milking? Dennis had better not go home without his boat. Whatever this cockamamie outfit had planned for him would be better than his reception, arriving empty-handed at Leigh.

Dennis shook the overalls out and spread them over his knees for warmth. After another couple of appeals to passers-by had failed he decided he would try to pull the suit on over his pyjamas. He took a can of tomatoes from the shelf with his good left hand and in spite of the pain, put it under his knee, to raise the foot. At the third attempt he was able to get the leg of the garment over it and gradually work it up as far as the knee, but then realised further progress was impossible. He couldn't get the other leg on, or hoist himself up and at the same time drag the garment under him with only one good arm and no knees. He pulled the tin out, thought of hurling it at the next soldier who went by, but then had a better idea – *Anything for a Joke* being the motto of all ditch-digging families.

He put the can back on the shelf with part of the overall sleeve spread underneath it. Then he stacked other cans beside it in a row and arranged another row on top, each can a bit forward and a little further left, like the eaves of the Ming temple at Flat Bush – in the process noticing that every can had the word 'Polska' on it somewhere. He had to work very carefully when adding further rows to avoid sudden strain on the overalls and always stopping when he heard people coming close. He was quite pleased with his handiwork by the time the orderly reappeared, sidling in to get behind the chair. As the man let off the brake and shoved the chair out Dennis gave him a resounding blast of "What have you done with my boat?"

Simultaneously the left-wing Polish tomatoes attacked from the side and rear. The orderly stumbled on the cans that were rolling underfoot and fell onto his patient.

"You bastard!" they shouted at each other.

Chapter 26

News from Tokerau Beach
(Northland,NZ) & Bamiyan (Afghanistan)
5 November 2006

Rosalie sat at the table in the Tokerau Beach bach, sorting out Jim's pills: two thickeners and two painkillers and an antibiotic, ready for him with milk and the newspaper. Waiting in another plastic dish to be taken three hours later were three heart pills. Thank goodness she'd found the thickeners last night before dinner – it was the biggest bottle of all yet it had gone completely invisible. It was Jim who first discovered it missing.

"Funny thing for a burglar to choose," they both said, as usual, but the bottle couldn't be found. They'd begun to wonder if the district nurse had packed it in her bag by mistake the day before. Being Saturday evening they would have had to drive to Kaitaia and beg some from the hospital clinic - otherwise Jim wouldn't have dared eat anything for the rest of the weekend for fear his colostomy bag might burst. It took more than an hour of increasing panic before they found the bottle, lurking among the glasses where she must have left it at lunchtime while getting Jim a drink to take with the previous dose.

In the crisis she'd almost forgotten about the kids in London, but the now the dread had come back. She and Jim had tried to phone again. Couldn't even get his relations in Scotland. They'd lain awake most of the night, turning on the radio every hour for little scraps of news about England under the poisonous cloud that might already have killed their daughter and her family.

Rosalie thought of Jessica, when she came to New Zealand as a three-year-old. How she'd loved the swimming! Absolutely fearless she was then. They had a terrible job keeping the sun lotion on her and despite their efforts she still got spots of sunburn. Lovely English complexion she had. In the first roll of film they'd all three of them came out pure white - Hiria and David as well as Jessica - but by the time they went home even Hiria was covered with freckles. And to think Jim might have been dead now if Hiria hadn't insisted on sending money to have his operation done in a private hospital. It had arrived six days after Hiria heard the doctor had said it needed to be done within the next three months.

Rosalie shut the bedroom door and turned on the radio again: "Country Life" featuring a West Coast entrepreneur trying to sell bottled wasabi to the Japanese. She turned on the TV as well: *Charlie and the Chocolate Factory*, when the whole world was going to pot. CNN would be better but they didn't have cable TV at the beach - had never dreamt it would be needed once the Americas' Cup was lost.

Jim called out, "I've got the BBC broadcasting from France!" His Noisy Friend, the little transistor, to the rescue!

"...where civil authorities are dealing with fires at many locations near the five bomb targets. Two trains

collided in southwest London this morning. Victims have all been taken to secure facilities. Many hospitals have had valuable equipment destroyed in the EMP blast and others are damaged or on fire. Refugees are fleeing the city on foot as the transport system has broken down. Authorities are warning people that if they are in the open they are exposing themselves to a high risk of radiation disease from the dense clouds of ash still hanging over London. Residents have been advised to stay safe in their own homes and seal all windows and doors to avoid even limited exposure. Gas, water and sewerage can no longer be used until damage to these systems has been assessed. Electricity supplies have also been cut off for safety reasons in England, except in the counties of Cornwall and Devon. In Scotland north of Dundee power supply is secure."

"How many have been killed?" asked Rosalie.

"We must have missed that. They haven't said who did it, either. Probably the Americans, since they're mad the British are thinking of pulling out of Iraq," said Jim. "Al Qaeda is the obvious thought, but I bet it'll be the Americans trying it to give the Brits a bit of bottle."

"...radioactive ash cloud is now drifting over the Channel, approaching France and the Netherlands. French and Netherlands Air Forces replaced the British in defensive patrols along the continental shoreline, watching to destroy any more missiles. The five smaller nuclear bombs are believed to have been detonated by suicide bombers in the United Kingdom. The electromagnetic pulse missile is thought to have been launched from a secret terrorist base in the

Netherlands or Denmark. No group has yet claimed responsibility for the attacks. Al Jazeera Television, however, applauded the 'successful strikes' fifteen minutes after detonation.

"Bloody wogs! I told you it would be them!"

"That doctor who saw when you were first ill, he came from Iraq. He drove two hundred Ks from Whangarei to save your life. You'd have bled to death if he hadn't guessed what the trouble was. 'Ali Something', he was."

"Hmph. I suppose there wouldn't be many of his sort at the Tikipunga pub. I wonder why he came so far? We had a Chinaman in Kaitaia one time, remember? About the end of the war, but he went away - too lonely. The only friend he had was the insurance man."

"It's a beautiful clear day here." Rosalie pulled the bedroom curtain and stared out at the bay. "I could see all the way to Hihi at sunrise."

"I reckon it's lucky it happened early in the morning. At least David and Jessica would both have been at home with her," said Jim.

"How do you think they'll be managing without power and water?"

"They'll be OK for water. You can drink the water out of toilet cisterns and they've got three. David will be more worried about his beer supply."

"Good job! That'll be one good thing that's come out of it!"

"Don't be bloody silly, woman! The whole three of them are probably dead right now! Roasted to a crisp with their lungs bust! Or poisoned by-"

Rosalie's wail rose and rose to burst into the little sunny room. Jim struggled out of bed and hugged her. He was sobbing too.

At two o'clock the Rural Delivery van stopped at their letterbox. Among the junk mail - not even nuclear war could stop that - was a letter from their son in Afghanistan. He was with the New Zealand Army in Bamiyan Province, or he still had been on 20 October.

New Zealand Army,
Provincial Reconstruction Group,
Bamiyan Province, Afghanistan.

20 October 2006

Dear Mum and Dad,
How are you? Is Dad doing OK with his bag? We are doing fine here. The people are quite friendly, but it is getting bloody cold. We went to Bagram Airport to meet a new lot and send some boys home. Picture us doing a haka in boots on the tarmac in snow. There was a lot of snow on the pass (4,000 metres) and we nearly skidded off the road several times - the roads on Banks Peninsula are pretty good practice but they're not high enough and there are too many bridges to match the real thing. We're supposed to be rebuilding a few of their bridges. Did you see us on TV blowing up a dud Russian bomb they found under one of the last Buddhas? The Taliban missed out on destroying that one, probably because the fuse didn't go off. One of the locals spotted it. He thought it was just a bit of old junk

but it made a pretty good bang. We pulled it out with a block and tackle. Just like Grandad, eh, in Omahuta Bush?

How are Hiria and David? I got Jessica a stone top for Christmas. There aren't many toys in Bamiyan, but they've got plenty of rocks. We have built a new police station out of concrete blocks and a few houses too. One of the families was living in a gumdigger's tent exactly like the one at Matakohe Museum only it had a flat roof. They throw up a mud wall round the bottom to keep the draught out – and believe me they have good draughts here. The chill factor is -20 degrees Centigrade. Good for drying meat though – or fish, if they knew what that was. They string bits of meat up from one roof pole to another. When you get the kontiki going again, Dad, can you post me a few snapper and we'll try stringing them up on the old house.

The people are all nice. One family invited us to a feast (just rice with a few dried apricots and a few specks of goat that we ate with our hands, no plates) for the house-warming and to meet their cousin, Zaheed, from Pakistan. He looked like Imran Khan with a bit of a red beard. He was only passing through. Nice-looking girls too. They don't wear bags over their heads round here. The Governor is a woman. Looks quite like you, Mum. Captain Gauldi has painted her portrait.

Hope you two are doing OK. We are fine. See you in February. Get the fishing lines sorted out!

Love,

Barry

Chapter 27

Travel Preparations,
Poland, 5 November 2006

Dennis was pleased to observe that the Polish tin-canning he'd arranged had put his captors, all ranks, into a bad mood. His wheelchair was pushed through the rolling cans of tomatoes, down the hallway into a white room where he was hefted by strong hands onto a plinth, on his side. Mercifully it was his good side. Was this where they had fixed his shoulder? There were pipes and nozzles coming out of the wall and plenty of stainless-steel gear.

Someone hauled the overalls from his leg and then dragged off his pyjama bottoms.

"Hey! What are you up to? I haven't stolen any of your tomatoes!" He kicked out and his legs were grabbed and bent back. Excruciating pain lit up in both knees.

A suppository was shoved up his anus. Dennis screamed at another burst of pain in the right knee as gloved hands hauled his right leg up in the air. Something was slapped on him and secured with sticky tape across the small of his back. More agony when he was rolled onto his back and the diaper was fastened across his stomach with more tape.

His shoulders were forced against the plinth while his ankles were stretched down and clamped together. Dennis screamed all the obscenities he had ever heard, trying to punch the orderly holding him down and kick those gripping his feet. He received a punch in the face in return, and at the same time two other men handcuffed his right hand to his left, but inside the sling– respecting the professional work done the night before on his shoulder? The cut on his nose was bleeding again.

There was no lack of staff here. Someone was counting down very slowly from ten, in English with a suspiciously Polish accent. As he got to three Dennis's bowels erupted.

Somebody cheered and others groaned.

They held him down for another minute and then the diaper was ripped off and he was rinsed down. The smell would have been embarrassing anywhere else but today Dennis was pleased. Another diaper was slapped on and the orange overalls were hauled up his legs. Dennis kept on swearing as he was lifted clear to have someone behind him pull the suit up his back. Then the orderly in front pulled the zip up to the neck leaving the arms inside. You had to admit, they were efficient. It was like gutting fish on the *Westcoaster* with Skotty in command.

"First time you've done this? S'pose it's a university subject in Poland?"

He got two more blows, to nose and ear, and then a cloth bag was pulled over his face and closed around his neck with a string.

Dennis felt like a tuna, netted and bagged, off to the Tokyo fresh market. Death to come next? But no mess wanted. He'd show them!

Strong hands dragged him off the plinth and back into the wheelchair.

"Get him out of here," said someone older. Sounded like the American - Fruit-Salad Man.

They were sending him home!

Chapter 28

Confession,

Beckenham, S. London, 5 November 2006

That afternoon at his refuge in London, Dennis's cousin Sergey found himself in the hands of well-meaning amateurs. David brought down a mattress and they made the visitor a bed on the dining-room table.

"Being so high, it will be kinder on my back," said Hiria, leaning backwards with hands on her loins as if she hoped the kindness would commence immediately.

He was tall enough to sit on the edge of the mattress but unable to use his hands to help himself move further back and they had a job to get him into the middle of the bed. David told him to lie back on the edge and he helped Hiria heave him over, using the sheet.

"Dank you," the man croaked. His voice was improving but he had a fever and his skin was breaking out all over in angry blisters. No doubt he also looked pretty ugly inside. The burnt arm was weeping and soaking the bandages, and his cut leg showed signs of going septic in spite of the manuka honey.

"Are you watching for Doctor Lewis, Jessie?" Hiria asked. "It's very important that we catch him and call him in."

"I might have missed him. If I see him, do I open the window and lean out and yell?"

"No! Do not open anything, Jessica! The air is poisonous out there. You cannot go outside for a second. You'll have to wave something - use this." Hiria handed her a tray cloth. "Or just bang on the glass. If it's after dark you could wave a candle. I'll get you one."

"I'm going down into the cellar to start digging through to Lewis's," said David. "Remember after the flood we found there was nothing but gravel down there? It can't be more than ten foot between our houses, and the two asphalt paths will hold the roof of the tunnel together. Their house is the mirror image of ours so I reckon their cellar will be right alongside."

"But a lot tidier, I bet. I wouldn't want Mrs Lewis crawling into my cellar."

"Well, I've got to do something," and he disappeared.

Hiria gave her patient a sip of water. He spluttered over it and struggled to get up on an elbow to cough. A spurt of bloody mucus shot out of his mouth and a red dribble hung from his lip.

He gasped as Hiria wiped him up. When he lay back his eyelids were swollen and the eyes bloodshot but they were intent on hers through the narrowest of slits. He was making a great effort as he croaked,

"I made the bomb in the rocket." He said it again, and then, "I also carried a little bomb. In a suitcase, to Charing Cross Station. Eleven o'clock, four November. In the morning... on the train to the Channel ferry... I saw my big bomb explode... in the sky. It was a rainbow bomb."

He looked sad and ready to die, but not before he'd told his part in the history of the world. He gave her a little smile and nodded when he saw she understood what he said.

While he was speaking Hiria had almost felt sorry for him. Then she saw a great gout of blood arrive on his lip again and visualised Jessica, not even a teenager yet, dying the same horrible death at his hands. And millions of other people in London too.

"You're a murderer! A bloody murderer." She wiped him, then dropped the cloth, backed off and sank into the armchair, staring at the grey TV screen. "Who was the other man who came out of the station dragging you? The man with half his face blackened?"

She looked back at him but the bomber made no answer.

"Was he a bomber too? Or another victim? Someone who wanted to help you? You poor, poor man!"

Hiria got up and strode to the window, where she pulled out the edge of the curtain and peered at the empty street. She thought of the policemen marching into the station, of David whose lungs were probably about to burst into radiation blisters, and of herself - perhaps in prison, but even if she escaped that, marooned forever in this miserable grey country with its hundred-year grudges, and snobberies worse than gang warfare. Why hadn't she married her brother's crazy mate and settled for being a plumber's wife in Warkworth instead of landing in this mess in

London? Who knew what worse horrors were to come out of this man's murderous business - probably even reaching her innocent parents in New Zealand!

Hiria suddenly remembered her first bomb. She'd been in Auckland on holiday with her Point Chevalier cousins. The lady down the street took them with her when she went to deliver vegetables to a little ship called the *Rainbow Warrior*. Hiria had two heavy cabbages to carry aboard but the ship's photographer wanted to take a picture of her and her cousins and said she must swap the cabbages for carrots because of the cousins having red hair. She could still remember how the ridges on the gangway hurt her bare feet while the photographer fussed about. Afterwards they were allowed to run all over the ship, hoping to spot the crock of gold.

"Look, but don't touch!" said the veggie lady.

In the morning they told her the photographer was dead and the boat had sunk, still tied up to the wharf. They told her "Frogmen" had done it. She never did see the photographs of her and the carrots.

"Why did you do it?" she demanded now of this London bomber. "Did you do it for money?"

"Oil. To make Russia strong again. Bush must go from Iraq, with no oil and no friends. My bomb today has ended his war."

"Or started a bigger one! Who are you?"

"I am Sergey Malyarovich Mikulitsin, Russian scientist." He closed his eyes as if that was all he had to say.

"You've probably killed me and all my family, you know, Sergey!"

The door suddenly opened and David, all enthusiastic, showed her his first bag of spoil. "I'm going to put this in the computer room. It's got to go somewhere!"

Hiria got up in a hurry, pushed him out and closed the dining-room door after them. She went to the front door and beckoned her husband to follow her. "That man is one of the bombers! He just told me he set off the bomb at Charing Cross and then got caught himself on a train under the Dutch missile. I think he said he made that, too!"

David put down his bag and leaned on the banister, incredulous. "Do you believe him?"

"Yes, I do. His name is Sergey Malyarovich Mikulitsin. He did it for oil from Iraq and to get rid of the Americans and their friends. 'To make Russia strong.' That's who you've brought home for me to nurse this time, instead of one of your drunken mates!"

"We need to tell this to someone. God, wouldn't they love this at work!"

"It's not a joke!"

"I know. The doctor could take a message to the police for us. Or: Jessie," he called out to his daughter in the living room, "are those vans that brought the policemen still there?"

"No, they went ages ago. And there are no trains, so there's been no one out there except for the old pram lady. She's still picking up rubbish. Though I did see the ASBO boy from my class, the one whose father hits him. Can I have a can of Coke?"

"Go and get one from the cellar. Bring up the whole box - I want everything out of there anyway. I'll keep watch here for a minute. Then I'll get on with the digging. God! A terrorist on my dining-room table! The dirty bastard!"

"What can we do about it? We should put a notice in the window that we need police help," said Hiria.

"I already put one in my bedroom window for the doctor," said Jessica, popping her Coke can. "Sophie will see it soon. We always used to do that before we got our cell phones."

The parents looked at each other over their child's head and smiled. What was left of the world might end up in good hands.

Chapter 29

Flight into Egypt,
Poland to Cairo, 5 November 2006

Someone in boots pushed Dennis's wheelchair swiftly down the flagstone paving and out into the cold. He could feel swirling snow on his toes, and for a few metres he could hear the suck of snow on the wheels as they jarred over rough concrete, then he felt himself being pushed up a steep ramp into a vehicle. He was turned roughly against a side wall, the brake was engaged and some form of seat belt was fastened across him. All the while Dennis was shouting through the rough blue material of the hood:

"Helen Clark is going to hear all about this. You'll be sorry. I want my boat in Auckland by the time I get home, and it'd better be in perfect condition. It's booked on the Estelle Maersk *in Rotterdam sailing for Malaysia and New Zealand tomorrow. I want to make a phone call to my lawyer, Gerald Brown and Co. in Auckland. And to Bill Sellars, 0064 9849 6007 and to my wife, Diane Bogdanovich, 021 673 44467, and to James Nash, the Auckland City Council Drainage and Sanitation Department, 0064 9 376 2020. I have a very important contract due to be signed at the end of November..."*

The door slammed and the vehicle started off. Dennis attempted a few despairing thumps with his head on the metal of the truck wall behind him. He felt tears coming and let them drip. It was entirely appropriate behaviour, and conditions inside the hood were perfect.

What the hell was going on? Who could want his boat this badly? And what did it have to do with Serge and Zaheed? Were these scum an American Al Qaeda cell? With Dutch connections? What was all that about a bomb?

He could hear a jet plane getting closer. Just as the plane was right on them the vehicle swerved and stopped. The doors were flung open to admit clouds of aviation spirit and the scream of a jet engine at an unbearable pitch. Someone - who must have been travelling with him - unbuckled the seat belt, kicked the brake and had the chair on the ramp before it stopped its juddering descent. At the bottom he was picked up out of the chair like a baby by someone huge, carried up seven steps, to have his feet scraped, knees jarred, head bumped, and be dumped into an upholstered seat. Two seatbelts were snapped across him, one normal and one across his neck. He heard other seatbelts clicking, one right beside him another a little way left and one behind. He was on a small jet plane. The door was shut and the plane at once moved into take-off. Dennis screamed along with it.

When the plane's flight levelled off he felt someone undoing the hood. Dennis blinked around at the pale luxury fittings of a private jet with blinds pulled down.

A female soldier in camouflage with a pistol on her hip stood beside him holding out a glass of Coca

Cola. She had brown eyes behind glasses, and her hair was pulled back under a cap. "You fancy a drink?"

"I expected champagne."

"Hurry it up, bud," said a Black corporal, visible all the way round her as he approached. He had a roll of parcel tape in his hand.

Chapter 30

Hamburg Barman Watches the News,
5 November 2006

Carl got the last of the patrons out the door of the bar at 1.30 am. The atmosphere tonight had been grim. Schadenfreude about England under nuclear attack went only so far when marketing beer in Hamburg. Remembering that the 9/11 bomber gang had a staging-post in Hamburg, people had too much anxiety about who might have done it and where the next strike might be. No one had wanted the Sports Channel. Carl poured himself a vodka and set about cleaning the bar, keeping one ear on the television high over the counter.

News reports about the London bombings were almost continuous, all coming from outside Britain where *"...radio blackout is almost total. However minor effects are showing up in Brittany and northern Spain as the pulse drifts southward in response to Earth's magnetic lines. Radioactivity from the five dirty bombs continues to cripple daily life in southern England and in Scotland. Supplies of blood serum are being dropped to London hospitals coping with burns victims, but no food can be dropped for fear of attracting people out into the open where radiation levels are still high. Dead bodies have begun to appear in suburban streets all over London. Foxes, dogs and cats have been seen attacking the remains in broad daylight.*

Rain is expected to lessen the radiation risk in coming days, according to experts from Chernobyl. Other experts warn that rainwater will then be as dangerous as the dust is at present.

There is as yet no United States missile response to the attacks but there are plenty of statements from President Bush and other American politicians, mostly Democratic, saying that whoever wins the election, America will stand firm against terrorists.

"If only you knew who they were," said Carl and began wiping tables. Millions of people slowly dying in London, two thousand dead already, and at any moment that mad dog, Bush, could push a button just to win an election in which he isn't even a candidate. Then Germany and the whole world would go up in smoke! Anyone can buy a bomb in Russia these days and fire it at anybody for any reason. Just because you don't like the neighbours' cat! He didn't fancy being chewed by a cat.

"I don't think I'll buy a lottery ticket this week," he decided.

The next news report stated the EMP rocket had been launched from the Netherlands. The launch vehicle had been found in the dunes near Rockanje, a small town south of Rotterdam. A suspect apprehended in Amsterdam a few days ago was now thought to be one of the terrorist gang. Their getaway vehicle was a boat impounded after it was found in a canal in central Amsterdam on Wednesday. It is a glass-bottomed hydrofoil made in Russia.

Carl sat down to watch.

The driver - Xavier Hollander, who claimed to be a New Zealander - said he was taking the boat to Thailand, to show coral reef fish to tourists. There was a photo of him, beaming and waving from his boat. There was also an interview with a yacht owner whose craft had been swamped by the hydrofoil on the Ijsselmeer on 25 October. Again they showed the video that Carl had seen a couple of nights ago of the boat being launched.

This time Carl was transfixed: on the big screen he could see that the man pushing the boat out was Frits Breijer! He had just the same long face and the frill of reddish beard. Though the cigarette lighter could have belonged to his friend. You couldn't see the face of the other man pushing the boat - he wore a cap. So had the man who'd been sitting in the bar that day when Frits Breijer came in to join him. One or other of them must certainly be the owner of the lighter!

Then he realised Xavier Hollander could have been the third chap - the one who'd been chased into the bar by the Turks and Armenians but left without buying a drink. He'd been a big, good-looking man like this Xavier Hollander.

Carl forgot his cleaning duties. He had plenty to think about. What should he do with his information? He wasn't inclined to run to the police every few minutes – he'd seen too much of them since last summer when those two little girls were snatched out of the bouncy castle at his front door. It made his flesh creep every time detectives came into the bar, no doubt looking for free beer, but probably also hoping it would be the day he broke down and confessed to running a white slave racket or a paedophile ring - or a sausage factory!

No, he wouldn't bother to help even the Dutch police with their enquiries. His customer, Frits Breijer or not, was possibly just a passerby who'd kindly stopped to help launch the boat. Yet it was curious that there was a Dutch connection. Funny, too, that the German TV, on the day when he'd first seen the fat blue boat, was already taking such an interest in a traffic-control problem on an Amsterdam canal, even allowing for the glass bottom. If it had first appeared on a popular Dutch news programme the item was probably a police plant. At least it would be a talking-point for his customers. The old boys, who all saw the fuss over the underpaid prostitute the day Frits dropped the cigarette lighter, would be amused, since they would all know the original 'Xavier Hollander' - they had not yet lost all interest in sex, even at such a remove.

Maybe he should try to get a few euros for a photo of the lighter. He might be able to sell it on eBay. Would anyone believe him? Who else had been in the bar that day? Those same three old sailors! They would back up his story.

Tomorrow morning he would look for them. About nine o'clock they'd be getting stiff in their beds and want coffee. He would go round the stalls in the square, see if he could find one of them, or another regular who might know them and tell which cafés they patronised.

Then he would take the lighter and go visit his friend who had a good camera. He knew someone who did shipping news for *Die Spiegel,* too.

He turned off the blower, pushed the wilting castle inside, locked the door and pulled the rollers down after him. He stood his coat collar up and hurried home in the damp fog.

Chapter 31

The Afghan Rug,
Beckenham, South London, 6 November 2006

That morning, the second day after the London bombs went off, Serge's whiskers appeared among the blisters on his chin. The sprouting moustache was lifting the scabs above his mouth like a porch roof. Hiria felt revolted as she spooned mashed Weetabix between the cracked lips. She was wasting the last of their milk on this disgusting creature!

Serge spluttered and shook his head at Hiria. They both knew it was hopeless. The blisters were inside as well as out and the food hurt him all the way down. He figured his stomach was probably useless anyway. Even so, he wanted a bottle, to pee. When the man came in again he would ask. He would point with his bandaged hand. Or he could try to get up and walk to the toilet. There must be one downstairs somewhere. But then he wouldn't be able to undo his pyjamas! The man might help, though he seemed hostile and kept away. They were his pyjamas, however.

It was freezing cold today. Jessica came in wearing two jackets, with leggings over her trousers and an Arsenal cap on her head.

"Do you want a hat?" she asked, offering him a red-and-white knitted beanie.

Serge nodded enthusiastically. He missed his old leather cap more than anything. Never mind "dying with your boots on", it turns out all a man really needs is a hat – that and a last piss.

Jessica moved to the end of the table and tried to pull the hat on to his head. He lifted up on his good elbow to help. She was no taller than his mother.

"Danks." He sank back, thinking how his mother would fuss over him if he were as bad as this in St. Petersburg. She would be yelling at Natasha all day long to bring warm wash-cloths or milky coffee or more pillows.

No, not Natasha - he'd forgotten - but the agency would have sent round another girl straight after the accident. They had plenty trained.

If only he hadn't left the letter with Bernardin's signature in the scanner – Zaheed had just been so anxious to get the whole translation ready to show the boss. That stolen page summarised Bernardin's proofs about the EMP action. It had clinched the deal.

It was a pity Natasha had to be killed. She'd been a good little servant until August when his mother foolishly let her go to Lake Seliger for Putin's Youth Camp. Anyone would know Nashi recruiters were bound to spot her there. He'd tried to keep everything clear and clean in the apartment while he was summarising the Iraqi documents, though probably Nashi had all the time been laboriously hacking into his internet record. Yet anyone could have looked up the originals. The 47,000 boxes of papers brought out of the Baghdad cellar and put on the net by Bush's supporters had only recently been taken off when someone must have realised how useful they were. Ah, it was great work he'd done there at home last summer.

And if he were there right now Natasha, or whoever the next girl was, would be trying to feed him chicken soup and scrambled egg, perhaps with caviar. He could fancy something like that. Just a taste.

Perhaps the Elizarova Prospect apartment had already been damaged in reprisal attacks by American missiles? His mother might have been arrested, or killed.

Could anyone know so early that Russians were part of the organisation?

Apart from the Nashi and their handmaidens, there was his bitch of a wife to worry about: she would come crawling around straight away once she heard he was missing, sniffing for any mention of her name in his will. She'll be mad when she finds out how he has tied up the boy's legacy.

Suddenly he needed more than a piss. He rolled to get his legs clear of the bed and fell in a stinking heap. "Obosratsya!"

He was weeping with the pain of his arm as well as the stomach cramps when everyone came rushing.

"Corr!" said David. He was covered with dirt. Serge didn't want his raw flesh touched by those hands but David hauled the pyjamas off and carried them away. Hiria covered him with a towel and had started to wipe him up when more violent diarrhoea arrived.

"So much for the Afghan rug. Do you notice the nice pattern? See - rocket launchers and departing Russian tanks, on a ground of blazing helicopters." Hiria glared at the patient.

"I'll have to ask my brother…oh well… It doesn't matter anymore, does it?"

David reappeared with short pyjamas and clean sheets and helped dress the patient. They put newspaper on the mattress this time. Sergey struggled back onto the improvised bed.

"I've put the pyjamas down the ash-pit in the living-room fireplace, but that rug won't fit. It'll have to go in one of the bags of spoil from the tunnel."

Sergey was groping at his money belt. He produced a cigarette lighter and held it out to David.

Hiria laughed. "Flick it," she said. "He wants us to burn away the smell!"

Two almost identical girls appeared at the door, observing the scene. Sergey thought he must be getting delirious.

"Sophie came through the hole. Her father's ill," said the one in the cap.

"I told him about Sergey. He said to give you this," said the girl with the black hair and dirty face. She stayed in the doorway, but held out towards Hiria a plastic bag holding a bottle and a syringe.

Hiria took it. "How did your father know about Sergey?"

"Jessie wrote me a window notice about him."

Hiria pushed her hair back behind her ears. "Thanks. How much do I give him?"

"There's a note," said Sophie.

So Sergey the Bomber had a nicer morning than was expected, though Hiria didn't give him the full dose. She was thinking economy in every move now.

Chapter 32

Stopover,
Cairo, Egypt, 7 November 2006

After his hospital experience in Poland and mercy flight out, Dennis woke next day in a windowless room with mud walls. Light came through a grille on a metal door. It was stinking hot and his diaper was full. He was very thirsty but his mouth felt crusty and sore. The tape had been pulled off his mouth sometime and had taken some of his whiskers with it. He must have been well drugged. He rubbed his chin as much as he could on the collar of his overalls. Both elbows, still zipped inside the suit, had pins and needles and the handcuffs were chafing his wrists. The shoulder was either better or completely numb.

So much for luxury travel. They could keep their Lear jets if that was the way they treated passengers and this hut, their standard accommodation.

Sitting up was a major, or even a brigadier. Eventually he managed it by inching down the bench, dropping his legs gingerly over the edge and throwing himself at the side wall. The diaper squelched. The room he surveyed was completely empty. Not even a bucket. And no insect life.

There was faraway conversation outside. It could be in English. Those bloody Brits have a lot to answer for - they've spread everywhere, and if this place is theirs, the mud walls are horrible. Dennis waited a good while before he called out.

Unfortunately his "Oi," came out croaky. He was still thinking about repeating it when a face appeared behind the pattern of the door grille.

"Awake, are ye?" The man had an Australian accent. He had a good look and a sniff. "About ripe for a shower, I think, mate."

Several locks and bolts were undone, the door creaked open, and the Australian came in wearing generic khaki.

"Where are we? Is it Darwin? I'm going home!"

"I'm not authorised to answer any questions until you've spoken to my superiors, but I will clean you up a bit. Can you walk?"

Dennis was curious about that himself, but standing up made him totter. The Aussie caught him and lowered him back on the bench. He went to the door and yelled, "Chair!"

A wheeled plastic chair with a hole in the bottom was delivered by an Aborigine in a long white dress and a little round cap. He went away and the Australian pushed Dennis down a low-ceilinged hallway lined with more cell doors. Dennis studied the curvy grilles and decided he was probably not in the Northern Territory after all. Though the man in white could have been an Indonesian boatperson, but he was too big and too clean.

"What the hell are you doing here, Digger?" Dennis asked the Aussie pushing his chair.

"Secondment," was the only reply as the Australian turned into a big wet room, just green tiles everywhere and a hose coming out of the wall. In one corner there were a couple of stools and a few bits of what looked like gym equipment.

The soldier unzipped Dennis's overall. "Phwoor!" he said, and grabbed the running hose to stick it down the back of the collar as an advance measure.

The water was cold, the best Dennis could remember. "Give us a drink, will you?" he croaked.

"You can't drink this water! You'll be having a proper drink afterwards. I'll leave the sling on but the rest of your clobber can go." The soldier was about to hand Dennis a cake of yellow soap when he saw the handcuffs. "Okay, then," and he dropped the soap on the floor; then kicked it further away.

He held out one empty sleeve and considered the twin problems of getting the overalls and the diaper off. First he pushed the top of the overall down till he could rip the diaper tape off at the back. Then he tore the front tape off, and rocked Dennis side to side to ease the suit down a bit more. Finally he grabbed the ends of the trousers, and with one foot on the side of the chair yanked the whole filthy mess out and flung it at the wall. The chair spun.

"Qantas trained, I can tell," said Dennis in all his glory, slithering luxuriously in the water on the seat, "but I do reckon you should get another brand of suppository- those ones stink."

The Aussie used the hose to blast him clean. Then he dumped the overalls in a bucket, hosed the floor and left.

Dennis didn't bother to thank him. Instead he bent down to rub first at his stomach where some of the midline hair had been ripped out, and then his poor knees, using his forearms inside the sling, and avoiding the handcuffs as much as possible.

Left naked and alone in the green room, Dennis studied the copper drain hole. It could do with a good clean - he had a vision of his wife and mother circling it competitively, spray bottles raised.

He could have licked up the trickles of water snaking towards it, following cracks in the tiles. In his career he had made a study of low points and this he recognised as the lowest point of his life so far. What next?

Who would care enough to come looking for him? Not the Fish Club boys - next week was the Coastal Classic. His wife? Pass. The police at Matakana? Not after the pursuit car landing in the pig pond at Whangateau.

Something big must have happened when he wasn't looking - in St. Petersburg or Hamburg or Amsterdam. Nothing had happened in Marken, and for Frans's and Johanna's sake he hoped it never would. Sergey and Zaheed kept getting mentioned. And a rocket attack on London. Serge had probably drowned but it was ridiculous to ever see him as a mad bomber. He might be half Russian but he'd turned out quite a good chap – a lot nicer to his mother than some people. And Zaheed could never have been a terrorist, not with those little fuzzy red whiskers – he'd hardly make a bad-tempered school caretaker.

What about the Turkish gang in Hamburg? Could they have been working for Zaheed? And the dirty prostitute as well? Too far-fetched. Zaheed's the sort never looks at any kind of woman except his wife. Poor bastard.

Then he had another thought, something his mother once said: *"Sergey's been plumbing-out rockets as long as you've been scraping fat out of sewers."*

The Natasha business was a bit of a worry too...

Get a grip: I saw them. They couldn't even organise a fishing trip.

They're probably all drowned.

Get a drink.

Chapter 33

David Goes for the Doctor,
Beckenham, S. London, 7 November 2006

On the third day after the London bombings the two girls were up in Jessica's room trying to decide which CD they would play as soon as the power came back on. Justin Timberlake's *Future Sex/Love Sounds* would be the likely winner but Sophie was wistful about Fall Out Boys. She yearned to hear their latest song, *"This Ain't a Scene, It's an Arms Race"*.

She looked at their first CD, holding it out to catch the light from the window. "They're so lovely!" she said.

"Come over here by the mirror," said Jessica. "I reckon we should cut your hair. You don't want all this cruddy old black stuff anymore!" She picked up a fat strand and they watched it fanning slowly downward in the mirror. "You've been an Emo far too long. It's way out of fashion."

"I'm not bothered but my mother would go spare! She's only just got used to this."

"Come on! What you've got to have these days is big at the front and short at the back. Your fringe will come in handy, and you can keep some long bits – I could cut some out of mine. We could knot it on!"

Much giggling and oohing followed as the black lengths fell to the carpet from Jessica's courageous scissor work. The transformation was completed with spangly eye shadow and sprinkles of stardust. Sophie had turned into a Now Girl.

"You need some real shiny lips. There: look!"

"Ooh! Fierce!"

"We should give you some bling. Try this." Jessica took up a necklace of bright-blue glass beads, stretching it wide to get it over Sophie's head without spoiling her hairdo.

The two girls studied the result. Then Sophie shook her head. "Nah. Too skinny and the wrong colour."

"I know where there's some real bling. Bring the scissors and keep quiet."

Jessica led the way out to the landing. From the window Sophie looked over the trees and down into her own garden. Her mother's new outdoor table and chair set looked like doll's furniture. Jessica's two fir trees, where her father had always promised to put up a hammock, had gone nearly transparent. No use even for a squirrel gym now – no privacy.

"There's a plane coming!"

Jessica scrambled up to look out the window, holding a long baton of rolled newspaper she had pulled from the corner of the skirting board.

"It's very low. And look at that thing sticking out the back – it could be a bomb!" said Sophie.

"Nah, that's just an Orion – we call them O'Briens. Dad says they are made to fly slow and low like that to sniff out submarines. They're probably just looking for more bombs and stuff round here."

They watched the plane till it disappeared over the eaves above them and Jessica dropped to the floor. "Scissors," she whispered, holding up her hand. Then she was hunched in the corner, prying under the panelling with the scissors.

Changg! Part of the wall was peeling outward from the bottom! A tall door opened and Sophie got a glimpse of a little dark room with piled with books. Something was moving.

"Rats!" they both shrieked, and Jessica banged the door shut and pounded on the upper part to seal it.

They rushed into Jessica's room and slammed the door.

"That was horrible," said Sophie. "Those little ones are mice, aren't they?"

"No, they were young rats." Jessica's horror was merging into embarrassment.

"Did you see them sitting up on those piles of books? Like it was a school for rats!" said Sophie.

They began to roll about on the bed, laughing

"What are you two little devils doing up there?" David's voice sounded smaller than usual.

Jessica sobered up at once and went out to peer two floors down at her father through the slit between the banisters. "Nothing!" she assured him, smiling brightly till he went back to the kitchen, grumbling

"Just as well!" in what he probably thought was an impressive manner.

David joined Hiria at the kitchen table for a war conference.

"Did you see the plane?" she asked.

"No, but I heard it. They're probably taking radiation readings." He shifted a bucket from under the table and nudged it in among bottles and jars and vases of water on the bench.

"Try to use up the small bottles first, will you?" said David. "It's driving me crazy, getting around in the dark with all these water hazards."

"I am trying. I've put cloths over them. You're kicking up so much dust since you've been digging - I never used to see dust but I hate the stuff now.'

"Don't worry about anything that comes out of the cellar - it can only be dirt. Without water it'll be the only way we have to clean anything,– and to use for a loo, once we've flushed all the cisterns. I think I'll put the next bag into the downstairs bathroom. And a half one to use there for sprinkling ..."

"Why don't you dig a long drop in the cellar?" asked Hiria

"Thank you, we're not in Tokerau now, Miss Heteraka!"

"Anyway, what are we going to do about *him*?"

"I suppose one of us could go next door and ask the doctor how to treat his sores. Lewis might even come through to look at him."

"Sophie says her dad's really sick himself after his day at the train wreck. He may be just as bad as Sergey."

"It makes me mad to hear you talk about that Russian bastard as if he were just an ordinary patient. He's a mass murderer – a war criminal, for God's sake!"

"You've hit the nail on the head there. I presume he did it to please Allah – though, come to think of it, the only motives he mentioned in his bit of a confession were 'oil for Russia' and 'getting the Americans out of Iraq'."

"It doesn't matter what his motive was: look what he's done!" David banged his fist on the table. "Only ruined England for a thousand years at least!"

"People sometimes do bad things for good motives." Hiria got up suddenly and turned away from her husband.

"Never mind any of that hypothetical rubbish, I'm going to go through the tunnel and ask to borrow the doctor's anti-contamination suit. I've got to go outside to find someone who's got a radio working and get them to tell the police or MI5 to send someone to take away our boarder."

"Of course you might find a bottle of beer too?" Hiria filled herself a glass of water from a flower vase shaped like a swan. She leant back on the bench to drink, took one sip and held the glass up to the window. "I think I'm missing the taste of fresh chlorine. Where will you go?"

"I do want to see how Dad is at Lewisham, but while I was tunnelling like The Great Escapers in the cellar I remembered we found that radio set tucked into the wall of the storeroom upstairs. I reckon the mother of the old biddy who sold us the house might have been a spy in the Second World War."

"Do you really? I was told her mother was a famous spiritualist. People keep peering in at us, as if they think we're living in a haunted house, but she couldn't have been a spy as well." said Hiria.

"Aw, no. Not even Hitler would have paid for that sort of information." said David. "They're probably just two women from a tragic family where housekeeping skipped a few generations. Though we did dig up those queer, devilish tiles and plates in the garden. Some of the books upstairs were pretty weird too. So maybe the radio..."

"If you couldn't get it working twelve years ago it won't be any better now. And remember, we didn't block up the cracks around that window on Saturday night. It looks straight out to Croydon; it wouldn't be safe in there," said Hiria.

"Yeah, I know. What we need is a shortwave radio in good working order. I'm betting those funny old chaps at the Radio Club at Kechill Gardens will have got their soldering irons out by now and repaired their crystal sets. They'd need some butane to do it but they'll always find some way under the radar – under the radiation, this week - to reach their friends."

"My dad's got a crazy mate like that up the beach at Tokerau. He's always boasting about being able to reach Alaska."

"Sounds like Mr Coggin and Brownie Johnson, going on at the pub about their ethereal adventures. I'll use the doctor's suit to go round to Brownie's. He's just the other side of the railway underpass. All right?"

"You might get contaminated – or someone might kill you for the radiation suit. But you might get some news."

"Bound to, and we've got a prime piece of news to tell, ourselves. Could you write his name down?" David jerked his thumb towards the dining room.

"I've got it here." She handed him a piece of paper. "I was going to put it by the phone…"

"This won't last forever, kid. You can send the girls through after a bit to ask what the Lewis's know. Do you think he'll sleep for a while?"

"He's well out to it. We'll be fine. You be careful, now."

They kissed at the cellar door. It was strange: in spite of their dreadful situation the bomb seemed to have freshened up their marriage. If the crisis lasted more than two weeks she would have to go through the tunnel herself to ask the doctor for another packet of contraceptive pills. They'd long ago decided to do without a son and certainly didn't want one that might come out with two heads, courtesy of the bomb.

David descended into the trench between sacks and bags and suitcases of dirt. The last she saw of him was his left running shoe, rather worn on the outside edge. She hoped his descent wouldn't have to do them for a funeral.

She took a deep breath of damp cellar air and closed the door.

David had a bit of trouble enlarging the hole in the Lewis's foundations to make it big enough to admit him, but emerged into their wine cellar and was reading labels and dusting himself off when Mrs Lewis came down her cellar steps at a gallop.

"Hello, Mr O'Brien! I thought it would be Sophie. Is she all right?"

"She's fine. They're up in Jessica's room doing girlie therapy, same as usual."

"This must be a dreadful disappointment for you. I suppose you thought, when you started digging, you would come out in New Zealand."

"Well, no, but just now, reading these labels, I did think I might have struck Australia. How's the doctor?"

"It's frightful! The rash is starting to come out all over him. We expected it on his hands and face but he seems to have breathed in radiation as well."

"Are you giving him plenty of fluids? That's about the only thing Hiria can do for our patient."

"Yes, I am doing the same, with plenty of emetics – but he's being sick anyway now. Do come and see him."

The doctor was in his bed on the first floor, a towel on his chest. He was flushed and tossing about with fever.

"I itch everywhere," he moaned. He wore cotton gloves on his hands to prevent him tearing his own skin.

His wife had obviously been sponging him when she heard the intruder in the cellar. She lifted off the towel and revealed his chest, covered in the same purple-red, lumpy weals as Sergey's. She resumed gently patting her husband dry and then applied a white cream.

"It's only zinc and castor oil but it seems to help a bit, perhaps just by keeping the air out."

"Didn't the de-contamination suit work, Doctor?"

"Yes, but through goggles you can't see well enough to get glass out of wounds. I couldn't stitch properly with the gloves on. Some of the people were horribly cut about. There were shards of glass, you see, sticking out of the walls and seats of the carriages from the blast, and then the train turned over on its side. People were thrown onto the glass. There was a lot of bleeding to stop and there are no ambulances. It might have been ages before they got to theatre and you really need to suture within four hours. A drink, please, Miriam."

"I'd like to borrow your suit," said David, holding the glass steady for him while Mrs Lewis removed the wash bowl. "I need to go outside to get a message to someone about our man. We think he's one of the bombers."

"What did you say?" Mrs Lewis turned in the doorway, water splashing onto her shoe.

"We think MI5 would like to know our patient's name. I'm going to see if there's a ham radio working anywhere. There's a chap called Brownie Johnson who might know."

"Vale Road, about Number 24," said the doctor, eyes closed.

"That's right! I'll be as quick as I can. Thank you. I hope you can get a bit of sleep."

Mrs Lewis took David downstairs, stopping outside a closed door. "We're using the front hall as an airlock," she said, pointing through the glass at a white suit. "First do up the snap fasteners and then the zip. Good luck. Bring us some news."

Outside, David clumped down the steps in his too-big shoes. The suit had been made for a taller, slimmer man than him but the zip was a brave one. Hiria, Jessica and Sophie waved out to him from the dormer window at the side of his house. He did a little dance for them and almost tripped in his clown shoes. He went to look at his car, though he knew it was useless. He brushed at the dust on the roof, gave the front tyre a token kick and waved to his audience again.

It was now about two in the afternoon but dark as four o'clock. The country club clock still said five to twelve as it had for at least eight years. He felt comforted by this reminder of English stickability, but could feel cold biting through the white plastic suit and set out for the station at a clumsy trot. *Never thought I'd wear white shoes. The boss would have made me go home and change, on suspicion I'd joined the Mafia. Wonder how he's doing out at Hampstead Heath with no one to make his coffee?*

There was no one about. He went a few steps into the railway station. The crash must have happened up around the bend of the track, level with Tesco's. The fence was pulled down flat from there nearly to the start of the platform, and newspapers and rubbish, and on this side leaves, were plastered to the station walls from bomb blast. He went down the stairs under the tracks and found a dead body. It was a boy of fifteen or so with an oozing, puffy face and peeling hands. He hurried through the tunnel and up the other side.

Brownie Johnston came to the front window of his house, looking worried by David's knock. David shouted his name as loud as he could. He held up the note Hiria had written and wished he'd brought a bigger one. Brownie signalled he should go round the back. There David found a shed with a tarpaulin tunnel connecting it to the back door of the house. Brownie was coming through the tunnel and calling him to keep going down the side by the fence to a shrouded door. Brownie had clearly been preparing for this day.

David fought through the folds of canvas and found Brownie lighting a paraffin lamp.

"Oh, it's you, Dave! Take off your suit, will you, and put it out the door, Thought I might have a pint or two hidden out the back in the shed, did you?"

David managed to get free of his headpiece. "Wouldn't mind if you had, but I've got a job for you. How's your radio feeling?"

"Awh, I had a bit of trouble with it but then I thought of an old transcender I used sixty years ago and I found the valve was as good as new. I've had it under the bench in a goldfish bowl, so I shouldn't have been surprised – glass is a good protector. It's nearly come right now. Got a signal from someone in Hungary this morning. Course I couldn't get much sense out of him. Told him how things are here. He seemed to be all right, just kept asking about us. What's your trouble?"

"We've got a badly burned chap at our place, came off the train wreck. Yesterday he told Hiria he was the Charing Cross bomber. Told her his name. It's Russian." He passed over the piece of paper.

"Well! It looks a bit Russian, don't it? Who do you want me to tell?"

"Can you pass a message to the police or Interpol? Anyone on the continent would do, surely?"

"Right then. You can do the pedalling and I'll have another go."

David studied the equipment. An old bicycle was cocked up on a sawhorse. The dynamo had been shifted on to the rear wheel and David was apparently expected to power the Morse transmitter by pedalling.

He climbed up and tried it. "Mind if I adjust the seat? I feel as if I'm going to fall off."

"Fine, fine." Brownie handed him a spanner. "Mind you, I had to pedal and transmit this morning both at the same time and I'm twice your age!" The old man sat down on a stool at the workbench and twiddled the knobs of his set. He reached under the bench and produced two brown bottles. "Open these first, will you? Then you tell me what you want me to say. You'll have to be pedalling for a few minutes while I try to rouse somebody."

David got off the bike, and found a bottle opener on the cluttered bench. On all four walls, banks of shelves stretched from floor to roof, filled with radio sets and computers, valves and nameless gear of every age. Books of radio call signs and manuals were stuffed into crevices. The beer was never better.

"Do you think The Prince would still be open?" he asked, as he fixed the bicycle seat.

"Lucky devil, anyone who was caught there! Hornby would see you right. You could die happy. Got your message written down?"

David turned the paper over and wrote: *Suspected bomber, Charing Cross Station, 4 November. Six foot three, bald Caucasian, moustache, forty-five, fair complexion. Radiation burns and cuts. Condition deteriorating. Alleged name, Sergey Malyarovich Mikulitsin. At 201 Lennard Road, Beckenham, Kent, BR3 IQN. David O'Brien.*

"Right, get on your bike! Keep it going...steady... Here we go!"

"*Dit dit dah, dah dah dit dit, dah dit...*" came through the set.

"It's Switzerland. Adligenswil, Lucerne." Brownie began to tap away. "I don't think they'll need the postcode. They won't be writing, will they? You'd better say 'Tell Interpol or the army.' Do they have an army in Switzerland?"

"Yeah, I think so. I knew a young chap who was in the Swiss Air Force. Apparently they keep their planes in caves in the mountains."

"Good idea. There you are: sent. I'll try a few more calls if this one doesn't answer. Keep pedalling!"

"Peep, peep peep peep, peep, peep peep peep peep, peep peep, peep."

"What'd he say?"

"Message received and understood, wilco - or numbers to that effect. They'll be using text language next. You'd better wait here for a while. I'll make us some bacon and eggs. Keep pedalling, though - there might be another reply."

"I was going to ask how you're surviving but you seem to be doing better than us. How do you cook?"

"I've got the barbecue over there."

Sure enough, Brownie only had to shift a box of tools off the pan and few books off the egg packet, unzip the bacon and he was soon cooking up a miracle.

As he pedalled, David marvelled at the happy life this old customs officer had created in a shed at the back of his house. It made David's IT job in the City look a miserable waste of twenty years.

He was allowed to dismount to eat.

"Your family all right?"

"Yes, but Dr Lewis next door got radiation burns from being called out to the train smash, though he doesn't look as bad as our bomber."

"Oh, dear. He was very good to the wife, Dr. Lewis."

"I don't know how either of my parents is. My father was in hospital at Lewisham. Fortunately my mother was probably babysitting at Richmond."

"Lewisham isn't too good. The whole of London and up to Sheffield in the north and much further south and to the west is knocked out as far as radio is concerned. I've got a friend in Bristol I was hoping would have got on the air before this. We've often talked about the day when we would have the BBC on the ropes and here it is, but he can't have kept his gas bottle full. Though you can always heat a soldering iron on a paraffin lamp. I've even done it over a candle when I was stuck out in the country. Here..." He passed David a cup of tea. "Sorry there's no milk. Have some sugar instead."

They sipped their tea.

"Would you like to borrow my car?" said Brownie.

"Will it go?"

"Yes, good as gold. I had it out last week. Went like a bird. You can crank it, you see. It's a Morris Minor - best car they ever made in Britain, and about all you'll see on the road this week. I'll keep watch here for your answer and send the message out a few more times whenever I can raise anyone."

"Thanks. I would like to get out to Richmond."

Brownie fished the keys out of his pocket. "It's on the other side of the shed. I'd try the South Ring Road, if I were you. Not that there'll be much traffic, but there'll be less physical damage away south.

"Here, take your wife this ham I dug out of the freezer. It's already cooked but I'd never be able to eat it all."

So David rolled up to the Lewises' door in the Morris Minor with a handsome bit of booty for both families. Mrs Lewis received the ham into her house, notwithstanding the little brass plate on the doorpost, but looked as if she'd rather have had anything else. She said she would tell Hiria "the message was sent" and that he wanted more leave to check on his

mother. She gave him another great send-off in his
little green tortoise.

Chapter 34

Preliminary Enquiries,
Cairo, Egypt, 8 November 20006

Dennis Bogdanovich was still sitting in his bottomless wheelchair at his unknown, hot green place of captivity, reviewing his prospects for rescue. He couldn't blame his friends or family for not rushing to find him. He'd been a bit of a shit all round - though surely his twenty years' services to sewerage must appear on the credit side of someone's ledger?

As for his personal resources, one arm and both knees might be buggered but his sex tools seemed OK, and if he could still think, he wasn't finished yet.

What was it Skotty held up as the first rule in fishing? *Know your enemy.* Where they lived, their breeding season and their preferred food and depth, because those things all determined what bait they'd take. The second rule was, *Don't forget: you know more than they do.*

What did he know? Did he even know where he was? Somewhere hot and Muslim-flavoured - the tiles were patterned with blunt Arabic squiggles and civilian staff came to work in their nightgowns. Could be anywhere in the Middle East or Pakistan or...

What breed were these mongrels he'd met? Various: Dutch, American, Polish, a possible French slimeball and one Australian strain had shown up so far.

What were they hunting? His boat? No, they had that already. They seemed keener on bombs and rockets now. So what sort of burley did he have to interest that sort of fish?

His mind-mapping was interrupted by the sound of approaching boots. The door creaked and then hit the wall. Four men in unmarked khaki came round in front of him. Two stomped back, rigidly "at ease" against the wall, while another two stood glaring at him beside a little table, waiting for seats to be brought forward for them.

The older man looked American: large, grim, self-important, with a crew-cut and whiskers. A catfish. The one who was Dennis's age could also be American, but that wouldn't be determined till he spoke. He looked more neutral and had wavy, light hair plastered down, a rosy forehead and prominent lower jaw – a snapper.

The Australian came hurrying in with clothing for Dennis and apologies to his superiors. He carefully placed two stools for them behind the table and then dropped a white tee-shirt over Dennis's head, pulled it down at the back and worked it over the arms inside the sling. For the rest, he flapped out a khaki towel and spread it over Dennis's knees and what had been intermittently kept private. The big fish then sat down on their seats with some care for their trousers while the Aussie joined the school of sprats along the wall.

Dennis took the initiative. "Who are you? Why are you doing all this to me?"

"You have been brought here to help us find and identify your co-conspirators," Catfish said, and his mouth shut in a straight line under the moustache. He was from Alabama all right.

"Why am I in handcuffs? Take them off!" Dennis poked the right elbow out and shook it carefully under the sling. "Who's got my boat? Where is my money belt? And my watch? I want a drink right now and a feed. And proper clothing. The New Zealand Government is going to take a very poor view of this, the way I've been treated, by the Dutch Politie and the Poles and all you other mongrels."

"We have been asked by the Government of the United Kingdom to examine you, urgently, and determine your part in the plot that has this week, paralysed electronic communications in England and Scotland by means of a High-Altitude Electromagnetic Pulse bomb and five dirty suitcase bombs. Any information we can obtain from you, we will be reporting to the United Kingdom government."

"Well I can't tell any of you anything about bombs. In New Zealand we don't even dynamite fish any more– it's considered an environmental crime these days." Dennis turned to eyeball the Australian whose eyes shifted to study the door grille.

"Where's that drink you promised me?"

"Who is Frits Breijer?" Catfish was holding out, close to the prisoner, Zaheed's lost cigarette lighter. The bulgy red eyes either side of it, fixed on Dennis, made it look like a hideous engagement ring.

No reply.

Catfish put down the lighter. "What is your relationship to Sergey Malyarovich Mikulitsin?"

"Serge? He's my mother's cousin's boy. A first cousin once removed, I suppose."

"I mean your professional relationship. Did he intend to use your hydrofoil as a getaway vehicle?"

"To get away from what? He took me to the Zuider Zee last week, and the only time I've seen him since, he took me on a fishing trip and nearly killed me. He's probably dead himself. He's got nothing at all to do with my business, and it wasn't my boat that capsized."

"What is your business?" asked Snapper. He was English, though not the over-educated kind.

Startled, Dennis began his usual spiel: "I catch rats for Auckland..." But he did want to get all this over and have a drink. The hole in the bottom of the chair was getting uncomfortable too. "I design drainage systems in Auckland."

"Did you help assemble the rocket?" asked the Englishman. He must be the techie.

"Hell, no! The week before last, I was busy in Bangkok and the week before that, finishing a drainage contract for Waitakere City. And burying my father."

Suddenly Dennis was ashamed. He had a creepy feeling his father could see him right now, sitting virtually naked in this green hellhole.

"On the 23rd of October you received a message from New Zealand requesting some 'acid-wrapped rods'. Are these radioactive devices?"

"You have no right to be looking at my private emails. Mind your own bloody business!"

"Sir...?" said the Australian.

Catfish raised one finger at him but kept his stare on Dennis. Snapper turned and quelled the colonial with a disdainful look.

"On the 17th of October you sent a message on the internet from Bangkok to friends in New Zealand, offering to buy them 'nuclear chickens'," Catfish told him.

Dennis snorted back a laugh.

Catfish sensed weakness and changed tack. "Tell us about Zaheed."

"I don't know anything about him. He just travelled with us to Holland. He's a grumpy bugger, I can tell you that much. Look, I don't believe you've got anything to do with Britain or the New Zealand Government. You could have contacted the Auckland City Council days ago and found out all about me from the engineer or the treasury department. Or Basil Carter Corporation. I just won a big tender with them and they're getting the contract ready for me to sign at the end of the month. You're nothing but a bunch of bottom-feeders - especially you!" He spat at the Aussie. "I'm not going to tell you another thing about anybody."

"That will do for today," said the American and left without another word.

"Take him back," said the Englishman, following his master.

Chapter 35

Hiria Alone,
Beckenham, London. 7 November 2006

Hiria heard Mrs Lewis's voice coming from the cellar, shouting like a girl at Ascot with money on a good horse. Hiria went down to her end of the tunnel, and hollered back – like a Kiwi mother rounding-up her kids for tea. Then she went gingerly into the dark to receive the amazing ham and learn that David had gone off on another mission, to check on his parents.

Her husband had escaped.

She took one deep breath of the dank cellar air and then let it all out, before shutting the door and banging the frozen ham down on her kitchen table.

The girls were still happy on hairspray upstairs, the bomber on the dining room table was snoring off his morphine; there was no reason she should not lie down on the couch in the front room and have a rest and a think - without benefit of caffeine, liquor or chocolate. She blew out the candle, dragged the throw from the back of the couch and covered herself. Her nose was freezing. Since the explosion and with the bomber groaning all night, she'd had very little sleep. Beneath the throw she pulled her hair across her face, slipping a strand into her mouth.

She could hear the girls upstairs, singing into their hairbrushes, and remembered her own happy hours at that age, capering on the coffee table at

Tokerau with a trumpet shell for a microphone, roaring out across the ocean to

"LA International Airport, where the big jet engines roar. LA International Airport,

I won't see you anymore!"

She wept at last.

It had been good to hear the plane go over this afternoon- you suddenly felt hope spurt. It was the same as if you'd been lost in the bush and heard one- but when it was gone you felt lonelier than ever.

Still, she was glad to be alone for a while, not be obliged to keep up a cheerful adult pose. It reminded her of that first year as a mother, shut up alone with a baby. Where were her neighbours then? She knew a few of them now, and this week David had been home more than he ever was in those days.

Prison would probably be like this – except it would be warm and they'd feed you, whereas in this house, thanks to their monstrous guest, the dreadful daily question "What's for dinner?" had become irrelevant. The answer could only be "ham" from now on and there was no knowing how long she would have to make it last. Oh, for a nice foam-plastic box of butter chicken and rice! Or a lamb kebab.

When would they be able to go out for takeaways again - or outside at all? Apart from the Lewis family they hadn't seen any of the neighbours, even at windows, except for old Mrs Whittaker this morning. Hiria had seen her waving quite bravely from her bedroom across Kings Hall Road. She wouldn't be hungry yet – she was bound to have plenty of tinned food left over from the last war. Like Hiria's old aunties in New Zealand with their rust-spotted tins of lamb tongues and bully beef, sardines and Canadian salmon, sliced beetroot and tinned peas! She'd be game for anything today. When David came back with the suit she might go over the road and enquire – but what will Mrs Whittaker say when she hears about Serge?

And what is she going to say when she hears about my arrest for embezzling?

What will David say? What is he going to do? She'd known from the beginning it would be a negative factor in his career, having a wife who was not only Kiwi but Maori. She'd told him what the locals told Captain Cook, that it meant 'ordinary.' He disagreed, said her body and her honesty were extraordinary and she had believed him –until she secretly changed her status. It was like having your credit rating downgraded but only you knew it.

Yet how could they have let her parents come to England in 2002 and not been able to even feed them, let alone show them the sights? And how could she this year have left her father bleed to death on Whangarei Hospital's wretched waiting list, and not have given him the chance of private surgery?

Was David right in saying, before he left today, that this bomb had destroyed England? Did that mean all business too? Had Serge made her crime undetectable?

She had saved three thousand pounds since her promotion and every Monday night, while David took Jessie to swimming class, she would religiously take the new instalment upstairs and put it into the old plastic bag still holding the contents of the fatal safe deposit box. It had been the secret high point of her week, noting the new total. Sometimes she tried the rubies on afterwards. But even before the bombing, and before her father's surgery, she had known it would be impossible for her to buy back and replace Mrs Inister's three rands because the price of gold had gone up so much since she sold them. The old vault officer who scribbled the release for Hiria knew Mrs Inister and believed she was mad enough to insist on keeping her valuables about her - but then he died. Hiria would have to set up a new deposit box and there would be questions. David was bound to find out, then. He'd wanted to rush up to the storeroom today in search of the old radio set. If she hadn't been able to stop him that would have been the end - worse than Sergey's bomb.

She had to admit she'd really kept the money handy so she could leave England quickly if/when she got found out. At the same time she ached to pay it all back - return the goodies to the bank and be free again. If her father hadn't been stricken with cancer, or even if after that she'd just had another year to save...

Maybe she could have taken out a loan. Bank managers lent money without blinking these days for things like cruises to the Greek Isles!

Poor, loony old Mrs Insister. What must she have thought about being fingerprinted to give them access to the strongbox? The boss said she looked all right but her signature for the release had been quite indecipherable. It turned out there was no need to touch the rubies or rands, since the realisation from selling the Boots shares was so amazing. If only she had taken the other valuables back right away... Then she never would have touched the gold.

Hiria groaned, working at the strand of hair with her tongue.

There was an answering groan through the wall. She'd forgotten about Sergey the Bomber. She sat up.

Deal with the presenting problem first and long-term goals will fall into place.

There was no long-term any more.

Her mother would have said, "*Do well and God will reward you.*"

She threw off the blanket, twisted her hair into a knot, got up stiffly and went slowly in to see him. The groaning was getting more desperate. If David's trip was successful the police might soon come to carry him off. Would there be a prison hospital for him?

"They're screaming at me. Kill them!" he implored as she came in the room. In the wavering candlelight she saw him rearing up and shuddering on the edge of the bed, pointing his bandaged arm at each of the dining chairs in turn.

"Kill them all."

"It's all right, Sergey. It's only the morphine," she said.

She used his red plastic cigarette lighter to light another candle on the mantelpiece and saw something she had never noticed before – the carving on the high-backed chairs, was pure Regency from behind, but seen from the front it was Munch's '*Scream*' exactly. Sergey had six girls standing around his bed, hands up to their ears, mouths stretched open. Londoners in agony.

Serve him right, but she turned two of the chairs sideways. Some smart artisan's idea of *Dread the Dinner Party?* Or *Night on the Marae* - sleeping with the ancestors in a carved house?

She dropped sleeves from the armchairs and sofa on the others.

"It's all right, Sergey, they've all gone now. Move over on the bed. Lie down."

What a scream.

The blankets had fallen off him. She covered him but he was still squirming, just conscious enough to know he'd been in danger. He was uncomfortable, though. Next thing he'd be getting bedsores to add to his troubles. Where had they put Jessica's old sheepskin rug? The New Zealand remedy for pressure sores was supposed to help invalids as well as babies. It always was a filthy idea.

The money belt was troubling him, too. It'd be like trying to sleep in a brassiere. He was hitting at it with his bandaged left hand as she prepared to spread the blankets over him. She managed to quickly slide his covers underneath as he raised the arm in another bumbling gesture.

"Would you like me to take your money belt off, Serge?"

The big hand with the loose bandage thumped down on the mattress. "Niet!" His scabby face turned to her with a jerk but he couldn't get his eyes to open. Ah well, slacken the buckle and he'll shuffle it looser, himself. It would really have been better put under his pillow. Perhaps he was trying to close the zipper after producing the lighter for them this morning. That was a funny moment.

She lifted the blanket to pull it up a bit. Sticking out of the money belt were two packages of new banknotes. *Drop the blanket and don't think of it!* Twenty thousand euros? *Don't THINK of it!*

No wonder he was uncomfortable and concerned. And we thought it was all cigarettes!

"Muu-um," said Jessica at her shoulder, "we're hungry!"

The two girls did look peaky.

And Sophie Lewis has had her hair butchered!

Two lines quoted from "LA International Airport" by Leanne Scott,1970. Recorded by Dick Frizzel, Columbia 45 139

Chapter 36

More News from Tokerau,
NZ and Bamiyan, Afghanistan, 7 November 2006

Hiria's mother, Rosalie, was knee-deep in the tide at that moment, in front of the bach at Tokerau. It was a beautiful November day; no sign of nuclear winter yet. The sky to the south was cobalt blue with mounds of fresh cloud along the sandhills. Suddenly she was in a milky wave up to her waist, though still gouging the sand with her toes to find the shellfish she knew were hiding underneath - an army of terracotta warriors standing shoulder to shoulder, with green epaulettes,.

Ah, there they were! Between waves she reached down to grab two of them but the next wave lofted her away. She struggled back out to them. Jim might fancy a few fat tuatua for lunch. If the end of the world had started and her daughter and grand-daughter were already taken, her priority, to the last, must be to keep saving her husband's life. She had become very alarmed this morning when she saw him scraping his porridge into the scrap bucket. Hospital corners on beds might be beyond her but she could tell when someone was thinking of dying.

As if the trouble they'd been having with the leaky colostomy bag these last two weeks wasn't bad enough, hearing about the London bombings had finished him off. It's a terrible thing to lose a child and he fears he has lost not only Hiria, but her husband and the child too. He loved David as much as their own son and doted on Jessica. In the last year he'd even taken to watching rock videos on Saturday evenings, to have something to talk about with her on the phone.

Ooh, that was a cheeky wave!

Now he turned the TV off as soon as the news was finished. They never told you anything much about civilians anyway. It was all just Blair saying it didn't matter much about losing the submarines because they were only old ones and he was thinking of getting new ones for Christmas anyway. He was safely in Paris and probably didn't have much idea about how people were doing in London.

Ah, there they are. Three, each as fat as two fingers.

Barry heard more in Afghanistan than they did. The New Zealand Army there got news through the British Army, from America. When he phoned yesterday he told her how the British Army was mobilised after the first bomb and then immobilised by the EMP one. Information was being passed round England and Scotland by Naval Reserve men using semaphore flags. Bicycle relays took pigeons here and there in case a reply was wanted.

NATO planes were still dropping blood products and antibiotics to hospitals but not food - Barry said the British Army would have eaten all the food anyway. The Americans were sending de-contamination equipment to Germany to be delivered to England by sea. So their ships obviously still worked. The Russians were providing clean-up workers from Chernobyl.

Dropped one. Try to find it with my foot. Another wave and I'm shifted off the hole again. Struggle back. Luckily there's plenty.

The Queen was in France. Barry said she travelled to Folkestone in the Scottish State Coach - not the gold one. She and the Duke and the horses all wore de-contamination suits (the corgis were crated). The Duke must have insisted on driving, because they said he was rather hot and tired, pulling off his hood as he got off the jigger at the other end of the Chunnel.

The Netherlands Police had captured one of the bombers. He was probably Russian but he said he was a New Zealander. What a cheek.

Yikes! That was a big wave. Got me under the arms.

Jim doesn't care about the news - doesn't even seem to care about the All Blacks being caught in England under the bomb. I've been trying to perk him up by saying, "Wasn't this the best team ever?" Or, "What about Richie McCaw?"

He looks at me as if to say, "You've left it a bit late to get interested in rugby, my girl."

The only part of the paper he likes now is the Family Notices. He folds it up and saves it for an afternoon treat. Then he goes through it, reading all the deaths, marking with a cross those he knows, or any he thinks might be Catholic - likely roommates in the particular mansion he has booked into.

When she had half a bucket of tuatua Rosalie thought she wouldn't bother to get any wetter. She took them back to the bach and showed Jim.

He hardly looked into the bucket.

"That mad young mate of Barry's, Dennis Bogdanovich, is in the paper! He's been arrested in Holland. They've got the name wrong, but it's him all right. When Barry rings you for your birthday you can tell him." Jim was beaming. "Lucky Hiria didn't marry *him*, eh?"

Well, that was a quick cure! She needn't have bothered breaking her nails and getting her clothes all wet. Though she could have been worse off: when Jim's grandmother was dying, the old lady'd had a fancy for stewed shag! Jim's father went to all the bother of shooting one and cleaning and cooking it for her, and when she'd tasted one spoonful she'd had enough. That must have been about sixty years ago.

Rosalie stood at the sink and raised her eyes to the hills heaving at the craggy end of the beach.

"Here, let me do that." Jim took the knife from her hand. "I can still do something, you know! They're much more tender if you mince 'em up raw, eh?

Chapter 37

Lewisham Hospital,
Ladywell, S. London, 7 November 2006

David got the Morrie going again outside the Lewis's house He made a business of the cranking, waved the crankhandle to Mrs Lewis, leapt in and puttered off, tooting madly, down Lennard Road towards Sydenham. His headlights extravagant in dimming London, he found himself taking right-hand options familiar from late-night taxi rides home, but now reversed, led toward the Prince of Wales in Lordship Lane. The roads were empty except for dusty parked cars, many with broken windows. *Crime must go on!*

He parked on the footpath and banged on the heavy pub door. No reply. No one to be seen through the window but there were plenty of empty glasses on the tables. They must have drunk the place dry.

He went back to the gutter and called up to the second-floor windows, "Hornby, you miserable old bastard, I know you're up there. Come down and give a man a drink! This is thirsty work, saving the world! Hey, Hornby! Goose! It's Rhino!"

Still no reply.

He turned away. "Useless bastard."

Curtains were twitching in upper windows of other houses. Mostly elderly ladies, poor old scarecrows. Some were banging on the glass, but he couldn't help them all. Those who weren't fit enough to climb stairs would be the worst off. Stuck upstairs they'd have no tea, and would never be able to reach water in the high cisterns of those old bathrooms, and if they went downstairs they'd be trapped there and probably die of the cold - it was going to be freezing tonight. He got back in the car and turned towards Lewisham Hospital and his father. He knew it was hopeless but having the car and decontamination suit obliged a son to try to see how his father's life had ended.

In the dim headlights he saw people crossing the street, four young kids with hands in their pockets and heads wrapped like Arabs facing a desert duststorm. He tooted at them and gestured for them to go home. They turned and jigged about, kicking derisively at his ridiculous car. They would interpret his attention as general adult hostility - home was probably even more dangerous to them.

He remembered going home to face his father on a Sunday night when the beer had run out and the horses had let him down yet again: a smart man caught in the class trap, doing a job he despised. For the sake of his own education, mostly thanks to his mother and uncles, and for the food and shelter his father had grudgingly supplied, along with occasional kicks and constant insults - for all of that he would try to say goodbye to his father, The Unknown Victim in a world war without heroes.

As he drove north on the South Ring Road he could see very little damage apart from one or two burnt-out houses and an electronics factory that was still smoking from its upper floors. Buses, trains and a few delivery trucks had been stopped in their tracks. A Sainsbury's refrigerated truck had gone on fire at a Catford roundabout. David was tempted to stop and forage in the blackened wreckage in case there was anything edible but he kept on towards the hospital for fear the car might be stolen. Besides, if he stopped he'd have had to crank-start it again.

For once he had no trouble finding parking. He left the Morrie among ambulances at the casualty entrance. The renal unit was in an annex at the back. He clumped towards it with dread. There was no one anywhere to be seen - no white figures in either contamination suits or doctors' coats, no nurses, no receptionists, no busy technicians, no tea ladies, no mournful visitors. The piles of tattered magazines in the waiting rooms looked no worse than usual.

He opened the door to the dialysis department and was swamped by stench. Six corpses sat in armchairs between machines, none of them his father. The early shift. One woman, still attached by taut, coloured tubes to her machine, was on the floor, swollen and oozing blood and rusty urine. Bacteria and bodily decay were not going to be stopped by a mere EMP bomb – in fact their mission of endless procreation might even be enhanced by radiation. David let the door swing back and went upstairs to his father's ward.

Inside the curve of the staircase the lift had stopped short of the first floor within its metal grille tower. A faint tapping was coming from it. David banged on the grille, then kept climbing to find either his father or a fire axe, whichever came first. He saw the fire box opposite the ward office but went into his father's room close by.

All four patients were dead. Desmond O'Brien was curled up on his bed like a skinny brown prawn. The window he was always jealous of losing had delivered a searing blast to his skin from the nuclear explosion. His eyes were burnt white. Frailty and the shock wave had no doubt stopped his heart. David patted the bony rump with a gloved hand. He considered taking his father's radio but it would never be any use again. The three other patients were dead in similar poses to his father. One had his thumb in his mouth.

David took the "Desmond O'Brien" nametag from the doorplate, noting that his father had reinstated the O' and the E - the name had been 'Desmond Brian' for a few years during the Irish bombing. He slipped the card under the neckpiece of his radiation suit and went to break out the axe.

On the staircase again, he banged on the grille and called, "Hello, in there?"

He heard slow tapping. This was no time for Morse code!

"Hang on, I'm going to chop you out of there. I've got an axe."

He swung at the highest convenient point, and in four blows had split a long opening in the grille. If he climbed up inside it he might be able to wedge the axe between the solid doors and lever them open. Pity he'd never taken notice of how to get out of a stuck lift - he and his friends had only ever discussed savage opportunities the predicament might offer them, inside.

As he clambered up he used the back of the axe to knock down some of the spikes of metal he had produced, turning them into footholds. His feet hardly fitted the criss-cross pattern but once he was level with the lift cabin he was able to push the grille out a little, like a vertical hammock.

He had very little room to swing the axe. He tapped on the door with it and called, "Hello, in there. I'm going to try to open the door. Stand back."

There was a muffled answering cry and some thumping not far from floor level. He waited a moment, aimed, and flung the axe at the crack between the doors with all the force his elbows could give it. The steel doors grabbed the blade and the handle jarred his arms. He slipped and had to grab at the grille with one hand and hold himself out from the bottom of the lift with the other arm stiffened, till he could find another foothold. It was like Harrison Ford, with colder weather and without the sexy costume - but no shortage of doom.

Time for another attack: he grasped the axe handle and tried to twist the blade in the crack. No luck. It was fixed solid without having made any perceptible opening. He would have to find another axe and drive it in further.

"I'm going to get another axe. I'll be back soon."

A wail came from inside the lift.

"I'll be back," he yelled, climbing down to the stair rail. This operation required a higher level of fitness than David had ever supposed he had. As a temporary concession he decided to look downstairs rather than up for another fire-alarm box and axe.

He found one not far along from the bottom of the stairs. The glass was already broken here and the fire hose trailed on the floor, flat and useless. He took the axe and climbed the stairs again, got up into the cage and banged a greeting/warning on the lift doors.

Another swing and a clanging blow on the trapped axe, and the doors parted an inch. The first axe fell past David and crashed two floors below. A black eye peered at him through the gap between the doors, accompanied by more wailing and the same bad smell he'd met downstairs. Two black hands helped his two white gloves force the doors back. A Black nurse was kneeling in the lift beside a bed.

"He died yesterday. Arrythmia and then heart failure on top of kidney failure. At about five o'clock, I think. I couldn't see my watch. I'm thirsty. Who are you? Why did you take so long to get us out? Why are you dressed like that? I've been so frightened!" She cried all the time as he was helping her arrange her long legs so that her shoes fitted into the mesh of the grille on the climb down. They fell together over the banister and on to the stairs. David hit his head and his left elbow and the girl fell on top of him.

They sat on the stairs and David told her how the worst story in the world had begun at the moment the lift stalled. The girl, who said her name was Nancy, stopped crying. She said she had known about the first bomb at Charing Cross. They had sent home all the orderlies and junior nurses immediately.

David told her they would now have to do something to keep her safe from radioactivity. She sniffed and began to plan with him.

First they went upstairs and she got them both a drink out of the patients' fridge. There were also some sandwiches and apples. The girl ate sparingly but David pulled up his helmet and ate dry bread and drank all the milk and supped several pots of yoghurt and a piece of coconut cake.

David told her about the man in his dining room at home and his symptoms but didn't tell her he was probably the cause of his own disease.

"I know about radiation burns," Nancy told him. "I was a doctor in Nigeria, and we had lectures at Ibadan University about Hiroshima from a visiting professor. She came from the Tokyo Women's Medical University. I am only a Charge Nurse here. We should really try to get into the radiography department and get some lead aprons and things like that. That's where I was going with my patient. He was just here on holiday andgot ill. I was taking him down to have an X-ray because I knew his language."

David took her in to see his father and the other roommates.

"He was a nice old man, your father - very polite. They were all very good, just waiting and hoping. In this room they all had pacemakers."

Then Nancy did a ward round. There were five patients missing on the other side of the ward and some of the dead showed signs of dehydration. Several of them had got out of bed and appeared to have died on the floor trying to escape. "I could hear people on the stairs for about the first hour, and then nothing," she said.

Nancy unlocked the drugs room. She filled a bag with packets of pills and bottles and syringes, and gave David a box of blood product sachets from the refrigerator to carry. She took a drawer full of dressings and some masks and rubber gloves from a locker and then led the way downstairs and along many corridors to Radiography.

The huge cream machines stood idle. In the dark side rooms Nancy felt about and brought out a radiation-proof overall with gloved sleeves, and a protective apron to go with it, as a head covering. At David's suggestion she put another apron on backwards to protect the gap down her back.

"My father would be proud to see me dressed like a proper Muslim woman at last," she said as she fitted goggles over a surgical mask. She stood for inspection.

David looked at her feet but couldn't see anything to cover them. Those white gumboots surgeons wore would have looked right but would probably be no help against radiation.

Nancy took two aprons and wrapped them round her legs, then fished out her scissors and cut straps from other aprons to cross-garter them. "Right. Now where are we going?"

"Do you want to go home? I have an old car, if it's not too far," said David.

"There's no one there. I'd like to be useful if I can."

"Have you had any sleep?"

"Yes. I kept dozing off in the dark. I think I was locked up for three nights. It was like Ramadan except I was fasting in the dark. When my patient was coughing and dying I prayed for him and afterwards I said the Janazah prayers because I don't know any Christian ones. I was all alone after that. Desperate as I was, I still dozed off. I just trusted, if He had any more work for me to do, Allah would send someone to rescue me. If not, I would die and be happy. Thank you."

"You've had a terrible time, all right. I'm going out to Richmond to check on my family but I'll call in to the Horniman Museum on the way. I think there's a Civil Defence post in the basement there. They might be interested in our bomber and I should think they'd be glad to have a doctor-nurse volunteer."

"Especially one looking as smart as me," said Nancy.

"They'll probably kick you straight upstairs into the Modern Nigerian Clothing Collection!"

So Jack and Jill set off the way they'd come, carrying bundles of medical supplies, and out into a clear, cold evening with a full moon rising over abandoned ambulances.

David said, "The Man in the Moon will be looking down on London and saying, *Now what are they doing*?"

"In Nigeria he's got a twin. Long ago their mother put them both up on the moon to keep them safe from being killed by ignorant villagers."

"What a very enlightened idea!"

Chapter 38

Civil Defence, Horniman Museum, Sydenham, London, 6 November 2006

In the moonlight David saw the Horniman Museum high above the road and pulled into a gate marked with a banner saying "Homeland Protection" tied over part of the old notice, but still showing "Staff Parking ONLY". The yard was dotted with piles of bicycles. David found a clear spot and stopped short as Nancy called, "Look out!"

A large pinkish-grey bird was sprawled on the tarmac, flapping its wings out of sync.

Nancy got out and nudged it with her foot. It dragged itself under a bicycle, flaring its surprising striped tail and shedding feathers as it went. Nancy reached under and grabbed it with both gloved hands. The bird gurgled in protest.

"It looks like a fan," she said.

"It looks like a target to me - it's a dove. Come on, then." David indicated the entrance.

His banging eventually brought a big, tweedy woman to the door.

"Come in quickly. What have you got there? Looks like a wood dove. This is not Animal Refuge, you know! You want the Petting Zoo at Crystal Palace Park but I'm afraid it's been closed for renovations for some time."

David pulled up his headpiece. "We've come here to offer you help!"

"Have you, now? We'll have to see the colonel about that."

"I've got a car and she's a doctor," said David. "Put the bird over there, Nancy - in one of those Pigeon Post boxes."

Nancy pulled off her goggles and mask. The lovely receptionist blinked but held most of her face official.

"Ah, good. Take off your suits, please." She clearly enjoyed watching Nancy disrobe, especially her gaiters, but then found her too much like Naomi Campbell, slumming it in the Red Cross.

"Come this way, please." Tweedy Bird drew herself up and in as far as possible and led them out of the foyer's moonlight and down a circular staircase to a large basement lit by paraffin lamps. Eight or ten people were there stacking boxes.

The boss, directing them from behind a desk, was tapping a pointer on a large map of the British Isles. "No, no! Put Harwich to the right of York," he said over his shoulder.

Seeing David and Nancy, he lowered the pointer, holding it at his side like a spear. "Hello. They're telephone directories. We must have a system in place for when the phones come on again. The bigger boxes are full of tsunami handbooks we got last week. Are you from HQ?"

"No, we're civilians. I'm David O'Brien. Nancy is a nurse from Lewisham Hospital – though she's really a doctor."

Nancy held out her hand. "Nancy Adechi, graduated from Ibadan in 1999. I'm working towards BMA registration as a Nurse Supervisor in the Renal Unit at Lewisham Hospital. I wondered if I could be of any assistance here."

"How do you do. Robert Brabant, Acting Commander, Homeland Protection, Sydenham." He shook hands first with David and then Nancy. "Is Lewisham still operational?"

"No, it seems to have been completely abandoned," said Nancy.

"Too close to the blast, eh? Like us. How did you get here?"

"I wrapped up in radiography gear," said Nancy.

David told him, "And I've got a decontamination suit I borrowed from a sick doctor who lives next door to me at Beckenham. Another friend has lent me an old car."

"A car!" He dropped the pointer and then didn't seem to know what to do with his hands. "We're expecting German decontamination suits to be delivered any day, and hopefully some sort of field telephone. The Territorial Unit at Lordship Lane is supposed to be running this post, you see, but they all went off to Twickenham yesterday morning to help set up a demonstration for the rugby test match opening, abseiling from the new stand and so on. Of course they then hung around there, expecting to watch the rugby, didn't bother to rush back here when the bombs went off. Talk about weekend warriors! Of course they'll be quite happy - they're probably locked down in *The Orange Tree* at

Richmond right now. Yes, very happy while there are all sorts of desperate people out there - you know, needing our help!"

"Right. We've seen a few ourselves. Our car's full of medical gear - we thought you might be setting up an emergency centre where the doctor could help."

"Hm. I don't know about that. I don't think that would really be possible. It's not our mandate to be offering medical services. We just haven't got the personnel or the expertise."

"I'm a fully qualified doctor and used to coping with emergencies," Nancy said. "In my fifth year we did three months with a mobile fistula clinic in the far north of Nigeria."

"I'm afraid dealing with radiation disease is a bit more involved than treating tropical skin infections!" Colonel Brabant clutched his jacket around himself and did up two buttons.

Staunch beside her commanding officer, Tweedy Bird said, "I don't think you realise, either of you: this is not quite the Rwanda situation we're facing here!"

"No, indeed," the colonel agreed. "We... er...couldn't afford to get ourselves swamped down here by desperately sick people needing expert attention. As you can see, we really haven't got much room. This was meant to be just a command post."

"What about upstairs?"

"Oh. Well, we have gone through, but only into the director's office. There's plenty of coal here in the basement, we're making soup over his open fire in a copper pot. One of the boys went out to the greenhouse - under a zebra skin, I believe, because there are several panes of glass missing - and picked some carrots and parsley the Museum staff planted. Would you like some soup?"

"Thank you, no. We ate at the hospital."

The juniors had taken advantage of the lull caused by the visitors' arrival to settle on the boxes of directories around a tin of cabin bread, sipping their mugs of soup.

"Who dunnit? That's what I want to know," one boy was asking.

"The Pigeon Post fellow they said the perpetrators were unknown but I'm putting my money on the Pakistanis," said Mr Brabant, accepting soup.

"We do most certainly all need to keep our eyes open." Tweedy Bird pursed her lips. "My daughter had a little part-time job at a storage place in North London and she noticed suspicious comings and goings in one of the sheds. She thought it might be drugs and told the police but when they came they emptied out sacks and sacks of agricultural fertiliser and replaced it with something else and then watched the people going in and out and tapped their phones, and they ended up arresting twenty Muslims - all jihadists!"

"I'm a Muslim," said Nancy, "and my jihad is to be the best doctor I can. My mother always said her jihad was to raise her children to be healthy, useful adults."

"Funny thing, my mother says just the same," said a ginger-headed girl, "and she's as Irish as Paddy's pig!"

"Ahem! I would remind you all, this is a National Emergency!" said Mr Brabant, glaring at friend and foe. "We have British wartime strategy and experience to draw on and clear updated guidelines on Homeland Defence to follow. We are not helpless!"

"Look, I just called in to see if you needed some medical help," said David. "I was on the way to Richmond to check on my mother, but if you don't need us here Doctor Adechi and I will carry on."

"Yes, well, I could requisition your car and your suit, you know," said Mr Brabant, "but if you come back here in the morning..."

"Sure. I could take a message for you, if it's to go anywhere between Richmond and Beckenham."

"We haven't been in touch with the police yet. I could get a report ready."

"Do you know any radio hams? They could probably get something going for you. If you've got any batteries you could check them - get them ready for when the phones and radio come on again. My friend was talking to Switzerland by shortwave this morning."

"Switzerland? What about White City? The army is supposed to be bringing diesel train engines down from Scotland to get the BBC going, but I suppose they're having to alter the points on the track by hand, all the way from Dundee." Colonel Brabant turned to look wistfully at the top of his map.

"We'll be seeing you in the morning, then," said David, backing out.

"Very good. Be careful. Goodbye, miss."

Tweedy Bird escorted them up to the foyer. Once they were dressed for the road she handed them their bird in the box. Nancy poked in a crumb of ship's biscuit but the bird didn't seem to fancy it.

"I was lucky to get out of there alive!" said Nancy when they were in the moonlight again.

"They might at least have invited you to set up a Talking Drum network!"

"Or I could have made them a model mujahideen school, like an ant farm, to amuse them till the television came on again."

Meanwhile, out at Richmond, David's brother, Tim, was fiddling with a cat's whisker radio. Their mother, Pam, was tending her mung bean sprouts, tipping them about with a little water in a jar.

"Look, some of them are splitting! I think I'll take the bottle to bed tonight, to keep it warm and get them growing."

Four-year-old Jack was sitting at his mother's feet and Cath was reading him *When the Wind Blows* .

"'*Well, the Inner Core, or Refuge, looks quite cosy, doesn't it, dear?'*

"'*I hope those doors aren't marking the wallpaper, James!'*"

"Why is there a big cauliflower on top of the old lady and old man's heads?" asked Jack, looking up at the cover.

"That's not a cauliflower, it's an atomic bomb," said Pam, taking the book from her daughter-in-law and turning it over to have a long look at the cover picture. "We used to be afraid of them when I was a girl."

The baby was crawling round the kitchen in pursuit of a black cat with white paws.

"Oh, good. Look, the cat's come back," said Cath.

"Yeow!" said the cat as the baby caught up with him.

"Christ!" said Tim, throwing his pliers at the cat, which exited through the cat flap.

Cath looked shocked. Then she snatched up the baby and ripped her suit off, thrusting that out the cat flap also.

David pushed the Welsh dresser across the door. A blue spaghetti bowl smashed onto the tiles.

Meanwhile the poor baby was screaming and throwing her head around to avoid the bottle of salty water her mother was forcing on her.

David had a job to make himself heard at the front door and Tim, when he came, was loath to open it to such an extraordinary stranger in what was already a double crisis.

"It's me – Rhino - you short-sighted, spotty giraffe!"

"Hello. What are you doing here? Is that Hiria in the car?"

"No, it's my girlfriend, the Ward Sister from Lewisham. I went to see Dad. She'd got stuck in the lift."

"Bring her in."

"I said I'd be just a minute. Dad's dead, Tim. I've come to tell Mum."

"Ooh. Hell. Bring her in. I'll get Mum."

The tiny porch was an awkward changing room, but between umbrella stand and shoe racks and the cactuses on the windowsill they got out of their decontamination rig once again. Tim opened the inner door and welcomed them in. Pam was right there too, anxious to get her hands on her son, while Tim quickly took Nancy upstairs to see his baby.

"Wherever did you get that outfit – not that it doesn't suit you. We've been so worried about you all! How's Jessica?"

"She's fine. She and Sophie Lewis are putting on heavy makeup for when the lights come on again."

"How's Hiria taking it? It's terrible, isn't it? To think you could all have been safe now in New Zealand."

"Look, Mum: I went to see Des."

Pam blenched and sat down on the hall seat, her eyes on David.

"He was dead. Seems to have been killed instantly by the blast through the window. The three other chaps in his room were all dead too. So were all the patients on that side of the ward. He would have died the moment the light and blast hit him. It's fused everything electrical and electronic in England, you know."

"What about Scotland?" Des might have been a temporary thing in her life but Scotland was still deep in Pam's heart.

"We don't know for sure yet, but Radio Caernarfon was still working yesterday morning, and they said Scotland seemed to be all right then except for Clydebank and Glasgow." He handed her the crumpled nameplate he'd taken from the ward.

Pam tried to smooth it out on her knee. She had a tear in her eye when she looked up at her son. "I am sorry about your father, David. He wanted to be a good man but he kept losing hope, and I just couldn't live with it any more."

"I know, Mum. I was there, remember?"

"I'm very sorry for you and Tim."

"You were great. In fact you were super great. But just think – without him you might have been nothing but a dedicated follower of fashion."

"You are awful – just because I'm wearing this dreadful old Guernsey of Tim's! I did like the sound of your girlfriend's leggings, though."

"What was Tim telling her about the cat?"

"Oh yes! It had been outside since the bombing and when it came inside just now the poor baby started playing with it. Poor old Bootsie too – Tim terrified him and then locked him out. Listen to them upstairs: they're trying to make the baby sick. To think my biggest worry has been what to use for diapers when we run out of paper ones. I've been looking funny at the curtain linings in my room. It's marvellous that you've brought us a nurse at just the right time."

"She's actually a doctor - but they wouldn't have her at any price, those creeps at Civil Defence, the minute they heard she was from Nigeria. She offered to set up an emergency medical centre but they'd rather carry on doing absolutely nothing. They wouldn't have trusted her to cut a bit of sticking plaster for fear she hadn't washed her hands since she came out of the jungle. By the way, the decontamination suit you admired came from our Doctor Lewis. He was called to a train wreck, but now he's ill with radiation disease."

"Did the train crash into a power pole?" asked a little voice at waist height.

"No, Jack," said his uncle, scooping him up in his arms. "The train just stopped when the electricity went off and then it must have run off the rails - like your Hot Wheels set. And it fell over sideways - or that's what the train wreck patient we ended up with said." He added for Pam's benefit, "He's lying on the table where you had Christmas dinner last year. We think he's one of the bombers."

"No! Is he a Pakistani?"

"Sorry, he's Russian."

"Charming. So that's what they're spending their money on now!"

Tim, Cath and Nancy came back without the baby.

"She's gone to sleep," Cath told her mother.

"She might not have breathed much in," said Nancy. "We've washed her inside and out, given her laxatives and antacids, and sponged her with bleach. You should cover the floor where the cat's been."

Cath clung to her husband but Pam started hauling bits of carpet from the hall into the kitchen.

"Do you two want to sleep here?" asked Tim. "It's nearly midnight and I'm afraid we're running out of candles."

"No, thanks. We'd better go back to Beckenham. There's more room there and Hiria could do with some help with our patient - if you're willing, Nancy?"

Nancy said she was.

"You and your cat are making me nervous," said David. "Can you give me a big plastic bag? We've got a sick bird out in the car."

"What sort of bird?"

Nancy said, "David thinks it's some sort of dove. Its tail feathers are falling out."

Tim produced a Tesco's bag.

Pam brought Nancy half a box of chocolates, and Tim and Cath gave her grateful hugs.

Chapter 39

Jetlagging and Water Sports,
Cairo, Egypt, 7 November 2006.

A sprat of unknown – likely non-Australian – breed wheeled Dennis back to a different empty cell and heaved him out of the chair and onto the bench, wrenching his left arm in the process. This cell had a bucket in one corner but it was redundant as on the way back Dennis had used the opening in the chair to connect with his escort's boot – and received a swift kick in reply. Consequently there was still no drink but he'd managed to keep hold of the towel. He spread it over himself and went straight to sleep.

He was having a dream about snorkelling off the Hen and Chickens. The others - Bush Pig and Hans and the Matakana ballet teacher - were scattering frozen peas to attract the fish but Dennis put some inside his mask to ensure a real close encounter. A huge snapper zoomed in and bit half his ear off. At the same time someone was dragging him into the chair, wheeling him down the corridor and throwing him onto a bench facing the other way. The handcuffs somehow struck his mouth and his bottom lip bled onto the sling.

It was still dark but it took longer to get off to sleep this time. He had lost the towel and was thirstier than ever. These were the meanest mongrels yet. Also two flies were buzzing around the cell. Drive a man mad. Eventually he drifted off.

He was being shifted again, half asleep in spite of the pain from his shoulder and from having his sore knee banged on a doorpost. There was a horrible, rackety air-conditioning unit here. He'd been upgraded against his will but would rather have had the flies back - he was getting too cold.

Minutes later, it seemed, he was moved again, this time to a cell with two air-conditioning units. He was left sitting in the chair, listening to them vibrate. One of them was slowly dripping. In spite of the pain in his left knee Dennis put his feet down and clawed his way closer. He put his mouth up to catch a drip. It tasted oily. He waited for the next drop. The room was getting a bit light but he was freezing, his feet and balls burning with frostbite. Zaheed kept coming to peer at him through the door grille. Sometimes he hung over him, whistling a bit of the tune from the Warehouse advertisement. Dennis found he was crying tears he could not spare.

The next time they came for him he was taken back to the bathroom. The Aussie was waiting for him. He had taken some of the gym gear from the heap in the corner and assembled it into a tripod with an ironing board or a surfboard leaning against it. So that was the reason for his secondment? Aussies often travel with surfboards and sometimes with ironing boards.

"You're from Queensland, eh?"

No reply.

"Byron Bay, I bet."

Two other goons grabbed him out of the chair with no consideration for his shoulder and held him up against the surfboard while the Aussie roped him under the arms and around his ankles, and then fastened him and the surfboard to the tripod, head down.

The two big fish had come in and stood against the wall to watch the sprats in mass action. Belatedly modest, the Aussie dropped a towel over Dennis, left it covering his face as well. Dennis would have shaken it off but someone was holding the towel tight to keep his head firm against the board.

Catfish spoke close above him. "Today we want to know who organised the rocket and bomb attack on London. I am sure you can tell us their names. Let us know when you are ready."

Before Dennis could reply water was pouring all over his face. He struggled to get free but strong hands held his head and the water poured against his mouth and into his throat, choking him. He passed out.

"Thirty-five seconds. That is a record," someone was saying as he recovered.

He was lying on the floor, still roped to the board, looking up at his tormentors. They all looked very interested. Snapper was bending right over and poking at his right eyelid.

Dennis coughed and tried to spit. Snapper jumped back and swiped at his soiled uniform. The Aussie was clearly amused, and tipped the board sideways.

Catfish was champing his jaw. Gum? Dennis coughed again and nearly choked. Two sprats were trying to shove their way in closer. Together they turned the board to the other side for a minute, and then one grasped his ankles and they hoisted up the board so his feet were in the air and the top of his head was pressed into the tiles.

Then he was flat once more and had the towel again slapped over his face.

Right above Dennis, Catfish lifted one corner of the towel and asked, "You have something to say, yet, or do we go again?"

One of the sprats was standing by, ready to turn on the hose.

"Uurgh," said Dennis, waggling his elbow under the sodden towel.

"Is that Kiwi for 'yes'?"

"Urgh."

"Sit him up."

The sprats unroped him, hauled him up and dropped him into the chair.

"Gi's a drink?" he croaked.

Everybody laughed.

"New Zealanders! Never know when you've had enough."

The Aussie gave him half a glass of water from the hose. It was delicious, the best Dennis had ever tasted.

Catfish gestured for his seat to be placed on the other side of the drainhole from Dennis. Snapper brought his own stool, pad and pen and sat alongside his leader.

"Now, the names of those people who helped you get the rocket ready?" Catfish's moustache quivered.

Dennis considered the question. He knew nothing, he didn't feel very bright, and he didn't want to piss on his friends who seemed to be under suspicion - Serge might still be alive.

But he didn't want to go under the waterfall again. "I think the ringleader is called Zaheed Apiata."

"How do you spell that?"

"I don't know. I've never seen it written down."

"Who else?"

"I heard them talk about a Jerry Collins. I think he was American."

"What State?"

"Dunno. He was supposed to be a bit of a drinker but I never saw him drunk. Can I have some more water?"

"When we've finished. Where did the rocket come from?"

"I don't know. It might have been Khyber Pass. They talked a lot about that - and Karangahape too."

"How are those names spelt?" asked Snapper.

"Permission to speak?" asked the Aussie, red-faced.

Catfish turned and looked him up and down. "Yes?"

"He's talking about a footballer and the red light district in Auckland, New Zealand."

"Aw, right! We go again."

The goons grabbed Dennis while the Aussie propped the surfboard up to receive him. Dennis was roped and towelled in spite of his struggles, and then the water drilled at his mouth and spurted up his nose.

Choking, he shook off the hands holding his head and squawked, "Stop."

They tipped the board sideways and let him spit and cough, and spit again.

"Well? You've got something to tell us now?"

The board was propped up.

"I just...wanted...to...say..." Dennis retched and spat down his chin.

He opened his eyes and looked for Catfish. Snapper had his pen poised. "I think I can see...what...your trouble...is."

He shut his eyes. There was a long pause.

Then he said, "You should put me up the other way. This end's full."

Chapter 40

Tokerau Tuatuas,
New Zealand, 8 November 2006

Dennis was ignorant of having caused his first miracle - felt no residual power going out of him - yet after lunch at Tokerau Beach on the other side of the world, Jim Heteraka felt quite well enough to take a bucket of empty tuatua shells to the beach for the gulls to quarrel over.

"You should have tasted the fritters," he told them.

The sky was blue and the tide just on the turn, the wind veering to northeast. On a day like this he would have been putting the kontiki out if things had been different. Maybe after healing for another week or two he might feel up to dealing with the battery machine as it reeled in the flying hooks. It was always safer, though, with a mate to help pull off the seaweed and the fish. Might get a couple of snapper, perhaps – but even a gurnard and stingray would do.

If Barry were here, or if young Jessica and her friends could come running to help him again, it would be possible to haul a line in - but that can never happen now. Never.

The big-boss, black-and-white gull screamed over the tuatua, threatening the younger and smaller seabirds, but he kept his wingtips folded. It was only a token meal and a token threat.

Jim turned and walked up the beach, away from the sun. He thought of going to see his old fishing mate, Fred Greenwall. Fred was an electronics whiz as well as a cunning fisherman. Jim dropped the bucket by the steps and set off with purpose. Fred might be able to raise Barry on the internet or the radio. There might be fresh news from London too.

"I hear you were a bit of a hero last week, Fred - on both coasts?"

"Oh, yeah. Well, it's part of the pledge – I'm always scanning. I heard there was a big four-wheel drive tipped over on Ninety Mile. They had no telephone and the tide was coming in."

"How did they reach you?"

"Another vehicle stopped and they had a citizen band radio. A chap out on the other side of our bay, near Mangonui, picked up the SOS on his radio and relayed it to me - he had no telephone either. So I called the ambulance and had to do quite a bit of coordinating..."

"Do you think you could get in touch with my boy? He's in Afghanistan with the army."

"Well, it might be possible. I was fixing someone's radio the other day and Runway Control at JFK Airport told me to get off their frequency because they had a plane coming in to land. What's their call sign?"

"The army's a bit coy about that, but I've got a phone number here. I don't think we can call him direct, but I need to get a message to him."

"We could try that phone number first," said Fred.

Jim pulled an envelope out of his pocket and read out the nine digits. It reached a sergeant in Waiouru who said she would get Sapper Heteraka to phone them back.

"Tell him to ring his mother," Jim said, hoisting himself out of his chair. "Thanks a million, Fred!"

He was hobbling along the street, two houses from home, when he saw Rosalie come onto the deck with the phone up to her ear. She was beaming and waving madly to him. It must be Barry already.

"Tell him about Dennis!" Jim yelled. His voice was still a terrible croak after the hospital poking all their torture gear down his throat.

They met under the pohutukawa tree and she gave him the phone.

"How are you, Dad?"

"Nearly good enough to put a line out, I'm thinking. Did your mother tell you about Dennis Bogdanovich getting arrested in Holland?"

"Yes, but I didn't understand it. Something about a glass-bottomed boat?"

"That bit's true but they've got his name wrong, and they think he's one of the terrorist gang that bombed London."

"Wouldn't Dennis love that! I'll get our intelligence boys on to it. They've been trying to get news of Hiria and David for me too, but no luck yet. My time's up, Dad. Look after yourself. Love to Mum – and you too. I'll ring you back as soon as I hear anything from London."

Chapter 41

Close by the Sea but No Boat,
Cuba, 9 November 2006

Dennis was aching all over. So many parts of him hurt it was hard to think which had woken him.

Something new - his left hip - was sore. He was lying on his side on a hard floor, fastened back at the waist to the vibrating wall of a plane. It was still roaring along. How long had he slept? He tried to straighten his legs and shift onto his back but the elbow resented being asked to help. When he eased off it he fell on his face. The restraint and the handcuffs bit into his ribs, and both knees screamed.

"Lie still, El Terroristo." A kick to his ear through the hood accompanied the drawly American voice coming from normal waist height. Someone he hadn't heard from before. His ear burned, and the right knee now hurt more than the left.

The plane landed and the sun set through the hood, but those were the last words Dennis heard till he was trolleyed out of suffocating heat with cries of big birds above and a definite tang of salt air, into a cool, echoing space that smelt of chlorine. Then someone said, "Fourteen."

Hobnailed boots on steel floors, a door bashing metal on metal - and Dennis was hauled onto a hard bed. The hood was unknotted and the sling removed by blue rubber-gloved hands. He could hear boots moving in a measured tread across a metal ceiling and onward. Once the hood came off he saw two guards, who filled the cell with camouflage and a smell of sweat. One held Dennis's arms tight while the other unlocked the handcuffs. When the guard let go, Dennis's arms fell, weak and aimless as a baby's.

He saw his day-old daughter.

"Look, she's got your wandering hands," said Diane.

He reached for her huge breast. It was wet with milk.

The outsides of his wrists were raw under the fluorescent light. His diaper was removed - nothing to declare - and replaced by a clean orange jumpsuit. Boots in the ceiling ding-ding-dinged back again while the right arm was being tortured into a sleeve for the first time since Amsterdam. The left hurt even more when its turn came because there was less play in the garment for it.

"Where have you bastards brought me?"

No answer. One guard gathered up the laundry while the other held the door open, and then it clashed shut behind them.

The cell was little bigger than a Portaloo and made entirely of metal. There was a shiny toilet and attached sink less than a metre from the end of the bunk. Brand-new American hardware. With a tap. Undeterred by boots patrolling outside and above Dennis slid off the bunk and fell towards the sink. He turned on the tap.

No water.

Chapter 42

Sergey's Great Happiness,
Beckenham, 8 November 2006

Hiria was affronted when her husband crawled back into the house in the middle of the night and woke her to say he'd brought home a nurse from Lewisham Hospital. She had instant recall of her brother waking her long ago with a report on midnight adventures with nurses in parked ambulances behind Waikato Hospital.

Then Nancy came round the bedroom door with her hair sticking out in all directions and dirt from the cellar tunnel smearing her face and white uniform. She caught sight of herself in the dressing-table mirror and bent forward to look closer, with such a comical expression of exhausted incredulity they both burst out laughing.

"You look like someone who's been hit by a bomb," Hiria said.

"Actually, I missed it completely!"

The two women made friends at first sight.

After a long sleep, Nancy woke in a guest room decorated with blonde pictures of groups of bottles. They looked very peaceful. She listened to the noises of the house to confirm what David had told her about his family and their bomber patient.

Someone came running up the stairs and a young girl opened the door. "Hello. I'm Jessie. Dad's cooking a minger pie on the open fire in between two frypans!" With her two thumbs joined downward she made a figure like a mountain with two peaks. "I'll bring you a bit."

"Lovely. Thank you." She wondered what a 'minger' was. Some little wild English creature with pointed ears? Perhaps a fox? It couldn't be last night's poor dead pigeon they'd tipped out into a pile of fallen leaves at the gate? Jessie had looked disgusted but fascinated by her father's dish. She heard her go bounding on downstairs.

Nancy got up, brushed her uniform, put it on again, said fajr, and went down to join the family.

"Hello, you had a long sleep," Hiria said. "Feel better?"

"Much better, thanks. I hear you are cooking something special."

"You must have smelt it! David's gone through all the cupboards to cook an amazing pie for your dinner," said Hiria.

"Well, it's basically just a Spanish omelette without the chorizo. We've run out of potatoes too, so I've made a crust with crisps. They were a bit limp so I thought I'd toast them up." David waved his free hand and tried to look like a confident TV chef.

Behind his back Jessica was grimacing and making her mysterious sign to Nancy. It was possibly the letter M.

The fire in the grate smoked strenuously and he said, "Get the bellows going again, Jess. We need to keep plenty of smoke going up the chimney." He told the adults, with a serious expression, "I'll put the rest of the cardboard back soon. I haven't had to burn much of it because I had the Pigeon Post box to break up."

"Do you like ham, eggs, sardines, smoked oysters and apricots?" asked Hiria.

"I like apricots and eggs," said Nancy with an apprehensive look.

"Uh-oh!" said David, deflated. "No ham for you, eh?"

"I like potato chips. I'd really like a drink, if you have anything."

"Would you like red or white or purple?" asked Jessica, indicating a line-up of coloured buckets.

"Purple, please."

Jessica dipped a mug of water out of the purple bucket and presented it ceremoniously to their guest.

"Come and meet the patient," Hiria said to Nancy.

Jessica stayed with her father. "Dad, there's rats upstairs." She looked for her father's reaction.

"Is that right?" David gave the pie another turn. "Maybe we could go into business selling rat pie. I hear the rats on Bikini Island are still perfectly healthy."

"They wear togs?"

"No! Years and years ago the Americans tested their atomic bombs on some tiny little islands called Bikini, way out in the North Pacific Ocean. No one can live there now, but the rats are doing fine."

"I hate them."

"Ah well, I promise, as soon as the shops open we'll buy some poison - and a big Cinderella trap too. Shall we save some of this pie for bait?"

Jessica grinned and nodded energetically.

In the dining room Serge was too ill to be very surprised at meeting Nancy, who with her uniform and professional manner, won his confidence effortlessly.

She pulled on rubber gloves and felt for the carotid pulse in his neck to assess his general state. His heartbeat was erratic but fairly strong. She examined all his injuries. His gums were bleeding steadily and blue blotches had appeared all over his body in between his wounds. The left leg with the cuts was twice the size of the right and the wounds were suppurating. Nancy then tried to lift his burnt arm to look at the underside and inspect the glands in his armpit.

"Chert!" he said with white lips.

"May His name be praised!" said Nancy.

"I didn't know communists still went in for blasphemy," said Hiria, laughing.

"I'm sorry for hurting you," Nancy told him. "I brought you a little pain relief from the hospital." She produced a syringe and found a vein inside his elbow. "There. Now, you'll be much more comfortable if you let me release some of the fluid out of this arm and after that I will dress your leg."

Serge nodded assent but reserved the right to moan as Nancy began by swabbing the whole arm with lint dipped by forceps into a bowl of saline. She lifted the shirting strip covering it as much as possible, to assess the wound underneath..

"And now I'm going to release the fluid," Nancy warned him. "I'm afraid this is going to hurt a little, but I promise you will feel better afterwards." The straining in Sergey's neck muscles were an indication of how painful he expected the treatment to be.

Serge nodded, his jaw clenched.

Nancy took a scalpel from her tray and quickly punctured the crust, many places in succession along his swollen, burnt arm. Under the stained strip of shirting Hiria had left embedded there, Nancy now laid a trail of folded gauze to soak up the yellow ooze coming from her incisions. From the head of the table where Hiria stood, the ruptured blood vessels underneath the white skin either side of the burn made the arm look like a stout frilled lizard with blue spots. "Nice work," she said, grinning.

"Tell me what the bomb looked like," Nancy said to distract her patient while she swabbed and then bandaged the swollen leg. "I didn't see it."

Serge delivered his scientist's report in short bursts, accompanied by groaning as the treatment proceeded. "I was in the Canterbury train, at.7.01 am. We left Forest Hill. It was crowded. I was standing, holding a pole facing – Ooorrw!...north."

A drool of blood fell from the corner of his mouth. Hiria dabbed it away with a rag.

"The light blasted my arm. It tore through the carriage. This hand," he waved it, "got burnt by the metal pole. Screaming. People thrown in a mass. Glass flying...stabbing into the – *ooowh* - wall opposite. The train fell sideways."

He opened his eyes and looked up at Nancy and then beyond her. "Someone was pulling herself up...on my legs. Up through the window. I saw a brilliant white...*oooh!*...burning through the clouds. I climbed on a seat...to the broken window. I could see all around. A green ball was growing – oohoow! Iridescence...rising up into pale sky. Out of the green glow...long fingers, cirrostratus - *ooh-o-orrr!* - clouds. Rising to 40 degrees above...the horizon, in successive arcs. Turning down like feathery...plumes at the poles." He waved the motions with his other hand. "In seconds – aahowr! - they disappeared. Replaced by cirrus-like rings...moving outwards. Tremendous...velocity. Finally stopping. The outermost...ring - *ah-oow!* - 50 degrees overhead. Did not disappear. Hung...frozen. 45 seconds."

His eyes closed again but the report continued - well rehearsed, though never written, Hiria reflected.

"The green light turned to purple. Began – ooww-orf! - to fade...at burst point. Bright red glow...began on the horizon. 50 degrees north of east. Same time, 50 degrees south of east. Expanding inwards and upwards." He raised both hands, upsetting Nancy's tray of instruments and balls of lint, and the bowl of soiled cottonwool and water.

Grim-faced, Hiria did not move to pick up any of it. She remembered that glowing horizon over Bexley.

Sergey continued, "The whole eastern sky a dull, burning...red semicircle. 100 degrees north to south. Halfway to the zenith...obliterating - *oh-ooor!* - some of the lesser stars. Interspersed....tremendous white rainbows. No less than seven minutes."

"It must have been very beautiful," said Nancy, taking scissors from her pocket and snipping off the end of the dressing as she reached the ankle.

"While it...lasted I felt...no pain."

Chapter 43

Endless Life in Stainless Steel,
Cuba, 9 November 2006

By the time the fourth meal clattered onto the door shelf Dennis could feel himself getting stronger. The toilet and sink had gushed six times by then and the last twice he'd been quick enough to get a good drink from the tap.

The meal looked like porridge but it could have been a wet risotto since there were signs of guest appearances by peas and carrots. There was no telling day from night because of the perpetual fluorescent lighting. The tin soldiers patrolled every two minutes, but the choreography was so out of sync it sounded continuous; only the fading to the end of the corridors and the crescendos at his door and in the ceiling could have been counted, if you had the music or maths to do it. He did calculate that if his cell was three paces wide there must be twenty cells on each floor, two wide and stacked two high. He was quarter of the way from the end of the lower row. The same module was repeated beyond the wall at his feet, and probably beyond the cells on the other side of the corridor too, judging by faint, intermediate vibrations.

Apart from the perpetual clanging of the patrols, the worst thing was having no one to talk to. Guards stared through his window slot when they passed left to right – that was how he guessed there were cells on the other side of the corridor - but they showed no expression, even when they saw him sitting on the toilet; it might have been the same khaki-and-crewcut person with a crook neck every time, except that one of them seemed to be a woman. What a way to earn a living - worse than drainlaying.

Every few hours Dennis could hear other prisoners talking in unison. He lay on the floor to listen at the gap under the door but none of it seemed to be English. Could be Muslims praying. He also tried thumping on his side walls and shouting but there was never any response. The neighbouring cells might be empty.

Through the din Dennis concentrated on a physical audit and making a plan for rehabilitation. He could see by his reflection in the tap that his nose was better and his ear, the most recent injury, was scabbing over without infection. Unfortunately his hearing had not been damaged.

The water torture had left only mental scars: hatred of all Americans, Englishmen and Australians as well as Dutchies and Poles, with reserve categories covering all men in uniform and suspicions about the Treasurer of Auckland City Council and the Government of New Zealand. He'd spat most of the water out of his lungs into the hood on the plane but he would recognise Egyptian or Afghani or any wog water if he ever got to taste it again. The water here tasted plenty chlorinated. American, even.

The dislocated shoulder was quite good. It must now be more than two weeks since it was reset by those bastards with the cottage hospital in Poland or Austria or wherever. He could tell this because he'd had his last shave in Marken and his whiskers had now reached the bendable stage. He should get a gentle shoulder rotation programme going. Both elbows needed work but the wrists were healing well. Most of the barnacle cuts except for those on his fingertips, were gone - residual benefit of a lifetime on the Silverbeet Diet? He would thank his mother when he could.

They must let prisoners communicate with their lawyers, surely? And families? Blogs?

Continuing the physical assessment: his backbone seemed undamaged. He was not up to playing squash or taking on a marlin just yet but he would start press-ups as soon as his arms were ready. Sit-ups might be possible first, but the knees still needed plenty of rest. Those bloody Dutchmen - Dullboot and Shinyboot - and their truncheons, they'd put him off lifts for life, even ones with velvet seats.

Well, here he was, stuck on the ground floor with no luggage, and no contracts to bother him, but plenty of time to concentrate on physical improvement. Surely they must let him out for recreation soon? There had to be something about exercise for prisoners in the Geneva Convenience.

And about piracy: where was his boat?

He was somewhere near the sea with no boat. What torture.

Soon after the next water flush there was a ruckus in the corridor: first lots of boots, and some shoving and banging on the cell walls, and then all the prisoners started shouting in wog language and hammering on the walls, nearly knocking the place apart. A door clanged shut very close to him and the boots receded. He had a neighbour.

When the general noise subsided Dennis gave a few thumps on the wall and croaked out, "Welcome." It had been a long time since he'd spoken aloud.

There was no specific response, but the new prisoner began transmitting information about himself under his cell door and Dennis lay down on the floor to hear more easily. The man's name was Joe Farouki. Dennis hoped he wasn't Egyptian. He spoke good English and had a lot to tell since he'd been here a long time, in Camp 4 and Camp 3. Conditions were apparently better in the old blocks. There they used to have a dining room, and space for basketball – except, he said, "There were so many cripples they played like two teams of old men."

Dennis immediately decided to raise his left leg as he lay listening, getting on with his exercise programme. Though the floor was still too cold for safe physiotherapy it was so much warmer than his bed that he sometimes slept there. He immediately decided it would have been better to have started with the right leg.

The bulletin was continuing with a lifestyle section: this present block had been made so big, lots of low-risk prisoners like this newcomer, were being shoved in to fill it up but it had been specially designed to prevent suicides after three successful attempts last June: "Asymetric Warfare the

Americans called it. Unsuccessful attempts were called "Manipulative Self-injurious Behaviour."" These terms caused a lot of jeering and extra racket from all the cells, the guards adding an accompaniment by bashing the doors with coshes as they marched past at a faster pace.

Then the new man must have given out the names of the three martyrs. Dennis couldn't catch all of them but felt the vibration of grief and rage in the shrieks and blood-curdling ululation that came in response to each one. The boots of the guard passing Cell 14 regularly stirred air under the door but were soundless for several minutes in the drumming on cell walls and floors and ceiling as prisoners upstairs joined in the salute of grief.

When the shouting subsided the guard beat on each door as he passed and yelled, "One month suspension all privileges."

Dennis gave a few thumps on his neighbour's wall and again yelled, "Welcome." Then he added, "Kia ora," two words he would never have uttered at home, and asked, "What privileges?"

"Paper and pencil for thirty minutes once a month, one book a week, thirty minutes in the rec. yard every second day."

"What about shaving gear?"

"Not a chance," the new man told him. "Who are you?"

"I'm Dennis Bogdanovich from New Zealand. Where are you from?"

"I am from Clapham. They got me mixed up with my cousin from Yemen."

“How long have you been here?”

“Since 19 February 2002.”

“How long is your sentence?”

“They haven’t told me. There is an Australian who’s been here as long as me. He is in solitary.”

“What do you call this?”

“I call it Endless Life in Stainless Steel. I know the salt from Guantanamo Bay will rot it through before I die, but not, Inshalla, before Allah sends scorpions to kill all Americans and frigate birds to pick out the guards’ brains and pelicans to rot their hearts in their pouches and feed them to their young.”

“Sounds good to me,” said Dennis.

Chapter 44

Sergey's Happy Death,
Beckenham, 9 November 2006

In London, Sergey was very low. The infection in his leg was taking him over and his lungs were filling with fluid.

On Wednesday he roused himself and told Hiria and Nancy, in short gasps, with his eyes closed:

"Find my son and say I don't...
begrudge my wounds...
for having been...
part of the...
consummation.

My brain the father..
science the womb.
The world was proud to hold us.
I saw...
the glory that surrounded God...
resurrected...
out of Russia.

 All the sky and earth in simul...
taneous orgasm.

Serge did not open his eyes again.

Hiria and Nancy looked at each other. Their mouths went down and met their shoulders coming up, in one straight line.

"Should we write it down?" asked Nancy.

Someone was knocking loudly on the front door. They could hear David talking to someone bossy. Hiria went to look, and next thing two men in khaki decontamination suits pushed past her into the dining room.

"Sergey Malyarovich Mikulitsin!"

Serge stirred but didn't open his eyes

"We have come to arrest you for complicity in a plot to cripple the United Kingdom by means of six bombs on the nights of 4th and 5th of November."

There was no response.

"Is he conscious?" the second man asked Nancy.

"He is very ill," she told him.

"Don't bother reading him his rights," said the first man.

Then: "Casket, Sergeant," shouted the second man.

Two more khaki-suited men crowded into the dining room, carrying over their heads a black plastic box with a curved lid. It was very much like a coffin. When they set it down beside the table and lifted the lid Hiria was relieved to see it had a window at one end.

One of the newcomers took hold of Sergey beneath the armpits, another took his ankles and they swung him off the table. His head dangled back, bumping on the table and again on the edge of the box as they lowered him in. He was a tight fit.

Nancy pushed between the khaki suits to lift Serge's burnt arm and arrange it so that it wasn't being squeezed at the side of the box. "Goodbye, Sergey," she said.

The lid was lowered and spring clips were snapped down all round.

"It's a pity he's not conscious," said the first man as the box was being manoeuvred past the stairs. "He's going to be transported in a trailer behind a Russian tank we requisitioned from Woolwich. He'd have enjoyed that. Apparently Russian tanks have a pump action ignition system. Very nice!"

In the hall the coffin was shouldered by the other three. Then it went swaying out the front door.

The officer shook hands with Hiria and David, and bowed slightly.

"Well, thank you very much for turning him in, Mr and Mrs O'Brien. This man has enemies in high places and low. We got your address from the British Army in Afghanistan, one of his accomplices is from New Zealand, but the Netherlands Police caught him in Amsterdam. We were delighted to hear about this chap, thanks to your radio message to Interpol. We're very glad indeed to have him."

Turning to Nancy, he added, "Thank you very much, Nurse, for keeping him alive for us. We'll be in touch.

Then he pulled down the headpiece of his decontamination suit, patted Jessica on the head and boomed at her through his mask,

"You have taken part in world history today, young lady! Shut the door!"

Jessica shook her hair vigorously. "I hate that man!" she said, twisting a strand across her face.

"Don't suck your hair, Jessica!" snapped her mother.

David put one arm round his daughter and the other round his wife as they all moved into the front room to watch from the window. The soldiers shut Sergey into the trailer and then climbed down into the tank. One of them waved before he vanished inside.

"Sergey wasn't Russian at all! He was a Dutchman called Piet ten Broeke," said Nancy, coming into the room waving a passport. "And look what they've forgotten!"

From under her arm she produced Serge's fat purse, the belt dangling. The buckle was still done up but the leather strap had been cut clean through with a very sharp knife, or perhaps a scalpel.

"Don't worry about it - I'm pretty sure Sergey has given up smoking," said David.

"It must have got jumbled up with the bedding," said Hiria, quickly turning back to the front window.

The tank, grinding and clanking, started manoeuvring to turn in the street. It came towards them, the gun snapping off part of their plane tree. It startled Jessica when the bare branch clawed at their window and bounced on the paving. The gun then swung away and the tracks casually rode over part of the Country Club fence on the other side of the street as the tank made the turn. Serge's trailer rode up the kerb, bumped down again and then disappeared into the railway underpass.

It was a long time before the rumble of the tank faded.

Chapter 44

No Friends Like Old Friends,
Cuba, December 2006

Ninety dishes of food and thirty days later, Dennis was nearly asleep when the cell door opened on two guards. One guard stood rigid against the open door. The older one who filled the cell slapped a truncheon on his left palm above Dennis face as he recited: "All prisoners who have not offended for thirty days are entitled to one half-hour of recreation on alternate days. There will be no fraternisation with other prisoners, no chanting of slogans and no casting of offensive materials. On your feet: Recreation. Hurry it up. Prisoner, stand!"

Dennis clambered to the door by holding on to the plumbing and came out into the corridor. There were two cells between him and the end of the corridor, and as Dennis passed them, clinging to the wall, he slapped on each window slit. The new neighbour looked to be about eighteen. He waved to Dennis. The man in the last cell didn't look up. He was very old. The guard unlocked a door at the end.

The recreation area was almost dark after the perpetual glare of his cell. It was more like a chimney than a yard. Concrete walls ten metres high, stretched up to a dark purple sky. The area was divided into four by high mesh fences. His section was about nine metres square. Recreation?

In the pen diagonally opposite a shaft of sunlight slanted down the concrete at the corner. Some lucky bastard was leaning back there, face raised, soaking it up. He had greying hair and a red beard, a bit longer than Zaheed used to wear his.

Dennis clung to the wire and goggled. Hooked nose, skinny legs...

"Zaheed! Remember me? Dennis Bogdanovich from New Zealand!"

The man left the sunshine and stumbled towards him.

"Whatcha reckon, Zaheed: how did it go? You know, what Serge said –

"'*Without science, no torture,*' eh?"

Strong hands grabbed Dennis and tore his fingers from the wire.

THE END

Messages from Guantanamo Bay, 23 February 2007

Allah ihu, I call in the night.
His peace spreads to every cell.
We bow in our separate submission,
angels, not guards, observe us
report our perfect observance.
Our treasure piles up in Paradise
in ramps to surmount these walls.

By Noah Aswad, written on a foam plastic cup.

My First Poem

Every second day
They let me see the sky,
Five fathoms up,
Like a crayfish in a hole
At Guantanamo Bay.

I won't say it gapes
Dark as a cunt,
Send no more dirty pictures,
If only Cheryl would growl me again
And make me a bacon sandwich.

By Dennis Bogdanovich

PS Send squash gear. The guards are getting fat.

The Face of Allah

The Worship of Allah fills my days
and comforts my lonely nights.
I walk anticlockwise the exercise yard
as when I did the Hajj.
A black patch on the doorway
for me is Mohammad's stone
but here there is no Ka'bah
and here I walk alone.

Allah attends to my cry
as he hears each man in a Friday mosque.
He enters every cell and says,
"I hear you when you call My name.
I see you bow to this strange earth,
acknowledging My sovereignty:
remember I am Lord of Time
as well as Lord of All Space.
Tell yourself when you are praying.
neither ends till you see My face.

Zaheed Khalid

Untitled

My wife will not give way,
she knows my innocence.
Her sisters will find her work,
my brothers will protect her
from words the neighbours say.
The child I never knew
has grown and will learn to pray
for a father with a long grey beard,
a broken nose and a limp,
who will,
Inshallah,
be home
someday.

By Zaheed Khalid

Untitled

Misery without end
or death from sudden poison.
The locust zoomed into my cell
into the spider's web.
Its strength was useless,
its gleaming wings
cast down as debris.
The spider repairs her net.

By Yusuf Farouki, written on toilet tissue.

The Tawaf
(Encircling the Ka'bah)

The love of the ummah
bears me on
as the crush I felt at the centre of faith,
bore me up and then spun me out
as a particle of the truth,
sends me now on a spiral path,
encompassing the world,
leading inevitably
to home.

By Tarif Omis

The Stars and Stripes

Imprisoned by The Land of the Free,
"The Stars and Stripes" every morning
serves as my call to prayer.

My father came from Michigan
to see me chained to the floor,
hair grown to a curtain
my only privacy.

He weeps and says
"Get a haircut, boy.
Your grandmother is OK."
And "Everyone hates the war."

By Herman Emerick

A Simple Suggestion

An embarrassment to the United States
has washed up in Guantanamo Bay.
Among the other jetsam
young boys and broken men,
by-catch of a terrorist trawl
that catches only minnows,
held in hope of the chance of suspicion
they maybe
plotted against The States.

Too innocent for tag and release?
Torture
and mince them into sashimi.

By Dennis Bogdanovich

These poems by English-speaking prisoners at
Guantanamo Bay are to be submitted for inclusion in
a forthcoming publication by the University of Iowa
Press, August 2007.